The Summer Diary

Elyse Douglas

COPYRIGHT

ISBN-13: 978-1511830898
ISBN-10: 1511830891

I always say, keep a diary and someday it'll keep you.

—*Mae West*

For Susan, my beach sister.

The Summer Diary

CHAPTER 1

Keri Lawton sat on Brandy Beach in the white glare of heat, her crystal blue eyes squinting, lost in their own stare. She wore a blue and white patterned one-piece bathing suit and a wide-brimmed white hat, pulled tightly over her head. There was little wind and the sun pressed heavily on her back and shoulders, reminding her that she'd absently left the remaining sun block in the beach house, along with a bottle of water. She draped a towel over her bare shoulders for protection.

As she pulled her knees up to her chest and hugged them, gently swaying, she watched the curl and thud of waves. She didn't notice kids romping nearby, struggling to get a kite airborne; was not aware of teens engaged in giggly combat over a volleyball game, or lovers entangled under a flapping beach umbrella.

She recalled an old photo of her grandparents, taken sometime in the 1940s when they'd first met. They were riding a bicycle through a glowing summer day, her grandfather seated, pedaling, her grandmother sitting cradled on the handlebars, leaning back into her grandfather's chest, her legs outstretched. Both were laughing, joyful, happy. It was such a wonderful photo—two lovers captured in the bloom of first love, before real life intruded and changed everything. Keri wondered if true love really existed. Would she ever experience it?

Images of her best friend, Sophia Anderson, kept flitting in and out of her mind, like leaves sailing past a window. Keri saw the little, chocolate-haired Sophia at 8 years old, with her wide, adventurous eyes, standing firmly in her driveway, beckoning her over with little wiggling fingers. Keri hesitated, not sure she wanted to join this feisty little pixie of a girl. Sophia's family had moved next door only a few days before.

Sophia shaded her eyes, slanted a look of irritation and sighed out impatience. "Come on. I'm Sophia. Come on over and play."

Keri finally did.

Still lost in memory, Keri saw Sophia swinging from a tree branch, her feet dangling six feet from the ground, while Keri's black terrier was frantically circling the tree, barking and leaping up, snapping at her heels.

"Climb up, Keri!" she called. "It's so much fun to swing like this. Come on."

Keri just shook her head. "No way, Sophia."

In their early teens, Sophia's parents purchased a beach house on Brandy Beach. At night, under close stars, Keri and Sophia would sit cross-legged around a campfire, strumming guitars, singing folk rock songs and roasting marshmallows. Those were the best days, the days of easy friendship and parochial dreams.

When they turned seventeen, their conversations were dominated by boy-talk, clothes, painted finger-nails and movie stars. They'd escape to the beach and stroll the edge of the tide, their eyes narrowed, searching for their "boy types."

"I want to marry a rich guy," Sophia said, as they rambled. Her bleached copper hair gleamed in the full flood of summer sun and the big sunglasses made her appear movie-star glamorous. She was already curvaceous and confident. She had an aristocratic air, dancing green eyes, and a petulant little mouth.

"Rich guys tell you what to do all the time," Keri responded. "They have all that money and they can buy any girl they want. So what do they need you for?"

Sophia made an ugly face. "Like you know, Keri."

Keri was a honey blonde with good cheek bones, an attractive diamond-shaped face, long legs and an athletic build.

"I've read magazines, and it's always that way in the movies," Keri added.

Sophia shrugged, imperiously. "Okay, fine, so I'll be the girl they buy. I don't have to be the wife. I can definitely be bought for the right price."

"Okay, so I'll be the wife," Keri said, slinging her long blonde hair. "I'll get all his money when I divorce him."

Sophia lit up. "Yeah! Good! I like it! We'll have it all, Keri. Between the two of us, we'll take him for everything he's got."

They slapped hands, laughed, flirted with the boys and vowed to be friends forever.

As Keri came back to the present, tears were leaking from her eyes and sliding down her cheeks. She wiped them away, even as memories continued to flood in. The faces were so clear, the smiles so distinct, the smells and colors recalled with such crystal clarity, that Keri was swept away again, lost in the emotion of those days.

Keri and Sophia had been coming to Brandy Beach ever since they were 8 years old, even before Sophia's family bought their beach house. When Sophia's family moved to Coventry, Massachusetts, into the house next door to Keri's, the girls quickly became inseparable friends. They played together, then studied together, and finally double-dated together. They became as close as sisters, confiding in each other about everything, including their sexual encounters. They always discussed their boys.

Billy Towne was sweet but not so smart. Kyle was smart but not so sweet. Art was a jock who couldn't kiss worth a damn, and Mike Carse was the love of Sophia's life, until she found out he was having sex with Amanda Perez, a buxom girl who made sure everyone knew she had "caught" Mike.

Keri was in love with Stephen Hanley, the valedictorian of their high school senior class. He was smart, nice-looking and quiet. But Sophia didn't like him.

"He's so boring, Keri. Whenever I see the two of you together, you look so bored. Does he ever talk to you?"

"Yeah, he talks to me," Keri said, defensively. "He's not like Mike Carse, who's always showing off and bragging about what a great football player he is."

"Well, he is a good football player," Sophia retorted, sharply. "And he's built like a super hero."

"Okay, you can have him."

"Okay, so I'll take him. You can have boring, old man Stephen, with his baggy pants, black framed glasses, short hair and skinny neck."

"Okay, so let's double date on Saturday night," Keri said with a challenge. "You'll see me and Stephen in action. I guarantee you will not be bored. We'll be a whole lot sexier than you and your superhero."

Sophia threw her head back, laughing wildly. "You kill me, Keri. I love it. Love it! Let's do it! I've got to see you and skinny neck in action."

When a volley ball slammed into Keri's back, she was jolted from her memory. One of the teenage boys drifted over, apologetically. "Sorry about that. You okay?"

Keri nodded and turned back to stare at the wide, scintillating sea.

After high school, both girls attended Brown University, receiving their Bachelors Degrees in Business Administration. They moved to Boston together and attended U. Mass., Sophia studying for an M.B.A., while Keri received an M.A. in Human Resources.

In college, they shunned the sororities, studied together, dated frequently, shared their dating exploits and adventures, and spent as much of their summers as possible at Sophia's parents' beach house, hosting parties and living on the beach.

And then they were separated when Sophia took a job in New York City. She met a man at the Hedge

Fund where she worked. Instead of commuting home on weekends, Sophia worked hard, played hard and called Keri whenever she had a spare moment to update her on her fast-lane life.

"I'm a loopy, crazy bitch, Keri. If I don't burn out, I'll be the toast of New York. By the way, the guy I'm dating is worth 20 million."

"Does he have a name?"

"Marty."

"Marty? Doesn't sound like a rich name. It sounds like a character in a Muppet's movie," Keri said.

"Well, come to think of it, he does kind of look like a character from a Muppet's movie, but he spends money like it's nothing. Of course he makes like six million a year. He's a gentleman though. He treats me well, buys me stuff and always pays the check. Hey, I ain't gonna complain about that."

Keri laughed. "Yeah, so what's not to like?"

"Do I sound like a mercenary bitch?" Sophia asked.

"Yes, you do, and I'm sure he's madly in love with you, like all the guys are."

"Hey, girl, I bought you the prettiest necklace in the world for your birthday. You're going to love it."

"I can't wait to see it!"

"Now before I say anything else, tell me who you're dating."

"Thomas K. Cooper. He's the head of HR. I'm learning a lot from him."

"Sexy dexy stuff?" Sophia asked.

"Sexy dexy? What is that?" Keri asked.

"Are you sleeping with him?" Sophia asked, pointedly.

"No… "

"Wait until he sees you in that necklace. Look out, baby doll. He'll lunge for you."

"That's a pretty picture. What am I, a quarterback?"

Sophia's voice softened. "I miss you, Keri. I miss your calm energy and your advice. I miss our talks and our secrets. I'm coming home next week. We'll get all caught up. I'll tell you all about this guy and you can tell me what you think. Can't wait to see you."

When the girls turned 27, Sophia got engaged to Richard Nelson Haynes, Jr., the wealthy son of Richard Nelson Haynes, Sr., philanthropist, real estate magnate, and the founding partner of Haynes & Rodgers Investments, one of the largest mutual fund and financial services groups in the world.

Richard Jr. was handsome, intelligent and wealthy, and he would inherit most of his father's wealth and property upon his father's death. Sophia had always been attracted to the tall, dark, rich types, so Keri wasn't surprised when Sophia came home to tell everyone the news.

The wedding was held in New York in September, at a lavish rooftop restaurant with a stunning 360 degree view of the city. Sophia pranced about in her stunning, creamy-white, strapless wedding dress, a sharp gleam of satisfaction in her eyes. Keri had never seen her so pretty and so happy.

Servers in white coats and black bow ties presented silver trays of pheasant, beef, oysters and caviar. They circled and glided, then exited through high silent doorways, disappearing into cool shadows. Crusty brown domes of bread were presented, cut and served with herbed olive oil and French butter. Blooming salads appeared, along with sliced fruit, cheese, and nuts. Wine and champagne flowed. The 10-tiered wedding cake was cut and distributed. The room throbbed with extravagant celebration.

After dinner, toasts were made—the longest and most effusive coming from Richard. His eyes misty with tears, he toasted his "Darling, gorgeous girl," and then she rose and gave him a big, sexy kiss.

A string quartet played lilting waltzes and Sophia and Richard rounded the room, until Richard Sr. cut in. He danced like a master, fluid, airy and controlled. At the last cadence of the waltz, he stopped dramatically, turning Sophia into a spin. She finished breathless.

As the guests all danced, and drank from crystal glasses, and networked, and ate, Sophia linked her arm into Keri's and dragged her off to a private corner. They stared out into a rosy sunset, where purple and orange clouds bloomed and glowed and Manhattan looked like a magic land of glistening towers, glass buildings and secret highways.

"So who's this guy you brought, Keri?" Sophia asked. "He doesn't look like your type."

"I told you about him the last time we were at Brandy Beach," Keri said, trying not to get defensive.

"I know, honey, I've just been so preoccupied with work and the wedding. Is it serious?"

Keri turned to look at Ken. He was a tall, thinning blond, who looked like the physics professor he was, with long arms, stooped shoulders and a distracted manner.

"How old is he?" Sophia asked, not hiding her distress.

"He's forty-two."

Sophia lifted an eyebrow. "Really. I never thought you went for older men."

"We're just dating, Sophia. It's not serious."

Sophia looked at Keri, carefully. She was dressed in a blue, v-necked, charmeuse bridesmaid dress, with a ruffle bow at the waist. "Keri, you've never been serious with anyone, have you? I mean, now that I think of it, I don't think you've ever been serious with any guy, except maybe that guy you dated right after college. What was his name?"

Keri took Sophia's hand. "This is not the day to go there. What did you want to tell me?"

Sophia got animated. "Oh... Richard wants me to be the director of one of his family's philanthropic organizations."

"That sounds exciting! What does it do?"

Sophia thought and then spoke as if she were reciting from a script. "We'll be working to build energetic and tolerant societies whose governments are accountable and open to criticism. They'll be open to debate and correction, and open to the participation of diverse populations."

"Wow. Interesting."

"Okay, so it's not really my thing, but at least I'll be out of that dreadful hedge fund and financial world bullshit. Richard thinks it will show that I'm really a part of the family."

"Sophia, you *are* part of the family."

Sophia leaned in close, whispering conspiratorially. She nodded her head toward Richard Sr., her last dance partner, the distinguished silver-haired man seated at the center table. "Richard Senior is still a bit cold around me. I think he thinks I'm too pushy or from a basically poor family."

Keri studied Sophia, noticing a rare phenomenon. Sophia looked nervous and vulnerable. Keri squeezed her hand. "Don't worry. He'll come around. All your men always come around."

Sophia nibbled on her lower lip. "Yeah... well, I hope so. Sometimes I feel like a fish out of water with these people. They live in another world, Keri."

Keri nudged her forward. "Let's go get some more Champagne."

Keri's attention came back to Brandy Beach. She stood up, stiffly, stretched and yawned. She was unaware of how long she'd been there. The volleyball game was over, the lovers were gone, and the beach crowd had thinned out.

A misty haze had settled over the beach, obscuring the white blister of sun. There was a slight chill in the air. Keri wandered down to the tide line and allowed the spreading cold water to splash around her feet. As she strolled, the oozing sand felt good between her toes. On June 3rd, almost two years after Sophia's wedding, life as Keri knew it changed forever.

Richard Haynes had his pilot's license and he flew a Piper Saratoga airplane to business meetings, to ski vacations, to Caribbean vacations and to New Mexico and Arizona. He had a passion for western art and Wild West antiques.

Sophia accompanied him on a weekend jaunt to Tucson, Arizona to personally view some items at an estate auction: a black, double loop holster & Colt 45, a North West Mounted Police saddle, circa 1876, and various knives, guns and belt buckles. It was a simple flight. The weather was good. The visibility unlimited.

There were two witnesses to the airplane crash. They said the plane just fell from the sky, plummeting to Earth near the Catalina Mountains, northeast of Tucson. Richard and Sophia were both killed.

When Keri heard the news, she felt a burst of shock and pain so severe, she nearly fainted. When her mother asked her what had happened, Keri's voice was hollow, as if she had no air in her lungs.

Sophia was gone, just like that. She had just disappeared forever.

Keri would never forget their last conversation.

"Let's meet in Boston when I get back and catch up on things, Keri," Sophia had said. "I have so many things to tell you. So many crazy things have happened. Like always, baby, I need your advice."

And then Sophia had texted. "Near Arizona. So beautiful. Miss you. Can't wait to see you and talk."

After the funeral, Keri felt completely lost. She kept reaching for her phone to text Sophia. She went shopping and saw the cookies she loved, chocolate pinwheels. She reread emails and texts and watched old videos of the two of them when they were teenagers. Night after night, Keri cried herself to sleep.

Back on Brandy Beach, Keri watched the sun slide down into the cool, gray line of the distant horizon. It was as though a part of her had died along with Sophia. Keri felt as though she were stuck in a doorway, unable to move forward or backward.

Five days after the funeral, Sophia's father called Keri to ask if she'd mind returning to the beach house to look through some of Sophia's personal items that had been sent there by the Haynes family. Neither Sophia's father nor mother could bring themselves to do it. Their pain and grief were too overwhelming. He wanted to have a yard sale, sell the house and move to Florida.

Keri agreed to look at the items, although hesitantly.

After sunset, Keri returned to the house and climbed the stairs to the second floor where Sophia's room had been. Inside was a large cardboard box that the Haynes family had mailed. These were the items that Sophia's father wanted Keri to go through.

Keri poured a glass of wine, drank it down and poured another. She hesitated long minutes before finally peeling off the tape and peering inside. She saw CDs, old phones and adapters, makeup and birthday cards. The deeper Keri explored, the more she found: carefully packed antiques that included a gold Victorian hair pin that had a brooch with scrollwork and gold on the mount. There was a Victorian cameo, set in an ornate gold plated mount, with a highly detailed carved shell cameo of Zeus with his wife, Hera.

Keri smiled. Sophia loved the Victorian period. When they were in college, Sophia often bought vintage Victorian blouses, with white lace and high collars, and brooches and hair combs. She often wore them on first dates to surprise and shock.

Keri snaked her hand down the side of the box, gently moving picture frames, bottles of perfume and a silver candle holder. Then she saw it—a box with what looked like a blue leather diary inside. Keri paused to think. Sophia never wrote in a diary, at least not that she knew of, and she knew everything about Sophia. Maybe it was someone else's?

Intrigued, Keri removed the diary from the box with great care. It didn't look especially old. Keri turned it over and ran the flat of her hand across the rich leather surface. She turned it to the front and touched the creamy diary ribbon that parted the diary about a quarter way. Keri hovered on the edge of curiosity and anxiety. She eased down on the floor, sat cross-legged and gently touched the lock. She jiggled it. It didn't open. Was there a key? On her knees, Keri stuck her head in over the rim of the box, searching for one. No success.

She removed most of the items, feeling and probing, but there was no key. Finally, Keri returned to the diary, again working the lock with her index finger and thumb, struggling to free the latch. No luck. Fighting anxiety, curiosity and mounting impatience, she went to a chest of drawers where she knew Sophia had kept desk things: pens, paper, a stapler. She found a small pair of scissors.

She sat on the edge of the double bed and, using the point of the scissors, she wedged the tip into the raised hinged loop and levered it. She gently pried it open. Keri took in a sharp breath, waiting, staring in nervous anticipation.

Her index finger found the marked ribbon and gently peeled the diary open to the book mark. The writing was Sophia's. Keri focused on the dramatic ornate writing that took up most of the cream-colored page. Yes, definitely Sophia's handwriting.

Keri's wide, eager eyes slid across the page:

What is it about this guy that turns me on? All I know is that I'm in love with him. In love like I've never been before. So crazy, stupid in love that I don't know what I'm going to do. He doesn't know I'm getting married. Can't tell him. I tried. He's the kind of guy who'd walk away if I did. Can't let that happen. Damn, I can't tell Keri either. She'd think I was a complete bitch. So, I'll just keep seeing Ryan whenever I can. Ryan... Ryan... I'm like a stupid high school girl in love. My shrink said to buy a diary and write down private things. Get the demons out in the open in words. Okay, Sophia, just be careful that the demons stay private and on these pages. Just be sure Ryan doesn't find out that you're engaged—at least until I figure out what to do about all this. But I've got to have this guy.

Keri lifted her eyes from the page, staring with a blank, entranced expression. She glanced at the date. The diary entry was written a little more than two years ago.

CHAPTER 2

For a long time, Keri just stared at the diary in shock, unable to absorb what she'd read, unable to fit this information into the story of Sophia's life as she knew it. And then suddenly, an alarm went off. The diary was like a live thing, a threat, a Pandora's box that, once opened, would spew forth poison, pain and lies. She slammed it shut, wanting to entomb the words, the secrets and those private thoughts forever.

Should she burn it? Yes, certainly! If anyone else read it, there was no telling what the truth would do. It would slice at the hearts of both families, bringing un-necessary sorrow after so much sorrow had already been borne.

No. No one else should ever see it. They should never even know about it. After all, it was Sophia's personal thoughts, her personal therapy. It would be a betrayal, a breach of friendship, a disloyalty to read it, or to let anyone else read it. Keri didn't want Sophia remembered that way and she didn't want to remember Sophia that way.

Keri wanted to remember Sophia as the dear friend, the dear sister she had been. So what if Sophia fell in

love with another man? What did it matter now anyway? Richard and Sophia were both dead. That was the
end of it. The awful, final end. The man in the diary
didn't even need to be thought about.

Keri climbed to her feet, still clutching the diary
tightly in her right hand. She clutched it as if she were
trying to squeeze the life from it, to smother it, to kill it.
She snatched up her half-filled glass of wine, slid back
the glass patio doors and stepped out onto the upper
deck. She leaned into the wooden railing, gazing out
into the dark sea. Far in the distance she saw flash
bulbs of lightning and heard the roaring sea at near high
tide. She tasted the salty air and wished she had never
found the damn diary; wished she'd never been asked
to return to the beach house; wished Sophia had never
taken that plane trip to Arizona.

Keri shut her eyes so tightly they hurt, willing herself to banish the old conversations, the teenage giggles,
the discussed ambitions and the boys and the sex talk
she and Sophia had shared.

Then her thoughts stalled, as she mentally groped for
a different route of thinking, an alternate pathway to
explain an anomaly. She and Sophia had never kept secrets from each other, or so she believed. They trusted
each other completely. So why had Sophia kept this
secret lover from Keri? Because she thought she'd be
judged? Because Keri would think less of her? It
didn't add up. Sophia had told Keri aspects of her love
life that would have shocked most people. Sophia had
often been wild and experimental. She often said that
she wanted to live life to its fullest and that included
having sexual experiences with a variety of men.

"I've got to try things, at least once, Keri. Otherwise, I'm going to walk around moody and bitchy, feeling like I'm left out of the party. Needless to say, I do not want to be left out of any party. If anything, I want to start one."

Even after Sophia had met Richard, she dated Frankie Ocean, a professional gambler who swaggered about, wearing expensive suits and a cowboy hat tilted back from his forehead, so every woman could see his large, pool-blue eyes.

But Sophia was not in love with him. "He's a carnival ride, Keri. That's it, and he's not an especially good carnival ride at that. But those eyes, Keri. God help me, those eyes just pull me back in."

And then one day, Frankie Ocean was gone and Sophia declared that Richard Haynes was the one.

"He's handsome, rich and he's good in bed, Keri. What else can you ask for in a man?"

"You do love him, don't you?"

"Oh sure," Sophia had said, with a flippant flick of her hand. "Of course. I mean why not?"

Keri pushed away from the railing, as a realization struck. She cast about for some old conversation she and Sophia had once had. It was about love and falling in love. The conversation had taken place about three years back, as they were strolling along the beach one hot, summer day. Sophia had just met Richard, and when Keri met him, she thought he had that "I own the world" kind of self-assurance that Sophia often was attracted to.

"I don't know if I could ever really love a man," Sophia had said. "I mean, I love their bodies and the macho stuff and everything, but I can't say I've ever really been in love with one of them. Have you, Keri? Oh, yes, you were in love with that Justin guy, weren't you, that guy you met at your first job out of college? Yeah, I think you really did love him."

Keri did love him, Justin Powell. He was a short, well-built, sandy-haired man, who'd been on a wrestling team in college. He was in the sales department of the cable company she worked for. Justin made Keri laugh. He knew more jokes than a bartender and he told them well. On every date, he'd try out new jokes he'd heard, performing all the voices—including the women's voices—so well that he had her doubled over, almost sick with laughter.

Justin was also kind and thoughtful in small ways, holding doors for her, bringing her flowers for no reason, and complimenting her on the experimental new hairstyles that Sophia convinced her to try.

"Yes, I did love Justin," Keri had answered.

"But he married that rich girl... what was her name?"

"Kathy... I don't remember her last name," Keri said.

"Well... I guess he wasn't right for you."

Keri had hesitated, the hurtful memory still fresh.

"I never knew why we broke it off," Keri said. "One day he just said he thought we should break up. He was never very clear about it. I kept asking if I'd done something. He said, no. He said it was him. He said he was the problem, which just meant that he was tired of me. So we broke up and I cried for a few days."

A burst of wind tossed Keri's hair and brought her back to the Now. She raked a blonde strand from her eye. She drained the last of her wine and lay down on a chaise, fighting a mounting grief. They were all gone now, just shadows and memory, Sophia, Richard, Frankie, Justin. Sophia was gone forever, and she was only 29 years old.

Keri grew aware that she was still gripping the diary so stiffly that her fingers hurt. It seemed stuck to her hand, as if held there by a powerful glue. The longer Keri sat there, the more brittle she became, the more her will power weakened, the more she knew she'd never have the strength of will to destroy the diary. It was, after all, a kind of last will and testament of Sophia Anderson, her wild and wonderful friend.

The humid night wind stirred across Keri's face and she presented it to the sky, silently sending Sophia a prayer of thanks for her friendship and love. Keri prayed to God that he'd absolve her of any sins, although Keri was sure God was happy to have Sophia around, just for the fun of it. Sophia the adventurer. Sophia the aggressor. Sophia the impulsive.

Keri sat up abruptly, as a thought struck. If Keri had died and Sophia had found Keri's diary, what would she have done? No question. She would have read it. Every word. She wouldn't have even thought about it.

Keri the quiet. Keri the careful. Keri the righteous.

More thoughts crowded in. If Sophia's diary held her lover's secret, then what other secrets lay buried on that rich creamy paper? What other discoveries about her friend were waiting in that diary?

Maybe Keri didn't really know Sophia at all. Maybe Sophia had only pretended to bare her soul when, in fact, she'd kept much of herself hidden away and out of reach. Perhaps that hidden self was candidly and boldly revealed in the diary. If anyone should read it, surely Keri should. Who else? Maybe Sophia would have wanted her to read it. Of course she would. The last thing Sophia had said to her was "I have so many things to tell you. So many crazy things have happened. Like always, baby, I need your advice."

Keri got up and worked the kinks out of her neck. The diary was still in her hand, a pulsing, taunting thing. Feeling exhausted, she went back inside, and closed and locked the glass doors.

Thank God she'd taken a few days off from work. In the past few days, she'd given her job little thought, aside from absently monitoring the texts and emails she'd received.

Keri was the HR manager for Qualico Tech, a company specializing in producing corporate security software and maintenance. The company also partnered with their clients, documenting, identifying, isolating and reporting on any suspicious activity, a daunting task in this day and age of international hackers.

Keri was the liaison between the HR department and the company's administration, keeping everyone up-to-date on rules and regulations, as well as implementing HR procedures and offering advice on corporate policy. She was also responsible for new hires, a challenging task, since qualified candidates were being recruited by similar companies all over the world.

Keri went downstairs to the kitchen, scrambled two eggs, buttered some toast and whipped up a simple salad. While she ate, the diary sat beside her on the kitchen island counter, and it seemed to wink at her.

She was tempted several times to seize it and start reading. She resisted.

After she'd cleaned up the kitchen, Keri checked her phone for messages, emailed the colleagues whose queries couldn't wait, and then called her mother. The conversation was simple, mostly about how hot it already was and it was only the second week in June, and how Keri was holding up. Keri said she was doing fine. Keri's brother, Dwight, was visiting from Columbus, Ohio and they too spoke briefly, catching Keri up on her 4-year-old nephew and her brother's job as a restaurant manager. Keri's parents were divorced. Keri seldom spoke to her father and hadn't seen him in years.

After hanging up, Keri showered, slipped on cotton pajamas and crawled into Sophia's double bed. Her subtle scent still hung in the room. Roses de Chloé was her favorite perfume, smelling of roses, Bergamot, and white musk.

Keri switched off the light, pulled the sheet up to her chin and settled back into the pillow. She heard the soft rasping of the sea, heard the tick of a clock somewhere down the hall, heard the low hum of the air-conditioner. Sophia's diary was lying on the nightstand beside her. Keri glanced over. Was it glowing in the dark? Of course not.

Just as Keri was drifting off to sleep, a thought stood up inside her and demanded attention. She snapped awake.

Who was this Ryan, anyway? How and where had he and Sophia met? What happened to him? The only diary entry she'd read was dated August 2nd, almost two years before Sophia's wedding. Were there more entries? Must be.

Keri sat up, half-covered by a blanket, and propped herself up with pillows. She heaved out an audible sigh of resignation, switched on the light and reached for the diary. Yes, if the roles were reversed, Sophia would have definitely read Keri's diary.

Keri opened it and found the first page. It was dated June 15th, three months before Sophia's marriage to Richard.

My shrink said to write out my feelings. Anything that comes to mind. Well, guess what? Nothing comes to mind. Well, okay, one thing comes to mind. Richard and I had a fight last night. He wanted sex. I didn't. Why? He's a fast, selfish lover. Anyway, I didn't want to. Okay, so I'm a selfish lover too.

I can't get that other guy out of my head. No, I'm not saying who that other guy is, just in case somebody happens to find this diary. I'm keeping it locked and hidden in various places around the apartment. Richard's apartment is so damn huge, with so many rooms and closets and nooks and crannies, I don't think he'll ever find it. I'll lock it and keep the key with me at all times.

Okay, anyway, I'm in love... what do you think about that, shrink? I've never really been in love before. Richard? No. I like Richard and we're going to be married, but I'm not crazy for him like I am for this guy. Okay, so I'm a selfish bitch. I know I am. I don't give a damn. I'm writing all this stuff in this diary because I can call myself and everybody else names because I'm the only one who's going to know. Okay, anyway, I met the guy recently. On the beach... Brandy Beach. He took my breath away.

Keri sat up, rigid. Brandy Beach? Two years ago? Keri and Sophia were together on Brandy Beach for a week at about that same time. Keri thought about it. Yes, she remembered. Sophia had been so distracted by plans for the wedding. She had been on the phone constantly, talking to vendors, Richard and her friends. She was overly excited and she drank more wine than usual.

Keri's eyes gradually lowered on the diary and she read on.

...I don't know his name yet. But I will. He runs along the beach every day. What a body! He's all bronzed, tall and broad. Just my type, but then what good-looking guy isn't my type?

Two days ago, I saw him coming and I thought, "Hey, what the hell?" I shot up from the beach and ran after him...behind him. I couldn't keep up, because the guy was running at an impossible pace. I thought he was trying out for the Olympics or something. But I kept going, huffing and puffing like a freight train.

Then he sensed me and glanced back over his shoulder. I waved to him. He slowed down, curious. He probably thought we'd met or something. Anyway, I caught up to him.

"Hi, I'm Sophia," I said, extending my hand.

He looked at it, then at me. His sea-gray eyes looked sad, but they were so alluring, so captivating.

"Do I know you?" he asked.

"Sure," I said, with assurance. "I'm Sophia, we just met."

He studied me. I could tell he'd never met a girl like me before. At that point, I couldn't tell if that was good or bad.

So I said, "Can I jog along with you?"

Yes, he was a gentleman. I could tell he didn't want me to, but he nodded and said yes.

Now I was intrigued. Most guys I come on to can't wait until they can kiss me and go for my tits. Not this guy.

So we ran together for awhile. When we stopped and I thought my heart was going to explode both from the run and from being close to him, he said, "You're out of shape."

I said, "Can I train with you?"

I wanted to laugh. He didn't know what to say.

His eyes quickly slid over me. "Yeah, okay."

I said, "Do you eat lunch?"

He said, "Sometimes."

"Today?" I asked, being my usual forward self.

Like I said, he was shy, tall, broad, blond and he had a boot camp haircut. He turned from me and squinted at the sea.

"Yeah...Okay."

So there you go, diary oh girl. I'm in love. I'm gonna have this guy one way or the other. Hell, if he doesn't have much money, I'll marry Richard and keep this guy on the side for good sex.

Okay, that's it for today, diary. I've got wedding calls to make. September will be here before I know it and I'll be an old married girl. But I'm not married yet.

Keri stared into the middle distance with unfocused eyes. Maybe Sophia was right. Maybe Keri would have judged her. She sounded so mercenary. So cold and selfish. She was engaged to be married, and she sounded like a high school girl going after a football player. If she didn't love Richard, then why did she marry him?

Keri turned the page and read on.

CHAPTER 3

Keri noticed that Sophia's handwriting was clearer than her usual rushed script, when she often left out commas and didn't always cross her t's. The dots for the i's were usually far from the intended letter, or left out entirely.

In the diary, Sophia wrote with care and precision, seemingly enjoying the process of documenting her thoughts and emotions.

I'm going to call this my "Summer Diary," because when I'm finished filling all these pages, summer will be over, I'll be married, I'll fire my shrink and I'll toss this thing into the fire. For now, I'm having fun. I can write any damned thing I want and nobody will ever know it or see it. I can be crude or selfish, sexy or crazy. Who cares? It's only me talking to me, and when it's all over—into the fire, baby, and forever forgotten.

My shrink is right, it's very freeing to write down whatever you feel. Whatever you think. It's like being in a hot air balloon or skydiving or being in bed with a sexy guy who absolutely sends you into spasms of ecstasy.

Okay, I feel wonderfully wicked. I went to lunch with the guy—oh what the hell—his name is Ryan. No last name, though. We ate hamburgers and drank dark beer at the Main Street Café. He's quiet, doesn't talk much, but wow, he is the sexiest man I've ever met. He oozes with it, but he seems to keep it inside, which <u>really</u> turns me on. Never met a guy like him. He's like an unopened treasure chest, and girl oh girl, would I like to ride on top of that chest!

He says he doesn't like to talk about himself. So I said... now get this bullshit, "Neither do I." Ha! So there were periods of time we didn't talk at all. Imagine me not talking! That was okay. I loved just being with him...just looking at him. He is good for my eyes. I noticed so many other women staring at him, their eyes all hot with invitation. Eat your hearts out, girls! He's mine.

He's a soldier...at first he would only say he was in the Army. Only once he slipped and said he was a special ops soldier, but he was vague about it. Said he was home for awhile but that he may have to leave at any time. Guess what, friend diary, I began to feel an urgency—like I had to move fast or he'd be gone. So I tried to set up another date...subtly of course. I was afraid I'd chase him away. He took my number and said he'd call. He wouldn't give me his number. Is he married? I don't give a damn. I've got to see him again. So, I hope he calls. Meanwhile, the wedding plans are taking up all my time. I know, I know, what a wicked bitch I am. Bye for now, diary, my new friend.

Keri impatiently flipped around through the diary, finding much of the same. Nearly every entry was about Ryan. Ryan this and Ryan that. Ryan is the love of my life. Ryan is a mystery. Ryan won't talk about himself. Ryan won't make a pass at me or kiss me.

Keri thumbed the pages until she came to the last entry. She had to know what happened. How it had ended.

To Keri's surprise, Sophia had not finished filling all the pages. There were at least 10 near the back that were completely blank. The last entry was written on September 5, exactly one week before Sophia's September 12th wedding.

Keri's eyes were heavy and itchy from fatigue, but she read on anyway, unable to stop.

I feel so low...I'm getting married in a week and I feel like hell. People think I'm so confident and self-assured... well I'm not. I just come on strong so nobody will know how scared and messed up I am most of the time. I growl and roar like a panther to keep myself propped up—to keep the demons away—those awful dark demons that come in the middle of the night or when I think about my life and I don't know what the hell I'm doing. Hell, I've never known what the hell I'm doing. Does anybody? Yeah, Keri does. Keri always knows what she's doing. But I wonder sometimes about her. She's so damn cautious about everything. She always wants to do the good thing, the right thing. She seems scared to take chances or try something new. I can't imagine her ever going on any kind of adventure that would take her out of herself. Maybe it was because of the divorce. Maybe after her father left her mother, something in Keri never fully healed or something. Well, listen to me, the bitch psychologist, who hated Psych 101. I never liked facing the truth about myself. That's why I decided to go into therapy. That's why I bought this diary.

Truth be told... and that's why I'm writing in this thing... I wish I was more like Keri. She's kind and non-judgmental. She's good and true and that's why I love her and always have loved her. She's the dearest friend anyone could have. I always considered Keri to be my true sister.

I was never as good to Keri as she has been to me. I don't have the depth of feeling she has. I'm always chasing the next happiness, the next thrill, the next escape from having to face the darkness I feel inside.

That's what I told my shrink, Ms. Eberstark. She's as stoic and as hard as a 4-star general. Most of the time she just sits there staring at me with those big bulging eyes of hers, lightly tapping a pencil on her notepad, and sometimes not lightly tapping. Have I made any progress with her? Who the hell knows?

Anyway, Ryan is gone, and I'm low as hell. I feel like I've been kicked in the stomach. He left me. Imagine any man leaving me? Never happened before. Men always wanted me. Couldn't wait to get me into bed. Not Ryan. I thought, maybe he was gay. I mean, I'm not bad to look at. Hell, I'm a good looking chick! Come on! Most men think I'm hot.

I told Ryan I was in love with him—but then I'd told him that so many times. He never said he loved me. He broke my heart. He wouldn't sleep with me. Said it wouldn't be fair to me. He said he didn't love me that way. "That way?!" What the hell did that mean? So I asked him, "Well, how do you love me, then?"

He just stared at me with those wounded eyes of his. I asked him to say something to me. I begged him to talk to me. I told him I would go anywhere with him and do anything for him if he just said he wanted me, if he just said he loved me. I would have married him right there on the spot if he'd asked me. Yes, I was in love, and I knew I was in love. The first time for me. I would have done anything for him... I ached for him. I was so in love with him. I said, "Ryan, why don't you love me?"

His eyes clouded over. Then he said...in such a soft voice that I could hardly hear him, he said, "My wife killed herself when I was away... on a mission...back in April. She took pills. It had been a top secret, high-priority mission. No contact with anyone once we departed. We were gone for almost two months. I didn't know she was dead for days. When I got back to the States, her mother had had her cremated."

I stared into his gloomy eyes and tried to make a connection, but I could see it was hopeless. There was nothing there but pain and loss. It was terrible. He was lost and I had lost him. What a damned shame. I wanted to say something to help him. I wanted to do something to bring him back to life. I wanted to love him, and make him love me. I felt so damn helpless and defeated. The one guy I truly loved and he was going to go away and I'd never see him again.

He said he was leaving. He didn't tell me it was for another secret mission, because he wouldn't discuss it, but I knew from his tone of voice, and from what he had told me about his wife, what that meant. He didn't seem to care if he lived or died.

I still hadn't told him I was engaged and getting married in a week. Was I awful for not telling him? Yes! Was it fair to Richard that I was so much in love with another man and I hadn't broken off our engagement? Yes! Is it fair for me to marry Richard? Was it fair that whenever I saw Ryan, I felt depressed and panicky and cold and distant toward Richard? Like I said, I'm not such a nice person. I'm selfish and stubborn, just like my father always said I was.

Ryan thanked me for being his friend.

His friend!? I was so emotional, I couldn't speak.

His eyes were wide, vacant and unblinking. I don't know what is going on in this crazy world. Sometimes I think we're all in metaphorical strait jackets pretending to be normal.

I know he may not come back. It was the things he didn't say that scared me. Aren't all those secret missions dangerous? Of course, and the public never hears about them. I'll never know if he lives or dies. I threw my arms around him and begged him not to go. I begged him to love me... to marry me. I was a crying, whining out-of-her mind crazy woman.

I watched him leave me...walk away along the beach—yes, into the sunset. How dramatic and theatrical. How terrible. I feel sick. I feel dead. How can I present a happy face at the wedding? Over 200 guests will be there—politicians, hedge fund managers, Richard's family, Richard's father, who doesn't like me or approve of me. I guess he's one of the few people who can see me for what I am: a deceitful, shallow bitch. Ha, ha. Can you blame him, Sophia? Can you blame him for not wanting you to marry his son?

Worst of all, Keri will be there, of course, my maid of honor. She knows me better than I know myself. Will she notice how utterly sad and miserable I am? No. I'll put on the best damned happy face you ever *saw. I'll be ecstatically happy and contented. I'll be a good wife to Richard. He deserves that. We, as a couple, deserve that.*

But what if Ryan returns and somehow gets in touch with me? What the hell will I do then? I'll run to him in a New York minute.

So this is it, diary. My relationship with Ryan is over and so our relationship, too, will be terminated forever. I will not write anymore. Summer is over and I'll be married in a week. I plan to be the prettiest, most cheerful bride ever. No one will ever know about Ryan or about my love for him. I'll probably never know whether he survived the mission or was killed. Oh God, it hurts to be in love. Hurts so bad. I will never see my true love again.

And me? Well, I'm going to live happily ever after, of course. Isn't that what happens in all the fairy tales?

Keri slowly sank down into the bed, tears streaming down her face. She reached over and switched off the light and lay there, sobbing, the diary lying on her chest, her right hand resting on it, as if to touch some essence of Sophia's spirit.

Anguish and regret gushed out of her and she turned and pressed her face deeply into the pillow, weeping uncontrollably, her body shaking, racked with misery.

At some point, Keri was exhausted and fell into a deep sleep. She dreamed that she was running across the front of the diary—a massive blue leather surface like a beach—and that she was being chased by Ryan, a big imposing man who had no face, just blank bare flesh. Terrified, she screamed out to Sophia for help. The turgid sea boiled and roared in toward her. Waves crashed in and pounded the beach. Keri's legs grew heavy, and her feet struggled for traction across the suddenly glue-like surface. She glanced over her shoulder and saw Ryan closing in on her, his arms outstretched, ready to grab her.

Keri jerked awake and shot up, her chest heaving, eyes wide with shock. She blinked around the room, slowly coming back to reality, taking in deep breaths. Morning light was leaking in from beneath the drawn balcony curtains, and she heard the distant static of the sea. Still trembling, she glanced at the clock. The red digital letters said 7:42am.

The diary lay beside her on the bed. Keri stared at it, as if it were a murder weapon, an enemy.

Why had she read the damned thing? Why? Keri threw the sheet back, covering the diary, and sat up. She rubbed her tired eyes, thinking, remembering, struggling to push the diary words from her mind, shutting her eyes and shaking her head as if to shake away that awful dream.

After a shower, she dressed in a T-shirt, loose-fitting jeans and sandals. She piled her hair up with a clip, and went downstairs to the kitchen, turned on the TV and listened to the news, sipping coffee, checking her phone for emails and texts, eating Cheerios and a granola bar. While cleaning up, she decided to leave the house as soon as she could. It held too many memories and, now, too many ghosts. She just wanted to get out of there, forget the whole nightmare and get back to her life. She'd even forgotten what day it was. Oh, yes, it was Wednesday. She didn't have to be back in Boston until Monday morning.

Back upstairs in the bedroom, Keri opened the glass doors and stepped out on the balcony to view the beach and ocean. How many times had she and Sophia stood next to each other on this balcony? Here, they'd smoked their first cigarettes, drunk tequila, waved at boys and talked for infinite hours about life, school and their dreams.

Dark clouds were stalking the eastern sky and a cool wet wind came in bursts, scattering sand and pushing against the seagulls as they dropped and banked, struggling to find alternate routes over the beach.

Keri released a deep sigh. Thank God she'd found the diary before Sophia's parents had. Keri knew Sophia's father well, and she suspected he was aware that his daughter possessed certain wild eccentricities. If the box contained any unpleasant surprises, he was confident that Keri would find them and keep them to herself.

Keri knew she had to spend a few more hours at the house, taking an inventory of the remaining objects and emailing Sophia's parents the list. She was sure they'd want to keep most of the personal items, but she'd ask for the hairpins, some jewelry with sentimental value, and maybe the silver candle holders.

Off in the hazy distance, she saw a jogger advancing up the beach, gradually coming into clearer view. She straightened, suddenly alert. It was an impulsive thought—a silly thought—that absorbed her. What if it was Ryan? Sophia had met him on the beach. *He* was jogging. Keri watched, rapt, waiting as he slowly came into focus, wearing white running shorts and a blue T-shirt.

But this jogger was short and overweight, with long black hair and a kind of lumbering stride. He was not a natural runner or athlete. And as he passed, Keri saw that he was only in his early 20s. Her shoulders sank a little.

She mumbled to herself. "Don't go there, Keri. Don't!"

Keri spent the next two hours inventorying the boxed items and keying them into her laptop. After she'd emailed Sophia's father the list, she went over to the bed, threw back the sheet and saw the diary, looking back at her. It seemed to glow and pulse, like a throbbing heart.

"What am I going to do with you?" she whispered.

For a minute or so, she stood with crossed arms, staring at it, pondering it, drawn to it. Ignoring it, she went about straightening the room and packing her blue wheeled duffle bag. If traffic was light, she'd be home in Boston by 5pm. Maybe Mitchell was around. Mitchell Farmer was a guy she'd dated for awhile. After their relationship stalled, unable to go to the next level, they decided being friends worked just fine. Mitchell was nice enough, and he was good-looking enough, and he was successful enough—he was a software engineer—but Keri didn't feel there was a solid romantic connection. All the pieces were there but, somehow, those pieces just didn't quite fit together.

Nonetheless, Mitchell was a good friend and a great conversationalist, and he had passion for his work.

Before she stripped the bed, she placed the diary on the night stand. It couldn't stay there, though. She'd have to pack it in her bag, or she'd have to destroy it.

Gathering strength, she seized the diary and went downstairs. Her plan was to tear out each page, toss it into a large, cast iron pot and set it on fire. Then she'd take the ashes out to the beach and scatter them into the wind. That seemed right. It would be a kind of sacred offering, like scattering one's ashes across the sea or on the quiet surface of a pond, or high up into the mountains.

Keri tugged the cast iron pot from underneath the kitchen cabinet and set it on the stove. She hesitated again, and then finally grabbed the diary. She opened it and, with firm concentration, was about to rip out a page when a line caught her. She saw her name. She nosed down to read it.

Keri never knew I slept with Justin Powell...

Keri froze. Her face grew hot with swift anger. She read on, her eyes galloping across the page.

I sort of came on to him... and he let me. It was playful at first and then...well, we drove to his apartment. When it was over, I didn't feel anything. We didn't talk much. It was all just hormones and lust. It didn't mean anything. At least it didn't mean anything to me. He had a good body and he was an okay lover, but he wasn't my type. I couldn't face Keri for a couple of days after that, though. I told her I was sick and I didn't want to give her my germs. Why the hell do we do the things we do?

When Justin broke up with Keri, I never felt so cheap in my life. Then he called me and said he wanted more of me. Ha! More of me? No thanks.

I was going to tell Keri all this just a few weeks ago, because we never held back any secrets from each other, but I just couldn't do it. I know Justin was one of the only guys she really fell for and I just screwed it up. I hope writing this down will help me exorcize this demon.

Okay, diary, I can't go on now. I'm starting to feel disgusted at myself again.

In a sudden rage, Keri slung the diary away. It slammed against the wall and dropped to the floor with a thud, face down, its pages spread out awkwardly. Keri's breath came fast. She closed her eyes and ran a hand over her warm forehead. When her eyes finally opened, she glowered at the diary, wanting to destroy it. Annihilate it. Rewind to the day when she'd discovered it, and set it on fire. What else was in that damned thing?

CHAPTER 4

All afternoon, Keri sat on a low beach chair, absorbed in the diary. She wore jeans, a light yellow sweatshirt, and a Boston Red Socks baseball cap. It was overcast, a cloudy canopy, but the wind had died down and the beach was mostly deserted, the sea calm. It was nearly 7pm when she finally finished reading all the diary entries and, by then, the sun had cracked open the lumpy clouds and was shooting golden rays onto the beach and the sea.

Keri closed the diary and laid it on the sand. She stood up, gazing out into the gray, moving sea. She felt pressed down by disappointment, depression and loss. It was as though she'd lost Sophia twice: once in the plane crash and once because of the wounding entries in the diary. But it wasn't so much the words and the revelations that hurt—although they did hurt—it was Sophia's lack of sensitivity and loyalty that hurt her the most.

Sophia was not the friend—not the woman—Keri had believed in and trusted. The diary revealed a selfish, egotistical and callous person. Was this the friend she'd known for over 20 years? Had Keri been so naïve or myopic, or just so plain stupid that she hadn't been able to see Sophia for what she truly was?

Would a true friend, a true fiancée, betray the ones she supposedly loved with such disrespect and blatant deceit? Had Sophia ever considered the ramifications of her selfish actions if she'd been found out—what her actions would do to the people who loved her?

Well, she *had* been found out.

Keri mourned not only a friend that was physically dead, but also a friendship that was spiritually and psychically dead. In the end, their relationship had been a deception, a fraud. Now that Sophia was dead, a confrontation was impossible, and Keri was left paralyzed with anger and grief, without any opportunity to release the pain she felt knifing into her heart, leaving an open wound.

And then came the pangs of guilt for her own inability to forgive Sophia for an event that had happened so long ago. Keri made excuses. After all, Justin obviously wasn't worth her love anyway. Maybe Sophia was lonely? Maybe she was jealous? Maybe she had a low opinion of herself and she just couldn't help it?

As Keri strolled the beach, picking up shells and kicking at seaweed, she recalled another diary entry that had upset her.

Keri has always been so cautious about everything— so careful. So many times I wanted to shake her and say, "For God's sake, take a risk, Keri. Have an adventure. Step out of your comfort zone now and then."

A tall male jogger approached, looming out of the ocean mist into sunshine. He wore a hooded sweatshirt and a red bathing suit. His bare feet splashed through the edge of the rushing tide, as sandpipers flitted away around him. He was plugged into his phone, his head swaying to music. As he passed, he didn't look Keri's way.

She glanced back to see him fade into the glare of sunlight. Could that have been Ryan? Keri pivoted and shaded her eyes to watch him, now a dark speck drifting further away. She suddenly felt an odd, indignant contempt, as Sophia's diary-words echoed cruelly in her head. *"For God's sake, take a risk, Keri. Have an adventure. Step out of your comfort zone now and then."*

She headed briskly down the beach, agitated by anger, not noticing when the sky freshened and sunlight began to glance and glitter off the water, warming the air. She felt flushed. She unzipped her sweatshirt and rolled up her jeans so she could walk through the cool water.

Keri's pace quickened even more as her mind quickened. Had Sophia truly loved Ryan, or was he just some unattainable goal that gnawed away at her ego because he wouldn't bow down and worship her the way most men did? Was he just "the one who got away," or could he have been her true love? Sophia had written so tenderly about the man. Nearly every entry included a deep longing, or a warm feeling, or a declaration of love. Those were not the sentiments of the Sophia she'd known, the sarcastic, carefree girl with the biting wit and the need to shock.

So who was the real Sophia? The stained glass window of bold colors and personality she saw? Or was there a subtlety to her that only Ryan noticed?

Keri felt snappish and disoriented. Too many things had happened too fast. She stopped walking, turned, and stared out at the agitated surf.

And Ryan. Who was he, and what had happened to him? Did he survive the last mission? Did he try to get in touch with Sophia after he returned to the United States? Her head dropped in despair as she realized again: she'd never known the real Sophia. Perhaps Ryan had. Perhaps Ryan had seen something tender beneath the bravura and the façade of self-confidence and control.

Keri reached down and splashed water on her forearms. Maybe her friends and family had been too close to Sophia to glimpse the nuanced, the vulnerable, the painful truth. Maybe Keri's and Sophia's friends had seen only a dazzling shadow of her, while Ryan had seen the true, enchanted image—the real Sophia.

Keri stared at a flock of seagulls gliding through the sunset sky. Sophia obviously had a talent for guarding and hiding her real self from the world. But if she'd been touched by love, maybe that love had opened her up to new vistas of feeling she'd never experienced before, vistas she hadn't even known existed inside her. Real love can do that, can't it? Keri had never personally experienced it, but she believed it could happen.

Maybe in that one, short summer, Ryan had gotten closer to Sophia than anyone else ever had. Maybe he could help Keri see the true Sophia. Maybe Ryan's insight could help Keri slough off her disappointment and anger and hurt. Maybe he could tell Keri things about Sophia that would help her understand and forgive her friend.

Keri stopped, hovering on the edge of an absurd thought. Should she try to find Ryan? The thought gave her a sudden electric thrill. She stared down into the sand, seeing the eroded ruins of an old sandcastle that had been punished by the hostile tide.

"Ryan," she said aloud, the sound instantly swallowed up by the beat of waves striking the beach.

Keri circled the space, gently kicking at the sand castle, mentally kicking at "what ifs." What if he'd been killed? What if he'd moved away? What if he was married and didn't want to remember Sophia? What if Sophia hadn't revealed the whole truth about the relationship because there was some awful truth about him?

And how could she possibly ever locate Ryan without a last name? Sophia had never once mentioned it.

In an instant, Keri knew the decision had already been made: She had to find a way to track down and speak to this man. She whirled and marched back across the beach to where she'd left her chair and the diary. There had to be clues in the diary—had to be phrases that could help her find Ryan. At the very least, she could discover what had happened to him.

A half hour later, Keri slid behind the wheel of her blue Ford Focus and drove to the nearest Starbucks. She ordered a café latte and a scone and found a seat near the plate glass window that looked out onto Main Street. It was nearly 8:20 and, as daylight faded, the streetlight globes flickered on, spreading amber light onto the sidewalks. Keri opened her laptop, reached for her phone and called her friend Mitchell. He was smart. He'd know how to find Ryan.

"Are you back home?" Mitchell asked, in his usual droll, flat voice.

"No. Actually, I'm going to stay another day or two."

"How do you feel, Keri?"

"Bleh... Do you have a minute?"

"Yeah... I'm still at work, coding a patch to some new security module. A big bank we both know so well just got hacked into again."

"Sometimes I wish we could go back to the horse and buggy days, before cars, TV and computers," Keri said.

"Then you wouldn't be calling me. You'd have to send a telegram or hire the Pony Express or something."

Keri got right to it. "Mitchell, I need your advice on something. I'm trying to find someone and all I have is a first name. Was in the military. Once lived in Brandy Beach."

"What branch of the military?" Mitchell asked.

Keri quickly thumbed to the page. "Okay... almost there. Special ops."

"You looking for a guy? A soldier?"

"Well, yeah," and then Keri quickly added, "he was a friend of Sophia's. I want to find him and tell him what happened."

Keri heard her voice. It didn't sound convincing.

"Okay... Well, special ops could mean the Navy SEALs, Army Rangers, Delta Force or Special Forces. Which branch?"

"I don't know."

"Do you have a phone number?" Mitchell asked.

"No."

"No last name?"

"No."

"Name search sites require a last name, Keri."

"I know. I've been trying."

"Look, Keri, Ryan is a very common name in Massachusetts."

"I know, Mitchell. I don't know what else to do. I thought you might have an idea I haven't thought of."

"I was going to suggest government agencies for the military, but you have to have his full name. Also, you probably need his date of birth and, of course, the branch of service."

Keri sighed into the phone. "All I have is what I've told you."

"Do you have a photo of him?"

"No."

"And why do you want to find this guy again?"

Keri hesitated. "It doesn't matter, Mitchell, it was a bad idea anyway. Just forget it. I'll see you in a couple of days."

"Okay, hey, whatever. Let's hook up when you get back."

After Keri hung up, she leafed through the diary again, dispirited, searching for any clue she might have overlooked. A moment later, she was turning the last few empty pages when something caught her eye. She hadn't examined the last few pages very carefully. She'd just flipped through them, quickly, believing they were all blank. On the second-to-last page Sophia had jotted something down in pencil.

345 Mercury Lane. 12:30. Friday. Ryan.

She sat up, excited. She quickly keyed in the address and the location, Brandy Beach.

Ka-Bling! There was a Mercury Lane in Brandy Beach! Keri did a swift map check. Mercury Lane was only about a mile away!

She drained the latte, shut her laptop and shoved it into her bag.

As she drove away from the curb and merged into light traffic, she wondered what she would say to Ryan if he answered the door. She had no idea.

CHAPTER 5

Mercury Lane was a quiet, tree-lined street. Its simple bungalows had unobstructed views of the ocean, dune fences and distant secluded beach houses. With her hands resting on top of the steering wheel, Keri eased along slowly, searching the street-side mailboxes, finally spotting a green one with the address 345 printed on it.

She stopped, pulled over and parked at the curb, noticing a weathered old car parked in the narrow driveway. There was a light on in the picture window. Encouraged, she pulled a breath, took off the Boston Red Sox cap, flipped on the dome light and finger-combed her flattened hair in the rearview mirror. She smoothed on some light pink lipstick, made an ugly face when she noticed her small, sleepy eyes and pale face, and then she glanced out at the little house.

It was a welcoming bungalow with a charming gabled roof, a freshly mowed lawn and a generous front porch, complete with a porch swing.

Keri switched off the dome light, gathered her courage and climbed out, wishing she'd worn a more attractive outfit. What kind of an impression would she make wearing loose jeans, a faded old college sweat-shirt, and flip flops? Whatever.

She started up the front walk to the three wooden steps and paused, gathering her thoughts. As she mounted the stairs to the porch, she heard a TV. She lightly knocked on the frame of the screen door.

No answer.

She knocked louder. The TV went silent. A beach breeze stirred Keri's hair while she stood stiffly, hardly breathing.

A woman appeared—a chubby, middle-aged woman with short, curly, bleached-blonde hair and a harassed expression. She squinted out at Keri. She wore a simple yellow-patterned sun dress and she was clutching a can of soda in her right hand.

"Yeah? Who is it?"

Keri cleared her throat. "Hi... I hope I'm not bothering you. Actually, I'm looking for someone who used to live here and I thought... well, I thought he might still live here or you might know where I can find him."

The woman's dark eyes filled with suspicion. Her thin mouth formed an O. "Who?"

"A man named Ryan."

"Ryan who?"

Keri stammered. "I... I... just know his first name."

"Nobody named Ryan lives here. I live here with my son, Grant. That's all that lives here. I don't know anybody named Ryan."

"How long have you been living here?" Keri boldly asked.

The woman scowled. "That's *my* business. But it's been six months."

"Do you rent?"

The woman heaved out a loud sigh. "I told you I don't know anybody named Ryan. That's all I know."

"Yes, yes, thank you. I was just wondering if the landlord might remember him or have some record of him."

"Well I wouldn't know anything about that."

"Would you happen to have the name and phone number of the landlord? It would really be helpful."

"His name is Burt Walton. He's a lawyer. He owns the place. I don't have his number handy."

Keri backed away. "Burt Walton. Thank you. I'll look him up. Thank you very much."

The woman twisted up her lips in irritation and retreated back inside, while Keri reversed and returned to her car.

"Well, she was about as friendly as a snake," Keri said aloud, as she started the car.

She grabbed her phone and did a quick search for Burt Walton in Brandy Beach. She found Walton Real Estate. That must be it. She'd visit their offices first thing the next morning.

Keri drove back through town, her mind crowded with thoughts. Traffic was heavy, as vacationers packed the restaurants, ice cream shops and burger cafes. As she searched for a place to eat, she realized that she didn't really know anything about the special ops soldiers, other than the usual movies she'd seen and things she'd read about in the news. Maybe some research would help her find Ryan, or at least learn more about what he was doing when Sophia met him.

She parked near a deserted playground, under the glow of a streetlight, and walked back through the night toward the town, past crowded restaurants, a noisy bar and a bustling T-shirt shop. She was looking for a sidewalk restaurant called the Main Street Café. According to the diary, Sophia and Ryan had often met there for lunch or dinner. It had a scatter of tables on the sloping pavement, with patio umbrellas and bright red chairs. She sat at a table for two, perused the menu, and ordered a chicken sandwich, french fries and a glass of Pinot Noir.

Keri began her computer research over the rising hum of conversation all around her. She found a site that gave generalities. She nosed forward and read about the SEALs and Army Rangers. Then she read about the Army Special Forces.

"The Army Special Forces are considered 'Sine Pari,' or 'Without Equal' in Latin. Also known as the Green Berets, they have adopted their own motto: 'De Oppresso Liber,' which is Latin for 'To Free the Oppressed.'"

That sounded impressive, Keri thought, as she sipped her ice water, hearing the cubes of ice clink against the glass. She read on.

She learned that the Army Special Forces are sometimes confused with the Navy SEALS or the Army Rangers. But Special Forces are in a league all their own. "In addition to learning combat tactics and reconnaissance, Special Forces, or Green Berets, receive training in language, culture, diplomacy, psychological warfare, disinformation—generating and spreading false information—as well as politics.

"The Green Berets operate with little oversight, working with native peoples in predetermined Areas of

Operation, and they serve as unofficial 'warrior-diplomats.'

"They exist in the haze that floats between the country and other nations, groups and peoples— and they're the nimble fingertips of the United States military, and 'quiet professionals.'"

Keri glanced about at the faces around her, all animated with pleasure and soft with relaxation. Every table was full, and she was the only one sitting alone. She studied the men and wondered what Ryan might look like. According to the diary, he was tall, blond and well-built. She didn't see any man who fit that description.

When her food arrived, she found a variety of sites, some with pictures of Special Ops soldiers. She ate while studying their faces, seeking some universal expression, some special quality that Ryan might possess.

Many were hard, determined faces, with cool, glittering eyes and firm mouths. She found photos of soldiers surrounded by mountains or desert, wearing olive green camouflage uniforms, shouldering rifles. Some were brawny, with lazy smiles but strong, lean faces. One wore a bandana headband; a camouflage jump jacket, unzipped at the front; and khaki bush shirt and pants, tucked in paratrooper's boots.

By the time Keri had finished her meal, her curiosity about Ryan had swelled into an intriguing mystery. She was more determined than ever to find him. She closed her laptop with an eager restlessness.

Keri spent the night in the guest bedroom, not wanting to return to Sophia's room, with its ghosts and memories. Besides, she'd stripped the bed and left the room immaculately clean. She caught up on emails and phone calls, leafed through the diary again, reread some entries and was asleep by 11:30. She slept restlessly, her dreams a jumble of confused phrases, beach images and faces of soldiers pacing before her, their eyes large, their faces haunted.

The next morning, Keri ate an early breakfast at the Brandy Beach Diner, and by 10am she was walking toward Walton Real Estate, dressed in designer jeans, a yellow T-shirt and red Keds sneakers. The sun was warm and the breeze alive with the scent of rose and honeysuckle. Butterflies were scattering across flowering gardens and lawns.

Walton Real Estate offices were surrounded by a quaint, white picket fence and a swinging gate. The building itself appeared more like an enchanted cottage than a real estate business. It was white, with blue shutters, a sloping tiled roof, many windows and a white door with a gold knocker. The lawn, hedges and flower gardens were carefully manicured.

As Keri opened the door, it "dinged."

She was greeted by an attractive, sun-bronzed woman, about 40, whose eyes seemed distracted and smile seemed distant. She sat behind a computer screen. Seated behind her was a younger man, fully engaged in his cell phone texting. Behind him was a silver-haired woman, talking on the phone in a soft, cottony voice, as if speaking to a lover.

"Hello," the bronzed woman said. "Can I help you?"

"Is Mr. Walton around?"

The woman seemed confused. "Harold Walton or Burt Walton?"

"Burt Walton, I think," Keri said. "I'm trying to gather some information on one of his former tenants, someone who used to live at 345 Mercury Lane."

"Well I'm afraid that would be confidential," the woman said.

Keri had prepared for this conversation and for the woman's answer.

"Yes... Of course. A friend they knew passed away, and I wanted to give them the news. Really all I need is a last name."

Keri extended her hand and smiled warmly. "I'm Keri Lawton."

The woman hesitated, then brightened and took Keri's hand. "I'm Donna."

Donna took Keri in, as if seeing her for the first time. Then she went straight to the point. "Keri...I wish I could help you, but all of that kind of thing is kept in the strictest confidence."

Keri's goal was to be able to speak with Burt Walton. "Yes, Donna, I appreciate that. Does Burt Walton have an office around here someplace? All I need to do is speak to him for a few minutes."

Donna hesitated, and then she reached for a business card and a pen and jotted down an address. She lowered her voice.

"His office is three blocks away. Please don't tell him I sent you. He wouldn't like it."

Keri took the card and winked. "I won't. Thank you so much, Donna. Have a good day."

Keri easily found Belair & Walton law offices. They were in a red brick, two-story building on a side street, shaded by trees, with a spreading lawn and a bright flower garden.

Inside, Keri stepped into a cool, air-conditioned room, with high ceilings and polished hardwood floors. There was a long mahogany receptionist's desk holding freshly cut flowers, and behind that were two doors on opposite sides of the room.

Keri drew up to reception and was met by a young redhead with a freckled face and lively green eyes.

"Good morning," she said, smiling.

"Good morning. I was hoping I could speak with Burt Walton?" Keri asked.

The receptionist blinked twice, but kept her smile. "Do you have an appointment?"

"No."

"May I ask your name and what it concerns?"

"I'm Keri Lawton and it concerns a former tenant of his."

The receptionist nodded her head, considering. "Well... if you wouldn't mind taking a seat, I'll see if he's available."

"Thank you," Keri said, her hands suddenly feeling sweaty.

She sat down in a comfortable, heavy oak chair and reached for a magazine. She leafed through it, her eyes blurring on the photos and articles, her mind drifting back two years, to June, when she and Sophia spent a week together on Brandy Beach. Perhaps that was the week Sophia had met Ryan.

Keri strained to recall the details of that week. What activities she and Sophia had done. What they'd discussed. Where they'd eaten.

She decided to use a meditation technique she'd recently learned in a yoga class. She gently closed her eyes, allowing her mind to relax and drift. She imagined she was descending white marble steps into a welcoming, blue, rippling pool. First her feet, then her torso, then her shoulders and then her head. She submerged, bobbed to the surface, and floated on her back, staring up into a silver blue sky, lost in deep silence.

Keri focused her mind on Sophia.

She saw Sophia's glowing face, tanned and youthful, and then she saw her jogging along the beach in slow motion, her pony-tail swinging, the sand kicking up behind her heels. Keri saw the beach house looming out of a smoky haze and she began to hear the sounds of the sea, the seagulls, the snarl of a jet ski.

An image bubbled up to the surface of her mind. She saw herself sitting on the second floor patio of the house, lying on a chaise with aluminum and plastic webbing, reading a novel. She couldn't see the novel's title. It had something to do with time travel. Keri loved time travel novels.

She lifted her eyes from the book and gazed out toward the beach. She saw Sophia there, toweling off after a late morning swim. She wore a sexy, coral-colored bikini, and as she stood, framed in the bright sun, Keri saw that she was talking to a man. Yes! Keri recalled that. She saw that in her mind. He was a tall blond! From the balcony, which was a good 70 yards from the beach, Keri could see the guy only from the back or in profile. She estimated he was in his late 20s or early 30s. Still in meditation, she removed her sunglasses and strained her eyes to get a better look. Keri breathed into the flow of memory, struggling to recall every detail. What was Sophia's body language?

She was standing tall with her shoulders back to emphasize her full breasts, making slow flirtatious turns of her head, drawing attention to her long neck. Yes, Keri could see that clearly! Sophia inched a little closer to the tall, broad-shouldered man and tilted a look up at him.

What were his features? Keri worked to view him from different angles, but the more she tried to zoom in on him, the fuzzier he became. He was too far away.

Keri's closed eyes fluttered to a time later in the day. She and Sophia were standing on the balcony overlooking the beach. Keri had asked Sophia about the man.

"Who was that guy you were talking to down on the beach this morning?"

Sophia shrugged her shoulders. "Oh, just some guy I see running on the beach sometimes. I guess he lives around here someplace."

Had Keri actually seen Ryan?

When Keri heard footsteps creaking the wood floor, her eyes popped open. She saw an attractive man in his middle-to-late 30s circle around the reception desk and come toward her. He wore a blue, pin-striped suit, a powder blue shirt and a red and blue striped silk tie. He had a prominent nose, short black hair and the relaxed expression of a smooth professional.

Keri replaced her magazine and stood as Burt Walton smiled a welcome. "You're Keri Lawton?"

"Yes... thank you for seeing me. I hope I'm not interrupting anything."

"Well, it's Thursday, it's June and I don't mind being interrupted when I'm dictating boring letters about taxes. Come into my office, Ms. Lawton."

Burt Walton's office was richly decorated, with a heavy, mahogany desk, rich brown leather chairs and an

Italian leather couch. There were three windows behind Burt's desk that looked out onto a lush green carpet of lawn and tall swaying trees.

Burt indicated toward a deep leather chair and Keri sat, as Burt eased down behind his desk, into his swivel chair. On his desk were a vase of fresh flowers and a photograph of two smiling kids: a blonde girl about 7 years old and a toffee-haired boy of perhaps 10. The lack of a woman in the photo was noticeable.

"They're a little older now," Burt said, seeing Keri's attention on them.

"They look adorable," Keri said.

"Especially when they're asleep," Burt said, grinning. "You love them more than your own life. Do you have any?"

"No… I'm not married."

Keri thought she saw a faint gleam of pleasure in his eyes.

He folded his hands on his desktop, lifting his chin a little. "So what can I do for you, Ms. Lawton?"

Keri summarized the situation, finishing with, "I know there are privacy issues, but I was hoping that perhaps you could, at the very least, be able to give me Ryan's last name."

Burt scratched his cheek and exhaled. "Well…of course I don't recall Ryan at all. I have little or nothing to do with the renters. That's all handled through the real estate business. And, as you mentioned, there are legal and confidentiality issues with regard to tenants."

He shut his eyes and pinched the bridge of his nose. Keri waited, apprehensively.

When his eyes opened, they focused on her. "Are you staying in town?"

"Yes."

"Well, it will take me a couple of hours to research this. How about we meet for lunch close by, say at the Main Street Café, and I'll see what I can do for you."

Keri thought that was a pretty smooth move, asking her out on a date with the pretense that he was doing her a favor. She could have easily returned to his office, or he could have even emailed her the information. You had to admire attorneys, she thought, remembering the one she'd dated a few years back.

"What time?" Keri asked, smiling brightly.

"Oh, say, 12:30. How does that sound?"

Keri climbed to her feet, hand extended. "I'll be there, Mr. Walton. Thanks."

Burt took her hand and held it for a few charmed seconds before releasing it. "You can call me Burt."

Keri offered a faint smile. "All right, Burt. Then please call me Keri."

Burt's eyes filled with delight. "That's a lovely name, Keri. That's Irish, isn't it?"

"Yes. It's the name of a county in Ireland."

"And Lawton?"

"Old English, according to my mother, who has done the research."

Burt lifted an eyebrow, grinning. "And do both names get along, the Irish and the English?"

Keri laughed a little, enjoying his humor. "The Irish has the temper. The English, the stiff upper lip. The American tries to be the diplomat, but most of the time fails."

He laughed, and it was a good and hearty laugh. Keri liked him.

CHAPTER 6

Keri spent the next two hours wandering through boutiques, picking through racks of summer items marked down 20, 30 or 40 percent, frequently glancing down at her phone for messages. She was too distracted to focus on anything.

Sophia's diary was in her purse and Keri kept hearing the dying fall of Sophia's words, "For God's sake, take a risk, Keri. Have an adventure. Step out of your comfort zone now and then."

"Okay, Sophia," Keri thought. "I *have* stepped out of my comfort zone and I *am* on an adventure."

Keri was at the café early and chose a table under a patio umbrella, away from the hot, noon sun. Burt was right on time, presenting an easy, confident manner. He was all smiles as he sat opposite Keri, laying his cellphone down in front of him, near the menu.

"Did you see anything tempting on the menu?" he asked.

"Yes. I ate here last night and I know the food's good."

"We can go somewhere else if you'd like."

"No, this is fine. I like it."

Burt pushed his menu away. "I always get the Cobb Salad. Today, I'm going to branch out and have the Salade Niçoise."

"The grilled cheese looks good to me," Keri said.

Keri had to admit that she found Burt attractive. He had a friendly, handsome face, dark, intelligent eyes, and full, generous lips. He must have plenty of girl-friends, Keri thought. He was certainly well off. She let her mind speculate on why the mother of his two children was not in the photograph.

After the sleepy, spiky-haired waitress took their or-der, Burt leaned back and glanced around. "Do you live around here, Keri?"

"No, near Boston, in Melrose."

"Yes, I know where Melrose is. What do you do there?"

"I'm the HR Manager for a tech company."

"HR… that's a challenging job, I would think."

Keri reached for a bread stick. "Yes. I like my job but it's good to get away from it now and then. I'm off this week."

Burt allowed himself the pleasure of studying Keri. He had always been a good judge of character, but as his law practice had grown, so had his perceptions of, and intuition about, people. He'd seen the many sides of divorce, the probation of wills, and the petty crimes of sons against fathers, mothers against husbands, and daughters against mothers. Burt did not always enjoy his profession, but it provided a good livelihood and it did increasingly help him understand the motivations, desires and fears of most people.

He suspected that Keri came from a good and loving family. Undoubtedly, she had an active, intelligent and curious mind, but she probably tended to be quiet, careful and introspective. When presented with prickly HR issues, she would most likely see the larger picture and be able to balance company and employee goals. She could probably be social, but she most likely gravitated to solitary thoughtfulness, which many would consider to be aloofness.

Burt found her thin, feminine frame, pretty face, and quiet manner both alluring and mysterious. Her full mouth, wide blue eyes and honey blonde hair were all very entrancing. She moved with an economy of motion, like a dancer. He sensed that there were exotic worlds behind those calm eyes, worlds that most people would never get to know—but, oh, how he would like to be the one who *did* get to know those worlds, and more.

Burt had researched Ryan with much more detail than he'd intended, simply because Keri's interest had interested him. What did she really want? What was she really after?

They discussed the weather, both summer and winter, and then they commented on how beautiful the area was in the autumn.

Burt complained about the chain stores that were trying to move in, and how large developers were lobbying the town board to allow them to purchase beach front property so they could erect high rise condos. Burt was strictly against it, speaking with force and irritation about those few and "greedy" board members who told him he was living in the past.

When their lunch arrived, Keri and Burt ate quietly, while beach people with kids filled the tables around them, traffic crawled, and the rising heat prompted Burt to remove his suit jacket and drape it around the back of his chair. Keri noticed that Burt had a bit of a paunch, but his meaty shoulders suggested he'd been active in high school and college sports.

Keri watched two teenaged bicyclists swerving through traffic, testing space, bumpers and tempers. Keri was fighting back impatience, anxious for Burt to give her the information about Ryan.

Burt sipped his water. "I've been living in this town for most of my life. I thought that after law school maybe I'd move to Boston or New York, but my father wanted me here, so here I am. It's a good place to live. Good town to raise kids."

"Does your wife agree that it's a good town to raise kids?" Keri asked, casually.

Burt suppressed a smile, impressed by the skill at which Keri had asked the question.

"My wife and I divorced about a year ago. Erika didn't like it here. She was from L.A., from an acting family. She moved back there, hoping to get into the business again. There wasn't much of that around here. She felt stifled, even though she'd moved here to get away from the frustration and challenge of the acting business and L.A. She thought she was sick of L.A., the plastic people, the traffic, the lack of any real culture."

"But she moved back to L.A."

Burt nodded, smiling ruefully. "Yes, she moved back."

"And the kids...?"

Burt picked at his salad. "I fly out there a lot, and I bring them here during vacations."

After Keri swallowed the last of her sandwich, she couldn't restrain her curiosity about Ryan any longer. She collected herself and spoke in an even, calm voice.

"Burt, were you able to find any information about Ryan?"

Burt nodded, blotting his lips with his paper napkin. He slipped his hand into his jacket pocket, drew out a folded piece of paper and opened it.

He scratched the side of his neck and cleared his throat.

Keri leaned a little forward, her eyes widening on him.

"His full name is Ryan Tate Carlson."

Keri swallowed, her pulse rising. She sat back with a little sigh, feeling triumphant. She had his name. Now she'd be able to find him.

Burt watched her. He saw the gathering excitement on her face.

"You said Ryan knew a friend of yours who recently passed away?"

Keri's eyes had wandered, as she was plotting her next move. Distracted, she nodded. "Yes. Yes... She, was my best friend. She and her husband were killed in a plane crash last week. Ryan knew Sophia."

"Did she know Ryan well?"

Keri glanced up, suddenly aware of what she'd said and the obvious implications. "Oh... no. I mean it was nothing like that. I mean, she met Ryan before... before she married Richard. I just think Ryan would want to know what happened, that's all."

Burt was intrigued. He didn't completely believe Keri, which made her mysterious and even more attractive to him.

"I wish I could give you more," Burt said, lifting a hand and then letting it drift down. "...But..."

"I understand," Keri said. "This is perfect. I'll be able to find him now. Thank you so much, Burt."

His eyes came to hers. "Will you be in town tomorrow or Saturday night, Keri?"

Her eyes darted across his face, then down and away. "I don't really know. I'll be heading home at some point."

"Would you mind if I called you, say tomorrow morning or afternoon? I would love to have dinner with you. Dayna's Grill has great seafood."

Keri slipped on her sunglasses, self-consciously. "Okay... yes."

"It might be fun," Burt added.

Keri paused before giving him her phone number. She watched him key it into his phone.

When Keri stood, Burt raised himself from his chair and gave a little bow. "I'll look forward to hearing more about Ryan," Burt said, "and seeing you for dinner."

That was an odd thing to say, Keri thought, as she strolled to her car. Why would he look forward to hearing more about Ryan? In fact, she didn't *intend* to tell him what she learned about Ryan.

But she'd probably have to tell him something if they had dinner together. After all, Burt had given her Ryan's last name. Maybe she owed him some information. Maybe not?

Keri rushed back to the house, eager to search Ryan's name, to see if she could locate him. But first, she forced herself to check the emails and text messages on her phone. Sophia's father had written, thanking her for the list of items in Sophia's box and telling her to stay at the beach house as long as she wanted to. There were a few emails from work—nothing urgent— and one from her mother.

She sat at the kitchen island counter, opened her laptop, and started with a Google search. She typed in his full name and waited: She saw Carlson Ryan. A Carl Ryan, Carlson High School. No Ryan T. Carlson. She checked images, but again no Ryan T. Carlson popped up.

Keri searched on, alert and unblinking. She found a site specializing in verifying people. She keyed in Ryan's full name. A minute later, 21 Ryan Carlsons appeared. Keri breathed in impatience as she scrolled through the list that contained Name, Age and City. She froze: Ryan T. Carlson. Was this it!?

No. Damn! This Ryan T. Carlson was only 23 years old. Had to be the wrong one. She kept scrolling, but came up empty. It was possible that his middle initial wasn't listed, just the first and last name.

Undaunted, Keri went to a military site and keyed in Ryan's full name. When it asked her to check off the branch of service, she selected Army. It asked her to register for free. She did. She keyed in Ryan's name and waited... She received the following message:

"You do not meet the necessary requirements to contact this person."

Maybe because he was in special ops, they wouldn't list his name, Keri thought.

Next Keri checked all social media sites: Facebook? There were only two listed—one appeared in his 50s, and the other was a teenager. Still, she jotted them down. It wouldn't hurt to contact them. Maybe they were related in some way. Keri got the same results with other social media sites. In the end, she found four overall possible candidates.

She went back to the previous site of the 21 Ryan Carlsons, and scrolled through the list looking for any and all who lived in or around Massachusetts. There was only one. He was 62 years old. One in Pennsylvania was 54 years old. Vermont, 50. New York, 23 and 70 years old.

Keri sat back with a deep sigh of frustration. She'd thought that once she had his name he'd be easy to find. Carlson wasn't that common a name. There had to be a trace of him somewhere. Or did there? What if he was dead? Keri sank at the thought. Somehow, she hadn't let herself consider that.

She got up, went to the refrigerator and took out a bottle of water. She screwed off the cap, took a long drink, and stepped outside. From the wrap-around porch, she watched the afternoon light play across the water. How much would it cost to hire a private investigator? Surely *he'd* be able to find Ryan, or at least find out what had happened to him. She lowered herself down into the nearest padded chair, feeling an irrational urgency, a gathering obsession to locate him, beating through her veins. Why did it matter so much? Was it just the mystery of the thing, or was there more to it than that?

She watched a sailboat drift lazily across the horizon—watched children rush the tide, screeching, turning, and scampering away when the cold waves charged them.

Keri drank the water absently, her entire calculating mind in motion.

Then an idea struck. She sprang up and hurried back to the laptop. This time she found the white pages for Brandy Beach and the surrounding towns and keyed-in just the last name. Nothing came up for Brandy Beach. Nothing for Bakersfield. Nothing for Dubane and nothing for Cottonwood. She kept going, nosing in closer to the laptop screen, her eyes scanning names, ages and towns.

Three towns later, one Carlson materialized. It was Sally Carlson, 59. She lived in Beechwood, a town about 20 miles north. Flushed with new hope, Keri quickly jotted down the phone number.

She stood, snatched her cellphone and dialed. She waited as the phone rang once, twice, three and four times. Keri smoothed back her hair and, as the ringing persisted, she drummed her fingers on the kitchen countertop.

Eight rings later, a woman's strong voice answered. "Hello... who is this?"

Keri blurted out, "Hi, my name's Keri Lawton and I'm trying to get in touch with Ryan. Ryan Tate Carlson."

The woman's voice took on an edge. "You're wasting your time. I don't want anything and I've told you people time and time again to stop calling me...So I'm going to tell you one more..."

Keri cut her off. "I'm not selling anything. I'm a friend... well, I mean I'm a friend of a friend of Ryan's."

There was silence.

"Hello?" Keri said. "Hello?"

The woman's voice was suspicious now. "What friend?"

Keri spoke fast. "Ryan knew someone a couple of years back. I'm trying to reach him because she was killed. I thought he'd want to know."

Sally Carlson's voice softened. "Was she in the service?"

"No... No, she wasn't. She was someone he met while he was in the service. They became friends."

"Was she a friend of Debbie's?" Sally asked, her voice taking on an edge.

"Debbie? No. I mean, I don't know who Debbie is," Keri said.

There was a long silence. Keri paced the room, straining to hear, suddenly concerned that Sally had hung up.

Keri finally spoke. "Are you there?"

"Yes, I'm here."

"So, do you know Ryan?"

"Well, I certainly hope so. I'm his mother."

CHAPTER 7

Keri felt weak in the knees. She slowly sat down. "Mrs. Carlson, is there some way I can get in touch with him?"

More silence

Keri waited.

"Ryan calls me sometimes. He lives alone and he likes living alone. I haven't seen him in weeks. I'm not so sure he'd want me to give out his phone number. He'd probably be very angry with me."

"Okay... Well...can you tell me where he lives? I could..."

"He wouldn't see you, and he certainly wouldn't want you turning up on his doorstep. Like I said, he's a loner."

Keri struggled to come up with the right phrase. "I do think he'd want to know about Sophia," Keri said, softly.

"Sophia?"

"That was our mutual friend."

"Well, I don't know anything about that. Did this Sophia know Ryan's wife?"

"No... No, I don't think so."

"What did you say your name was?" Sally asked.

"Keri. Keri Lawton."

"All right, Keri. I'll call Ryan and see if he wants to see you. Give me your number."

Keri did so. "Thank you, Mrs. Carlson. Thank you very much."

To distract herself, Keri spent the rest of the afternoon catching up on work emails and texts. Friends were concerned that she hadn't been responding to them in her usual rapid manner. Keri assured them that she was fine, she just needed downtime after her friend's death.

In fact, since Sophia's death, Keri had freed herself from the often necessary but relentless demands of social media, texts, emails and phone calls. She'd begun to reawaken to the fundamental value of silence and the recuperative power of spending time alone.

At 6 o'clock, when Keri hadn't heard from Sally, she wrestled with the urge to call her back, feeling a mounting dismay that she'd never hear from the woman again. She resisted. She left the house and wandered the beach in her bare feet, shorts and T-shirt. Her chic sunglasses tinted the world to a fascinating pink and, as she lifted her face into the hot breath of the wind, she felt her phone vibrate.

She stopped, turned her back to the sun and answered.

"Hello."

"This is Sally Carlson, Keri. Ryan just called me back. I'm sorry, he said he doesn't know you and doesn't want to see you."

Keri swelled with disappointment. "Did you tell him about Sophia?"

"I told him you were her friend. I didn't say she died. He's had enough of that news."

"Oh, I see." Keri bit her lower lip. "Did he say anything at all?"

"Not much. He doesn't talk much, Keri. He's been this way for nearly two years. Well, ever since Debbie—that was his wife—killed herself."

Keri heaved out a deep sigh. "Is he still in the military?"

"Oh, no. He left after his 10 years were up."

Keri seized on a thought. "Mrs. Carlson...I hope I don't seem too pushy, but can I come to see you?"

Silence.

"Why do you want to see me?" Sally asked.

Keri honestly didn't know. If Ryan didn't want to see her then what was the point? Keri made up something and it surprised her. "You could tell me about him."

Sally's voice deepened. "Keri, have you ever met my son?"

"No."

"Then why do you want to know about him? I don't understand."

Keri fished for a reason, carefully considering her words. "Sophia was like a sister to me, Mrs. Carlson. I knew her better than anyone else, including my own brother. It's difficult to explain. Sophia was very much in love with Ryan and she never told me about him. She kept it all a secret."

Keri kicked at the sand, desperate to get to Ryan.

"Maybe she wanted the secret kept, Keri."

"This is difficult to say, Mrs. Carlson, but I'd just like to know what he's like. Sophia wanted to marry him."

"Well, he certainly never told me about this," Sally said.

"Mrs. Carlson, I found Ryan's name in Sophia's diary—a very private diary. Please don't tell Ryan about the diary. I haven't told anyone about it. Sophia never believed it would be read. I found it by accident. I never dreamed it would have such a powerful effect on me. It's been a very difficult time. I guess I'm looking for some kind of closure. Some way of facing all this so I can move on."

Keri waited, looking up into the blue, serene sky.

Finally, Sally spoke. "Have you had dinner, Keri?"

Keri perked up. "No."

"Okay, I have a chicken in the oven. Come have dinner with me. It'll be nice not to eat alone."

From Sally's directions, Keri easily found the house, located at the end of a secluded street, nestled under trees. She parked at the curb, climbed out and took in the white, single-family, 3-bedroom house. The single car garage was closed, the lawn needed mowing and the hedges were a bit overgrown.

Keri cradled a bottle of wine in one arm and a bouquet of mixed flowers in the other. She started up the narrow cement walkway, her low heels clicking a rhythm, her right toes pinched in shoes she'd never liked but refused to throw away because they'd cost so much.

It was nearly 8 o'clock and the sun had dipped behind the trees, glinting gold off the rooftops of homes nearby. Keri climbed the cement steps to the porch, smoothed out her light blue cotton top and shimmied a little to allow her white slacks to settle over her hips. She rang the doorbell.

The door swung open and a tall, sturdy woman, wearing a white cotton top, blue capri pants and sandals, flashed a friendly smile. She had a broad, tanned face, long, silver-gray hair, and lively eyes. Sally seemed a formidable woman, made of hardwood and stone, a practical woman who faced life's challenges head-on, never retreating one step.

"Hello, Keri," she said, pleasantly. "I'm Sally. Come in."

Keri stepped across the threshold and Sally closed the door quickly, to keep in the air conditioning.

"Did you have any trouble finding the place?" Sally asked.

"No. Your directions were perfect. It smells so good in here, like Thanksgiving."

"Nothing so extravagant," Sally said. "Just chicken, potatoes and green beans. The chicken might be a little overdone, but it's okay. I also made gravy. That'll fix it. Good rich gravy with sweet sherry fixes everything."

Keri offered Sally the flowers, and she brightened, touching them, inhaling the scents.

"Flowers? How wonderful! I haven't gotten flowers in so long. What a treat. Thank you, Keri."

"And I brought some wine. I took a chance. A California Chardonnay?"

"I love Chardonnay. Well, now, it feels like a party, doesn't it? Come on into the dining room."

Keri followed Sally through the living room, a welcoming space with earth-tones of green and brown, a comfortable recliner, a 2-piece sectional sofa, throw rugs over a parquet floor, and an unexpected marble fireplace. Keri hesitated when she saw framed photographs on the mantel. Was there one of Ryan?

The cozy dining room was lit by an attractive, four-light chandelier and natural light from a wide picture window. Keri stepped onto a deep beige carpet, noticing the rose pattern twining across the wallpaper.

There were settings for two on the glossy walnut dining table, with white cloth napkins, white bone china and matching covered serving platters.

"This is lovely," Keri said. "I hope it wasn't too much trouble."

"Of course not. I don't often get dinner guests. Most of my friends have moved to Florida or the southwest. They're all running from the cold. I love the cold and I tell them they're all chicken shits. I'll put the flowers in a vase and get some wine glasses. Sit down and relax. I'll be right back."

Keri sat with her back to the window, directly opposite Sally's setting, taking in the pulse of the house. It was quiet and clean, and simply but tastefully decorated. Keri had the feeling that Sally, like her son, was sort of a loner, despite her welcoming manner.

Minutes later, Sally returned with the flowers blooming from an ornate blue vase. "Now aren't those lovely," she said, as she arranged them at the center of the table.

After the wine was poured and the food was on their plates, Keri stole occasional glances toward her hostess, searching for clues that might reveal aspects of her son.

Her gray-blue eyes were clear, her face strong, her cheek bones high. Although she was a large woman, she carried herself with a comfortable grace.

"The food is very good, Mrs. Carlson."

"Oh for heaven's sake, Keri, call me Sally. Mrs. Carlson makes me sound dowdy and severe. I'm glad you like the food. I'm a simple, practical cook, but I do put a lot of butter in the mashed potatoes. I learned that from Julia Child."

They explored each other with small talk: Keri's occupation, where she went to school and where she'd grown up. Keri learned that Sally had lived her whole life in Beechwood, and had lived in this house since she was married to Ryan's father.

"Is Ryan your only son, Sally?"

"My only son, yes. I also have a daughter, Lynn, who lives in Jacksonville, Florida. She has two kids and I get to see them in the summer and at Christmas, when I go down there."

"Does Ryan ever come to visit you?"

Sally cut into a piece of chicken. She took a bite and chewed, thoughtfully. "The last time was four months ago. And he's not that far away, maybe 30 miles. Keri… Ryan has lost his spark for life and I don't know if he'll ever get it back. I keep thinking that, one day, the dark cloud over him will pass on over, but I just don't know anymore. And he was such a fun little boy. He was always getting into things, like most boys, but he was curious and sensitive. He and his father were real close. His father worshipped him and Ryan thought the world of him."

Sally's mouth curved into a meager smile. "Those were good times. We were a close family."

Keri sipped her wine, waiting for more. She saw that Sally wanted to say more.

"My first husband was killed in a hunting accident when Lynn was 20 and Ryan was 15. Lord God, that was so hard on Ryan. He missed his father so much. And then I did a fool thing. I married a bastard of a man. Didn't know that when I married him, of course, but then I wanted another man for Ryan and, let's be frank, I also wanted a man. There's nothing wrong with wanting a man in your bed, is there, Keri? But he has to be the right man and, take it from me, Buddy was not the right man. Well, anyway, Ryan didn't take to Buddy, and Buddy didn't take much to anything but his boozer friends."

Sally shook her head. "I sit here sometimes and wonder how I could have done such a stupid thing and married that loser. Oh, Buddy was funny and all that but, finally, he wasn't worth kicking out the back door. But that's just what happened. Buddy took a couple swings at Ryan over something I don't remember. But Ryan was 17 years old by then and he was big and strong and he could take care of himself. When Buddy swung at Ryan the third time, Ryan hit the son of a bitch so hard, he knocked him out the back door, down the stairs and out into the yard. With one punch, Ryan knocked old Buddy down on his ass."

Sally reached for her glass of wine and took a long drink. She stared at the wine with contempt. "I grew to hate that man, and I swore I'd never have another. I divorced him after that. You think a woman would know better than to marry a knucklehead like that."

"You're a little hard on yourself, Sally."

"No, I don't think so and I'll tell you why. Ryan was never the same after that. And then when he was 18, he ran away. Didn't know where he was for a time. When he finally did show up, he'd joined the Army."

Sally reached for the gravy and poured it generously on every item on her plate. Keri watched with masked amusement as the gravy pooled around the chicken and the green beans, and smothered Sally's second helping of mashed potatoes.

Sally replaced the gravy boat and paused, looking at Keri carefully, her eyebrows raised in query. "You're a pretty girl, Keri. Are you married?"

Keri gave a quick shake of her head. "No..."

"Good for you." Then, as an afterthought, Sally made a sour face. "Well, listen to old, bitter Sally. Just because I had a bad second husband doesn't mean all men are bad. After all, Ryan's father, Nick, was a good man. A damned good man. A good husband and father. And you know what? Ryan was a good husband to Debbie."

Sally gave a little flicker of her hand. "Well, anyway... I blame myself for Ryan running away from home. And then he tried out for the Special Forces and that really scared me. I mean, the world is so crazy everywhere. He told me later he almost didn't make it. He said it was the hardest thing he'd ever done. But he wanted that green beret and he wanted to wear that Special Forces tab on his shoulder. Oh, I knew he'd pass. He was always smart as a whip and determined. He got high marks in high school. He could have gone to any college he wanted to. He was offered scholarships."

Keri ate slowly, listening to Sally gush out the words, as many people do when they spend a lot of time alone.

Keri pushed around a green bean. "Why did Ryan leave the military after 10 years?"

Sally reached for a roll, tore off a piece and wiped up the extra gravy on her plate.

"Well, you don't know about Debbie. Debbie Mathers was such a pretty little thing, with auburn brown hair and big brown eyes. But she was—how do you say it? She was fragile. She was so quiet and withdrawn. You'd never know she was around. If she was in the house, you'd never hear her. She scared me sometimes when I turned around. She'd be standing right there, looking at me—smiling at me with that peculiar smile she had. That fragile little girl destroyed herself and she nearly destroyed Ryan."

CHAPTER 8

Sally's voice thickened. "Of course I don't really know everything that happened. Ryan has never talked about it. I thought their marriage was okay. Ryan loved her like she was a princess. He treated her like one. Ryan is a good man, like his father."

Sally stopped to chew the bread. Her eyes filled with sadness. "That little girl… that fragile little Debbie got ahold of some sleeping pills and she just swallowed them down. I didn't even know she was dead for almost two days. Debbie's mother called me. Debbie lived here for awhile, then she just quietly walked out one day and went back to live with her mother. She never said a word to me except 'Goodbye.'"

"Well, of course Debbie's mother was a crying wreck when she lost her daughter. I think she's still a crying wreck. Maybe even a little crazy. Maybe that's where Debbie got her strangeness."

Keri listened intently, holding the glass of wine to her lips.

Sally continued. "What mother wouldn't be half crazy to lose a pretty little daughter like that? But Vicky, that's Debbie's mother, shouted and screamed at me, called me names, and blamed Ryan for everything. She said Ryan had killed her daughter. She said he'd made so many worthless promises. He'd promised roses and cream and, in the end, he wasn't even there to help her when she was all alone…when she killed herself."

Keri finished her glass of wine, her eyes lingering on Sally's somber face.

Sally clamped her eyes shut. When she opened them, they were stormy, filled with turmoil. "Imagine blaming Ryan for her daughter's death, when he tried with all his heart to help the girl. I know it nearly broke Ryan. That's why he stayed in the military. That's why he chose another tour, another dangerous mission. He didn't care if he lived or died."

The women sat in a long silence, as Keri looked at Sally with uncertain eyes. When Keri spoke, her voice was soft, whispery.

"How long did Ryan stay in the military after Debbie's death?" she asked.

Sally fortified herself with a breath. "Oh, it was another year or so, I guess. I never knew where he was or what he was up to. Ryan wouldn't talk about it. Well… you know, those Special Forces men are so secretive. They don't say anything. I do recall that he came by one day before he left for a long mission, and he told me it would be a difficult one. He gave me that narrowed serious look he gave me when he was a little boy, going off to hunt with his dad. He gave me a big hug and a kiss and I looked into his eyes and I thought I saw death. I worried for days and weeks when I didn't hear from him. I got a letter from him now and then, but no real news."

Sally picked up her napkin and absently wiped each corner of her mouth. "I half expected to get the visit that all mothers who have children in the military fear. The one they all dread. But Ryan came back. Of course, when he returned, he was changed. And he's never been the same since. Debbie's death really hit him hard, and maybe he'd gone on one too many missions. I mean how much can a soldier take? Battle after battle. You hear so many terrible stories about what goes on over there. Well, anyway, he left the military... and I never thought he would."

Keri took the wine bottle and poured them both a little more wine.

Sally forced a small smile, then it grew, and grew wider. Her voice took on strength. "Okay, no more depressing talk. I'm feeling a little buzzed, Keri, and I like it. I like this Chardonnay!"

Keri smiled and swallowed some mashed potatoes. She turned toward the window to see the last orange smudge of light fade into splotches of darkness.

"It would have been a beautiful sunset on the beach," Keri said, facing Sally again. "What is Ryan doing now?"

Sally stared, wistfully. "He's working on a lobster boat. He bought half and a friend bought half. It's called the Sally May."

Sally smiled, proudly. "Those are my first and middle names. Isn't it nice that Ryan did that? It pleased me so much. Anyway, that's about all I know. His grandmother, his father's mother, passed away a year or so ago, and she left him a big, old, Victorian house out on Crandall Cove. It needed a lot of work and I guess he spends a lot of time restoring it. He lives there alone—at least as far as I know. He sends me money every month, even though I've told him not to. I probably have more money than he has, although the land and that house are probably worth millions. And he sends me little presents, some earrings, chocolates and scarves. Things like that. I go see him now and then. He doesn't talk much. He just seems lost... just lost."

Keri gently swirled the wine in her glass. "You said he doesn't come to see you very often?"

Sally shook her head, frowning. "Not often. I guess this house brings back bad memories for him. Memories of his father—and like I said, Debbie stayed here when Ryan was in Afghanistan...before her death."

Sally sat there in perplexed reflection. "But I'm still here, and I try not to let it get me down or take it personally that he doesn't come. Ryan has to find his own way, doesn't he, just like we all do. Well..." Sally let the thought fade into a long silence.

After dinner, Keri tried to help clear the dishes, but Sally wouldn't hear of it. While Keri checked messages and texted her mother and Mitchell that she'd be staying at the beach house another night or two, she glanced up to see Sally come from the kitchen with apple pie and a pot of coffee.

"I bought this pie at the store so I don't know how good it is. Ryan always loved apple pie."

Keri tasted the warm pie and savored the crunchy apples and flaky crust. Sally was disappointed, saying it was too sweet. Half way through their dessert, Sally turned her eyes on Keri.

"About this diary...You said your friend wrote that she was in love with Ryan?"

"Yes. She wrote a lot about him. In fact, most of the diary is about how she felt about Ryan."

"When was this?" Sally asked.

"About two years ago, in June."

"Was Ryan in love with her?"

"No, I don't think so. My friend was very upset when he left."

Sally laid her fork aside, tilting her head a little, thinking. "But your friend married someone else?"

Keri took a sip of her coffee. "Yes, the man she was killed with in the airplane crash."

"Such a tragic thing and them being so young. So very tragic. I'm sorry, Keri."

Sally put her finger through the loop of the coffee cup, lifted it, then set it back down, as a thought arose. "You know, Keri, Ryan was very depressed at that time. Debbie had died in April. Ryan was almost inconsolable. How did Ryan meet your friend?"

"On Brandy Beach. Ryan had rented a place nearby."

Sally nodded, remembering. "Oh yes, I remember. He stayed there until he was redeployed. I stopped by once. It was near the ocean, right?"

"Yes."

Sally stared at Keri for a moment, her mind working on an idea. Her eyes suddenly widened with renewed interest. "Keri...I've just decided. I'm going to give you Ryan's address. I don't care if he likes it or not. In fact, I think it would be good for him to be visited by a pretty girl. It might do him a world of good."

Keri straightened, gazing at Sally with a combination of excitement and unease. Now that Keri knew Ryan's history, and now that the reality of seeing him was at hand, she was a bit apprehensive. Was he the violent type? Would he slam the door in her face? Maybe seeing him was a bad idea after all. She touched her neck, self-consciously.

Sally sensed Keri's misgiving. She stood and went into the living room. A moment later, she returned with an old family album. She set it down and opened it to a recent page. She turned the album around so that Keri could see it. Sally pointed.

"That's Ryan… so you'll know what he looks like."

Keri drew the photo album closer, her eyes expanding on Ryan's photo.

Sally reached across the table and touched Keri's arm. "Don't worry, Keri, Ryan is a good man. He's lost his way, but he's good. If he decides he doesn't want to see you, he'll tell you right out. He's not rude. Quiet, yes, but not rude. I've always been proud of him for that. And, of course, I've been so proud of his military service to our country. He looks good in his uniform, doesn't he?"

Keri nodded, but she didn't speak

At the front door, Keri took Sally's hand. "I had such a good time, Sally. Thank you for the wonderful dinner."

Sally's eyes fell tenderly on Keri. "Keri, I like you very much. I hope we can do this again soon. I hope you get the answers you're looking for and…let me know what happens with Ryan, okay?"

CHAPTER 9

On her drive back to Brandy Beach, Keri felt the strange urge to purchase a diary. A real diary, not an electronic notebook or tablet. It was odd, really. She'd never even thought about keeping a diary—at least not since she was 5 or 6 years old. If she wrote anything down, it was on her laptop or iPad. It had never occurred to her to write in an actual hard copy diary. At least not until now.

Keri found a gift shop that was still open. She parked and walked crisply inside, her eyes searching the shelves for address books and diaries. It was near closing time and she was one of only two people in the shop. From overhead speakers, she could hear James Taylor's recording of *You've Got a Friend*.

The young woman at the register was slumped over her cell phone, bored and impatient to close. When Keri asked where the dairies were, the woman didn't look up. She lifted a crooked finger and pointed to the third aisle.

"Over there," she said, flatly.

Keri examined the shelf. She saw a blue leather diary that immediately drew her eyes. It had a rich, leathery sheen. She picked it up, ran her hand across the surface and then opened it. The paper was a thick, creamy bond. Very nice. Strangely alluring. She thumbed through it, feeling the enchanting pull of it, as if she were being drawn into a potentially magical world of infinite possibilities. Maybe Sophia had purchased her diary at the same shop.

James Taylor was cut off in mid lyric, when the clerk shut off the power. *"You just call out my..."*

"We're closing," the young woman called, with an edge to her voice.

Keri paid for the diary and returned to her car, energized and anxious to begin her first entry. As she drove along Ocean Front Drive, she rolled down her windows so she could hear the rolling sea and smell the wet, salty breeze. It had been a busy day and she was tired, but also delighted that she'd met Sally, a wonderful woman. And, best of all, Keri had Ryan's address. What a thrill that was.

She would be on the road the first thing in the morning. Crandall Cove was only about an hour away. Would Ryan see her? Would he even speak to her, or had he closed the thick walls around himself so completely that no one would ever be able to penetrate them? Maybe she'd just watch him. Maybe she'd never actually meet him. It was her choice, after all. She didn't have to face him if she didn't want to. He might not even know she'd been there.

At the house, Keri showered long, warm and luxuriously. After slipping into pajamas and brushing her teeth, she made a check-in call to her mother and texted colleagues, who had HR questions.

She roamed the house, secured the doors, switched off the lights and padded into the guest bedroom, clutching her brand new diary. She slipped under the cool sheets and propped herself up with two pillows. Under lamplight, she ceremoniously opened the diary and turned to the first page, smoothing it out with her palm. With pen in hand, she paused, pondering, deliberating, wanting the first entry to be an important one, a revealing one, one that perhaps contained some fortunate revelation. It was, after all, the first step on a kind of journey.

The longer she sat there thinking, the sleepier she became. Her eyes grew heavy, her breathing slowed and, while her body sagged and her chin inched down toward her chest, she wandered in a soft sleepy haze, believing she was out on the night beach waiting for someone, under the intoxicating influence of a full buttery moon, the lap of the ocean and a soft languid breeze. Keri stopped, hearing the soft tingle of wind chimes. She turned slowly toward the sound. Ryan was approaching under drenching moonlight. She stood there, transfixed and waiting.

The last thing she heard was the shudder of the air conditioner. Lost in sound sleep, the blank diary lay on her stomach, riding the tides of her breath.

It was raining when Keri awoke, heavy drops striking the windows and drumming on the roof. A quick glance at the clock shocked her fully awake. It was 9:14! She flung back the covers and the diary sailed, landing with a thud on the floor. With sudden recall, Keri hurried over and picked it up, examining it with care, ensuring it wasn't damaged. She placed it on the side table and strolled to the patio doors. When she peeled back the drapes, she frowned out at the watery world, all gray with dark blotchy clouds.

Downstairs over coffee and her laptop, she checked the weather. It was supposed to clear up by around noon. Should she wait to travel?

At 10:30, as she was dressing with special care, her phone rang. She glanced over. It was Burt Walton. She hesitated, wrinkling up her face in conflict. Her hand hovered, and answered.

"Hi, Burt."

"Keri. How are you this rainy Friday morning?"

"Glad I don't have to go out in this."

"The weather people said we'd miss most of it."

"*The Farmer's Almanac* is more dependable, according to my father," Keri said.

"Do you read *The Farmer's Almanac*?"

"No, but I always get interesting responses when I mention it."

"Interesting… so you like to provoke?" Burt asked.

"Only on rainy days," Keri joked.

"Well… here I am asking you for dinner tonight, right on time, just as I said I would. And I promise the sun will come out, it won't be too hot or humid and, if you say yes, there will be peace on Earth and goodwill to men… and women. At least goodwill and peace where this man is concerned."

Keri laughed. She liked Burt's light and easy manner. She liked his baritone voice. "Well then, how can I say no?"

"Oh, you could say no, but then the world would be such an unhappy place and there would be no peace on earth or goodwill to this man."

Keri laughed again. "Okay...shall we meet or will you come by?"

"I will be delighted to pick you up... say 7pm. I'll make the reservation... well, actually, I'll let my secretary make it, because Dayna's Grill accepts calls only between the hours of 1pm and 4pm, and when they're full—they're full."

"I've heard about this place," Keri said. "The food is supposed to be excellent. There was a write-up in the *Boston Globe* a few weeks back."

"I love the seared sea scallops with leeks, mushroom sauce and tarragon."

Keri made an "Ummm" sound. "You're making me hungry and I just ate breakfast."

"See you at seven, Keri. I look forward to it."

At 12:30, Keri was on the road, driving south toward Crandall Cove. The storm had blown itself out by eleven and the dark clouds were rolling north, slinging rain over Maine, New Brunswick and Nova Scotia. Perched beside her was her brown Michael Kors drawstring purse, containing Sophia's diary and Keri's empty diary. She had still not managed to write even one line in the thing—not even one word—despite all her deliberation and mental ruminations.

And now, as she thought about it, she grew increasingly edgy and agitated. Why did she buy the thing in the first place? Why did writing in it seem so important? Why was she hesitating? Why did she have writer's block? Sophia didn't seem to have writer's block. She gushed forth like a fountain, with anything that bubbled up in her head.

The sun finally burned away the fleeing misty haze, sparkling on the newly washed trees, shrubs and flowers. Keri slipped on her sunglasses and followed the curving two-lane road until she broke out of a grove of trees and on to the bluffs, where she had a grand view of the dazzling Atlantic Ocean below. She rolled down her window and inhaled deeply, seeing the water crashing into the rocks below. She would stay on Highway 26 and arrive at Crandall Cove in 15 or 20 minutes.

She'd stop in town to eat lunch and get a feel for the place, and then she'd launch herself on her journey to find Ryan's house. Who knows, maybe she'd even see Ryan in town. Sally had said Crandall Cove was a small town, populated by fishermen; locals who'd lived there for years; and rustic vacationers who didn't want the razzle-dazzle noise of nightlife, snazzy boutique shops, or trendy summer restaurants.

Keri turned left off the main highway, following a winding asphalt road which descended toward the wide, shimmering sea and Crandall Cove. Gradually, a quintessential sleepy fishing village came into view. She saw three marinas packed with fishing boats, sailboats and cabin cruisers. There were weather-beaten, shingled beachfront properties tucked up into trees, and surfers carrying oversized boards beside their mud-spattered pickups.

Keri removed her sunglasses, shaded her eyes and gazed seaward, watching draggers work their massive nets. She wondered if Ryan was out there somewhere, with other lobstermen, lowering traps or landing their catches.

En route to town, she drove past a rickety-looking clam shack, where beach-bathers and locals were lined up at the window under a leaning, sun-bleached sign that advertised New England quahog chowder and fried clams.

As she entered the town, she looked right to see rows of two-story clapboard or shingled storefronts, a discount marine shop, a bait and tackle shop, and a corner diner, complete with striped awnings. On the left was a high-steepled church with a wrought iron fence, a manicured lawn and a graveyard. The tombstones were marble, gothic towers, some leaning.

She passed casual restaurants and shops that sat alongside well-worn fishermen hangouts. The one dusty hangout that caught her eye was at harbor side: Dan's Drink & Eat. *That's it*, she thought. *That's where I'll eat lunch.* Ryan probably ate and drank there.

Keri parked on a cobble street near the Crandall Cove Marina. She climbed out, stretched and saw a cabin cruiser approach, glinting in the sun. The pilot pulled the throttles back and eased the boat into the channel between the jetties, its engine purring as it drifted in toward the marina. She smelled the odor of fish and salt, heard the sound of creaking wood in the ocean wash, and felt the silky texture of a soft sea wind. Overhead, seagulls dipped and circled, looking for snacks. She heard halyards clinking against masts.

Keri turned her attention to the local hangout. She resettled her shoulders for courage, gave a little shirt-tail-tug of her fawn-colored blouse over white linen pants, and started toward Dan's Drink & Eat.

She climbed the wooden steps and entered. The screen door hissed, then slapped shut behind her. In the dim, dusty light, all eyes opened and stuck to her with scrutiny, as if she was the new gun slinger in town.

The wood floor squeaked under her feet. Ceiling fans turned lazily. The round wooden tables with ladder back chairs and the heavy oak booths were occupied with suspicious men and women in jeans and T-shirts, many wearing ball caps. There was a long, tarnished oak bar with wooden stools, and men and women were slumped over frosty mugs of beer or shot glasses. Most had swiveled themselves around to inspect her.

On all four wood paneled walls were black and white photos of fishermen hoisting up their prized catches, their faces weathered, smiles broad, eyes steely.

Keri swallowed. This was not a place for tourists. This was *the* local hangout and they did not want *any* amateurs. Keri was an amateur and a tourist.

She was about to pivot and run, when the wiry, silver-gray-haired bartender, with a waxed white mustache, motioned for her, indicating at the only barstool unoccupied—the one on the farthest end of the bar, near the jukebox that was playing Willy Nelson's *You Were Always on My Mind*. The bartender's smile was faint, his dark eyes watery but friendly.

She hesitated, lowered her eyes and then willed herself ahead, past the curious faces that were tracking her every high-heeled step. Why did she wear high heels? Vanity. Pure and simple vanity. If she saw Ryan—if she met Ryan—she wanted to appear sexy, sleek and fetching. Now she wished she'd exchanged them for the sandals back in the car.

Keri sat stiffly on the stool. The bartender stood over her.

"What can I get you, Miss?"

Keri's mind was a blank. She felt like an alien, dropped in from another planet. Her lips moved soundlessly. Actually she'd whispered her choice, a beer, but the bartender didn't hear it.

The bartender stared at her with the mild, tired patience of a man who'd seen almost every type of man and woman God had ever made.

"Would you like to see a menu or something, Miss?"

Keri nodded.

He reached over his shoulder, snatched one up and slid it in front of her. It had a big greasy circle on the *Drink* of Dan's Drink & Eat. There was a coffee stain on the *Crab* of Crab Cakes.

The heavy, barrel-chested man next to her turned. His middle-aged face looked rough, and his features were arranged in a haphazard way: a frank stone face, round nose, purposeful thin mouth and small stony eyes. He wore carpenter's overalls over a T-shirt. He whistled a tuneless, breathy song. He stopped, staring at her with cool wonder.

"Get the crab cakes, Miss," he said, in a rumbling bass voice. "Always good. The best in town, right, Doc?" he asked the bartender.

Doc nodded. "Yep."

Keri faced Doc, managing a cordial, shy smile. "Thank you... Doc. That's an interesting name for a bartender."

Doc shrugged a right shoulder. "Yeah, I guess so. Most folks around here think my medicine is better than

Dr. Mason's. I even make house calls," he said, with a little wicked wink.

The big man's eyes widened. "Get a shot of whiskey with the crab cakes, Miss. Hell, I'll even buy it for you."

Before Keri could protest, the big man ordered the shot—and the crab cakes for Keri. Doc seemed amused, as he poured the burnish whiskey into a shot glass and placed it gently before Keri. He stood back with his arms crossed.

She stared at the shot as if entranced. Her eyes shifted left and right. The big man waited, and the bartender waited. Everyone in the room seemed to be waiting for her. Even the jukebox was in between songs. All was quiet.

"Go ahead, Miss, swallow it down. Good for you," the big man said. "Good for the blood."

Keri had not had a shot of anything since college, and even then, it was a Kamikaze shot or a Jäger Bomb. She'd never particularly liked whiskey.

She lifted the glass to her lips, paused and then tossed it back, feeling the stinging glow of whiskey slide down her throat. She nearly gagged, but quickly recovered, as a blossoming warmth gathered in her chest. With as much poise as possible, she put a fist to her mouth and coughed, delicately, then replaced the glass on the bar, swiftly reaching for a glass of water.

"Good?" her barstool neighbor asked. "That'll fix you right up, young lady."

The jukebox seemed happy. It began to play Elvis Presley's *Burning Love*.

Keri nodded as she coughed again, and took another sip of water.

The big man extended his big, meaty paw. "I'm Big Pete."

Keri took it, her feminine hand disappearing into his. He gave her hand one mighty pump. It nearly dislocated her shoulder.

"I'm Keri," she said retracting her crushed hand.

There was a slow return to food and drink and buzzing conversation, as it seemed that Keri had passed her initiation. She was now tacitly accepted into the local chapter of Dan's Drink & Eat hangout.

While Keri ate the delicious crab cakes, bantering casually with Big Pete and the bartender, the juke box cranked out tunes by Johnny Cash, Credence Clearwater Revival and Nora Jones.

When Keri had nearly finished her lunch, she turned to search the room and the bar to see if, by chance, Ryan was there. He wasn't.

Keri asked for the check, but the bartender told her it had been taken care of. Astounded, Keri asked by whom.

Big Pete turned a large, gapped-tooth smile on her. "Hell, I have two daughters, Keri. I don't see them that much. They live in Illinois with their mother. You go out there in that big world and have yourself a good day on ole Big Pete."

Keri thanked him, insisting on buying him a drink. Big Pete frowned, taking offense.

"You're my guest, Keri. Maybe next time. Maybe not. We'll just have to see."

Keri thank him again and then hesitated. "Big Pete, do you happen to know Ryan... Ryan Carlson?"

Big Pete's eyes opened in mild surprise. "Do *you* know Ryan, Keri?"

"Well... I just..."

Big Pete cut her off. "Are you his sister...come all the way from Jacksonville, Florida!?"

"No... No, I'm just a... I'm just ..."

Keri locked up, her mind reeling.

Big Pete bellowed out. "A girlfriend? Does Ryan have a girlfriend we don't know about, Doc?"

Curious barroom eyes turned. Doc turned. He was gripping two mugs of beer with frothy heads.

"I wouldn't put it past him, Big Pete," Doc said.

"No, no, nothing like that," Keri said in a frantic rush. "I just..."

Big Pete cut her off again. "You said you live near Boston?"

"...Yes."

Expectation hung in the air.

Big Pete studied Keri, curiously. "Have you ever met Ryan?"

Keri spoke in a small, miniscule voice, feeling sweat roll down her back. "No."

Big Pete slapped the flat of his hand down on the bar. "Well, by God, Keri, this is a first. I've never known Ryan to *ever* have a visitor. This really *is* a first."

Doc was leaning, listening. "Me neither," he said. "Ryan's mother, Sally, comes once in awhile, but I think that's about it, isn't it, Big Pete?"

"That's it, Doc. Never a pretty girl from Boston, like Keri here. This, I gotta see."

Keri wanted to sprint away. "No, no...I'm just here because of a friend."

Big Pete nodded, his mouth working on a grin. "Well that is just fine, Keri. Fine. You'll find Ryan up at his house. Do you know where that is?"

Keri fumbled for her purse to get her phone. "Yes. I have the address. But I…"

"Well let's go, Keri."

Big Pete pushed away from the bar and stood up. He was a soaring, big man, a good head and shoulders taller than Keri in her 2-inch heels. She figured Big Pete was 6 foot 4 inches tall and weighed about 300 pounds.

"Hell, I'll take you up there," Big Pete said.

Keri stepped back, shaking. "Oh no… I mean that's okay. I'll find it."

"It's no trouble at all, Keri. No trouble. Let's go."

Keri's shoulders went rigid. This was not the way she wanted to meet Ryan. She wanted to observe him first and pick the time and place. She wanted to do it in secret. But Big Pete was nearly out the door. Keri breathed in her anxiety and started after him.

CHAPTER 10

Keri followed Big Pete's rattling pickup truck through town, past a tree-lined park and up a steep, winding hill. Keri swallowed back dread, wishing she'd just kept her big mouth shut. For all she knew, Ryan despised Big Pete. As generous and as kind as Big Pete had seemed to her, maybe people despised him or thought he was odd or crazy. After all, he had eaten two orders of crab cakes, french fries, a mound of cole slaw, a massive corn on the cob, an order of mussels, and a dish of vanilla ice cream. He'd washed all that down with three mugs of beer and three shots of whiskey.

They climbed higher onto the bluffs, 100 to 150 feet above the glistening Atlantic Ocean, gliding along a narrow lane asphalt road. The view of sea, surf and pounding waves was infinite and magnificent, the sky wide, the sun high and hot, shimmering off the road and the hood of her car. Keri breathed it all in, feeling revitalized and thrilled by the panoramic scene.

Minutes later, Big Pete's truck angled right onto a dirt road, and they bumped and ramped along until Keri saw a house loom out of a hot scrim of mist. It lay perched dramatically back from a tall, rugged bluff, surrounded by undulating dunes, sun bleached rolling dune fences and long, waving, electric green grass. In the distance were worn, sand-swept homes and the majestic tower of a lighthouse.

Keri's breath caught. Was this it? Ryan's house?

They turned into the winding drive, their tires popping across the gravel, and Keri drew up behind Big Pete's truck and got out. The air was still and hot.

Big Pete lumbered out of his truck and shaded his eyes, looking about. Keri heard the whine of an electric saw, followed by the echo of hammer.

Barking dogs announced their arrival. A floppy brown dog appeared from around the back of the house first, followed by a limping and shining golden retriever, both barking at the top of their lungs.

Big Pete turned to her. "That's Brownie and Tippie Toe, Ryan's two rescued dogs."

Big Pete patted them down. "Hey, stop it with the barking. It's only your old buddy, Big Pete."

Brownie skidded up to Big Pete, all wet tongue and bright eyes. He nuzzled his nose into Big Pete's hand as Tippie Toe came shambling up, finding his free hand and swarming his ankles.

"Ryan found Brownie all beaten up by the side of the road," Big Pete said. "He brought him home, patched him up and built a big dog house for him. About five months ago, Ryan found Tippie Toe with a broken leg and arthritis in both front legs. He fixed her broken leg and built another dog house for her, and you should see those dog houses. Nicer than my place."

Tippie Toe shyly found Keri's lowered hand and she stroked Tippie Toe's head gently. "Hello, Tippie Toe. You're a beautiful girl."

Brownie wandered over and sniffed at her. "Hi, Brownie. I love those ears."

Brownie's long floppy ears perked up and his tail whipped about when she lightly patted his head.

"Ryan's around back, I think," Big Pete said. "I'll go find him. You wait here. He can be a bit snarly if you interrupt him when he's working on the house."

That was fine with Keri. She sat on her haunches petting the dogs, and they luxuriated in her attention and affection.

Suddenly, they whirled and bounced off after Big Pete, Brownie barking out happiness and Tippie Toe struggling to keep up.

Keri stood up and swung her purse over her shoulder. She strained her mind, rehearsing the right words she'd use when she met Ryan. She couldn't just blurt out Sophia's name and blather on about what had happened to her. She couldn't just tell him, right out, that Sophia was dead. She had to finesse it, ease in slowly.

Keri stepped back on the smooth thick lawn, readjusted her sunglasses and appraised the house. It was an impressive 3-story Victorian house, painted a pale light blue with white trim. There was a finely carved figurehead of a mermaid jutting out above the front door, with a hand shading her eyes as she gazed out to sea. On either side of her were portholes for windows.

Keri started toward the house, drawn to the wraparound front porch, the turrets, the towers, the detailed scrollwork, the fanciful moldings and the gingerbread detailing. The views from every room must be glorious, she thought. It would make a fabulous bed and breakfast, or it could be rented out for weddings or family reunions, especially if there was a flower garden or a rose trestle or a gazebo out back.

Keri stood mesmerized by the gentle sighing of the surf below, by the sweet scent of honeysuckle and by the blue hydrangeas that embroidered the house. As she turned in place, she had the feeling that she was drifting in a beguiling dream, far from the real world. Yellow butterflies fluttered, bumblebees blundered into flowers and in that soft moving wind, birds darted and swooped over the bluffs.

Keri sighed out tension.

Seconds later, the tension returned. She saw Big Pete, and a tall younger man emerge from around the back of the house and start toward her. Brownie and Tippie Toe were right behind. She steadied herself with effort, and combed back her hair with stiff fingers.

Under the bold yellow sunshine, Ryan seemed to approach in slow motion, in easy unhurried strides. The playful wind scattered his long, sandy-blond hair, and he pushed a hand through it and removed his sunglasses, squinting her a look as he slowly closed the distance. He wore a sleeveless blue T-shirt, denim cut-off shorts and faded black Keds sneakers. He had considerable breadth of shoulder, a wide chest and gleaming muscled arms that suggested an athlete in the prime of his career.

This was not the same man Keri had seen in the photograph at Sally's house. There was a force about this fully present Ryan—an elegant masculinity that completely pushed Keri off balance. This big tanned man standing before her had impact, he captivated, impressed; he aroused intrepid desires. Keri felt a warm animal response. There were little tremors in her legs, her chest, her fingers.

Ryan stopped, standing five feet away from her, staring, waiting. He had a noble hero face, all sharp lines, sharp jaw, strong muscular neck.

Keri's thoughts stalled. She saw his intense sea-gray eyes probing her, checking her out. His expression was a blank page.

Big Pete spoke up. "Keri, this is Ryan. Ryan... Keri."

Tippie Toe and Brownie sat obediently on either side of Ryan, tongues hanging long, panting.

Ryan glanced at Big Pete, as if he were struggling to understand. He turned back to Keri, giving her a few seconds of curious evaluation.

"Well, say hello, Ryan," Big Pete said, staring at the two of them, perplexed by their silence.

"Say something, Keri," Big Pete said.

Ryan cleared his throat. "Hi." It was flat and lifeless.

Keri opened her hand to the wide ocean. "Beautiful place," was all she could force out. "Great view."

Ryan scratched the side of his neck. "Yeah, thanks."

Toward the back of the house, Keri saw whirling sprinklers, the spray of water sparkling in sunlight.

"Well, ask her inside, Ryan," Big Pete said. "Where're your manners? Offer us both some lemonade or something, for God's sake."

Ryan gave a quick, unsteady nod, ducked his head and managed a half-hearted grin. "Yeah, well, okay. Let's go in."

He turned to the dogs and pointed to the back of the house. "Go."

Brownie went loping off into the glow of sun, with Tippie Toe hobbling off behind him, her tail high and proud.

Big Pete looked at Keri. "Come on, Keri. Ryan's been out in the sun too long. He's been working on this house for weeks."

They strolled across the gleaming carpeted lawn and mounted the four wooden stairs to the porch. Keri noticed an old wooden rocker and she thought of her father. How he'd loved rocking chairs. Ryan opened the front door and ushered Keri and Big Pete inside, then he stepped in behind them.

Inside it was cool and bright, with knotty pine plank floors, tall ceilings and new crown molding. There was a grand staircase leading to the upper floors and pocket doors that separated the living room and dining room.

Ryan led the way into the dining room, with its spectacular view of sky and sea, and the wide expanse of craggy bluffs stretching away on either side. There was an antique farmhouse table, beautifully decorated with vintage silver pieces, straight back chairs, a scattering of antiques and a large stone fireplace.

Big Pete and Keri sat opposite each other at the table, while Ryan left for the kitchen. Big Pete folded his hands on the table and looked at Keri, pointedly.

"Ryan's kind of quiet, Keri. He doesn't hang out with many people. Mostly works that lobster boat with Charlie Bates, or works on this house. Sometimes when we're over at Dan's drinking a beer, he won't say three words. But he's a good friend. He'll give you the shirt off his back or do anything for you. Just don't ask him to talk about himself or anything about his past. He won't."

Keri sat awkwardly, her thoughts rambling, her emotions chaotic and on guard, as if she were expecting an attack. She recalled entries in Sophia's diary in which she described how Ryan seemed to look through her, and past her, as if she weren't there. Keri had seen that same look.

Ryan entered, gripping two glasses in one hand and a single glass in the other. Pete took one and passed it to Keri. Ryan sat on the far end of the table, with his two guests on either side. He slid the second glass toward Pete.

They sipped their lemonade, as the silence lengthened. The ice clinking against their glasses was loud. Brownie barked somewhere far away. Keri saw swallows swooping across the windows.

"Well this is nice," Big Pete said, after he'd drained his glass. "Did you make this lemonade yourself, Ryan?"

"No..."

"Well...It's still good, isn't, Keri?"

"Oh yes. It's very good. It has a nice lemony taste."

A big gray tabby wandered in, sleepy and silent. He lifted his head, searching the air for new scents.

Big Pete glanced over. "Hello, Max," he said.

Max's gray marble eyes were two slits of suspicion. He arched, turned and crept away into shadows.

"Max ain't very friendly, Keri."

"He likes the night," Ryan said. "He's not much for people."

Big Pete gave Ryan a knowing look. "Yeah, like you, old buddy."

Ryan ignored him.

It was Big Pete's air-whistling that filled the silence.

Keri was fascinated by his ability to whistle notes that didn't form a coherent melody. But somehow it was pleasant and comforting.

Finally, Big Pete stood up. "Well, boys and girls, I've got to be going. I'm a working man, and I've got a house to frame up the road. It's all about hammer and nails."

Keri froze. "Don't you want another lemonade?" she asked nervously.

Big Pete shoved his hands deep into his overall pockets. "Nope. Gotta go. Nice to meet you, Keri. See you around, Ryan."

Ryan nodded uncomfortably. "Yeah, sure. See ya."

"Thanks again for lunch, Big Pete," Keri said.

"Anytime. Come on back anytime, Keri. Maybe we'll go fishing or something."

Neither Keri nor Ryan moved until they heard Big Pete's clattering truck fade away into the still, summer afternoon.

Keri had the urge to leave. She had the urge to run. She'd never felt so ill at ease. Her façade of indifference melted away whenever she looked at Ryan. He was a magnetic wonder, whose reserve and mystery further amplified his attraction. She was about to stand when Ryan spoke.

"Big Pete said you live near Boston."

"Yes... Melrose. A little north."

Ryan twisted, uneasily. "Big Pete used to play defensive tackle for the New England Patriots. Everybody knows him around here. He's kind of the cornerstone."

Ryan's voice was soft and deep and to Keri, it sounded personal and intimate.

Keri's voice was tight in her throat. "He bought me lunch at Dan's."

Ryan avoided her eyes. "Did he? He doesn't usually take to strangers."

Keri finished her lemonade.

After another long silence, Ryan swallowed the last of his lemonade.

"It's so beautiful here," Keri said, unable to think of anything else. "You could make a fortune if you rented it out for parties."

Ryan didn't respond.

There was more silence.

"My mother called me about you," he said, softly, still avoiding her eyes. "Why are you here?"

Keri pushed her glass aside, searching for the right explanation. She decided to just throw it out there. "I know you said you didn't want to see me."

Keri waited for Ryan to respond. He didn't.

"I just thought you'd want to know about Sophia. She was my best friend. We grew up together."

Ryan folded his arms. "My mother mentioned Sophia. Sophia Anderson."

Keri's stomach knotted. "Yes...I only found out recently that you two met a couple of years ago."

Ryan searched Keri's face.

Keri held his eyes, seized by attraction and desire. The feelings were new. They were warm. They were unnerving. It was as though some secret cave of her heart had been opened, and she stood at the entrance, afraid to look inside.

Ryan gave her a small frown of concentration. "What about Sophia?"

"She was killed in an airplane crash. I thought you'd want to know. That's why I wanted to see you."

Ryan's face took in the news slowly, his face impassive at first. He lowered his eyes as they filled with sadness. "I'm sorry to hear that."

In the heavy silence, Keri played with the drawstring of her purse, aware that both diaries were inside. They seemed to be whispering to her—castigating her for coming, because at that moment, sitting alone with Ryan, Keri knew she hadn't come because of Sophia. She hadn't come to give Ryan the bad news. She'd come to see Ryan for herself—to see with her own eyes why Sophia had fallen so deeply in love with him—so head-over-heels in love with him.

Keri was also aware that anger and jealousy had played a part. Maybe she'd always been a little jealous of Sophia's bold sexual freedom and her easy attractiveness to men. Keri wasn't ugly, for sure, but she had none of Sophia's sassy allure and unconventional inventiveness. Keri was simpler and, yes, careful, and perhaps a little boring.

After she'd seen Ryan's photograph at Sally's, Keri's desire to see Ryan expanded into near obsession. There was something about his face—those sea-gray eyes—that drew her in. The full upper lip, the line of his jaw, the cool mysterious expression projecting a natural sexual energy that penetrated and pulsed with delicious agitation.

Ryan lifted his eyes. "Thanks for coming by to tell me."

His words held finality. Now Keri didn't want to leave. She wanted to talk, to explore.

He stood up.

Resigned and taking his cue, Keri climbed to her feet. "I just thought you'd want to know," she repeated.

"Sophia and I were just...friends, you know."

Keri relaxed a little, grateful for the confirmation.

"How did you find me?" Ryan asked.

Keri looked away. Should she lie? No. He'd know she lied. "Your mother. Online."

He was silent for a minute. "So Sophia told you about me?"

Keri stammered. "Well... she... She... Yes. She told me."

"What kind of airplane crash? Commercial?"

"No, private. She was with her husband."

He sighed, then nodded. Ryan shifted his weight from his right leg to his left. "Well, I need to get back to work. Thanks, again."

Keri reached for her purse. "Yes, of course."

In silence, they left the house and strolled to Keri's car.

"Do you know how to get back to town?" he asked.

"Yes."

Ryan slipped on his sunglasses and looked toward the ocean. "Okay... Well, goodbye then."

Before Keri drove off, she watched Ryan stride slowly around the back of the house and disappear.

She shrugged down a little into her seat, slowly letting out her breath. So that's how it feels, she thought. That's how it feels when every cell of your body awakens to the swift and absurd possibility of love. So that's how it feels to hurt and to feel joy at the same time. So that's how it feels to offer your heart to a potential lover, and take the chance that he won't smash it to bits.

Keri glanced at her watch. It was a little after 4pm. She had plenty of time to make it back to Brandy Beach for her date with Burt. She didn't want to meet him, but she had told him she would. She wouldn't back out.

She glanced through her rearview mirror once more, hoping for a final glimpse of Ryan, but there was none. Disappointed, she drove along the high bluffs road with that splendid view of ocean and sky, wondering if she'd ever see him again. He'd hardly seemed to notice her. He'd probably forget her by the next morning, or sooner.

So that's how it feels? Summer stops. There's a lightning strike. You dare to believe in the full warm breath of love. You feel half asleep with desire, and smell the pungent aroma of love. You give your eyes to it. Your body to it. You hurt and burn, and you thrill.

You drive away, empty and wanting.

CHAPTER 11

Ryan worked the electric saw, feeding a flat sheet of plywood into the spinning, grinding blade, sweat beading up on his forehead and arms. Thoughts and images kept cutting into his mind, distracting him. The sun was baking him, the hair at his neck was damp and sticky. A pesky fly kept diving in on him. Brownie and Tippie Toe were chasing, romping, wrestling and barking.

Ryan swatted the fly and spoiled the cut. He cursed and punched off the power on the electric saw. He slung the sweat from his forehead and stood there, hands on his hips, remembering.

Sophia was dead. It was hard to believe. She'd been so full of life and play; a little reckless, yes, but fun. She'd wanted to marry him.

"I'm going to marry you, Ryan. You'll see. I don't give up easily. You can't turn me down forever," she'd said, wagging a finger at him.

But she'd wanted more of him than he could have ever given, especially at the time. Especially after Debbie's suicide. Especially, when he was about to embark on another mission to Afghanistan.

She'd wanted to spend nights with him; spend her days with him; marry him. But whenever he looked at her appealing face, he'd think of Debbie's pretty, tortured face. He remembered her depression, the drugs, the booze. He remembered the brittle, emotional girl from a broken, dysfunctional family, whose mother was a religious fanatic—now a bitter non-believer—whose father struggled with booze and struggled to hold any kind of lucrative job.

And when Debbie got an abortion because of a date-rape her senior year in high school, her mother disowned her. She told her frightened, lonely, only daughter that she would go to hell. Debbie left the house, found various low-paying jobs and ran with a low crowd, low men and low self-esteem.

Ryan met Debbie three years later, when she was 21 and he was 26. She was a lost girl who drank too much and often took drugs. Debbie was working as a waitress at a local restaurant close to where Ryan's mother lived.

It was her delicate, fawn-like vulnerability that had touched him. Her sad eyes, pretty button mouth and thin shoulders brought out the protector in him. By that time, Ryan had seen so much violence and death. He'd seen mothers and children slaughtered. He'd seen women raped and beaten. He'd witnessed his buddies being killed or maimed. He'd seen unspeakable things.

After his first visit to the Country Kitchen Restaurant, with its paneled walls, checkered plastic table cloths and heavy wood furniture, he returned every night and asked for her to wait on him.

The second night she waited on him, she was shy and a bit clumsy, nearly spilling a mug of beer on him. He caught the thing as it slid off the tray.

She'd peeked out through a brown bang and apologized, her face flushed.

The fourth consecutive night Ryan visited the restaurant, he again asked for Debbie to wait on him. By now, her waitress friends gathered in the corners and whispered and giggled and escaped into the bathroom, reappearing with fresh lipstick and longer lashes.

Debbie took his order in a quiet, shaky voice. He noticed her face was waxen. Her eyes moved, seeking escape, then slowly lowered, when she realized there was no escape.

"Are you feeling all right?" Ryan had asked.

She nodded.

"You look pale."

"I'm just... well. I had a rough night. So you want the fried chicken?"

"No, I want you to go out with me," Ryan said.

Debbie stood like a statue.

"Will you?"

Her button mouth twitched. Her eyes brightened. "Sure."

They were married two months later. Sally never told her son that she thought he was marrying for the wrong reasons. She never let on that she believed Debbie was a very troubled girl, who needed a lot of professional help for a very long time. Sally liked Debbie and she wanted the best for both of them, but in her practical heart, she didn't think the marriage would last.

Ryan was convinced that Debbie needed him, and he needed that. As much as he loved his country and the team he fought with, he'd grown tired of fighting. The wars seemed to go on forever. There never was an end to the battles like there had been in other wars. There was no final celebration: "Okay, now, let's go home to our families and let the horrors of death, dying and destruction gradually get replaced by loving wives, good friends and peaceful times."

Ryan was a professional and when he was called, he went. That's what he had signed up for, and that's what he did.

Ryan found Debbie a receptionist job through a friend of his mother's. Ryan promised Debbie that he'd make a good life for them. He'd protect and love her, because he did love her, with all his heart. He loved Debbie more than he'd thought possible, and he sent her flowers and chocolates and stuffed animals. Their love-making was close and tender and never rushed.

Ryan had to help her—had to save her—had to help her forget her ugly past, her mother's harsh judgment, her father's weak nature and his meager affection. Ryan repeated—like a mantra—that they'd focus on the present and the future. *Their* future.

And they were happy for a time—wonderfully happy. Debbie laughed and danced and cooked and went back to school to learn book-keeping. Sally finally convinced Ryan to contact a therapist. The couple was trying to have a child, and Debbie sank into depression when she didn't conceive. She felt it was God's punishment. Her mother's curse.

"I hope we have a son, Ryan, and I hope he's big and strong like you and not so skinny and frail like me."

Ryan wrapped his muscled arms around her waist, lifted her up and kissed her long and deep.

"You're not frail, Debbie. You're getting stronger every day. We'll have a girl *and* a boy. The girl will look like you, all pink and pretty, and we'll name her Little Debbie."

Debbie laughed. "Like the Little Debbie snack foods."

But Debbie didn't get pregnant, and then Ryan was redeployed. Debbie moved in with Sally and grew lonely and depressed. She started drinking again, and she hooked up with her old drug friends, and fell into another down-hill spiral.

Sally tried to help, but Debbie refused. She grew weak and lost. There were days when Sally didn't know where Debbie was or who she was with.

Sally was shocked when she learned that Debbie had moved back in with her mother. That made no sense at all, but what could Sally do?

Sally's letters to Ryan were carefully composed, with the subtext of urgency. Finally, Sally told him, frankly, there was an emergency and he had to return home. She held back nothing. She told him everything.

At the time, Ryan was part of a nighttime special operation raid by U.S. Army Special Forces, Air Force Pararescue Jumpers, Army Rangers, and Navy SEALS. Their mission had been top secret and in the planning stages for weeks. A high level U.S. military commander had been taken hostage when his convoy was ambushed in the Paktika Province, Afghanistan.

Ryan Carlson was an SF Medical Sergeant trained in a variety of things, including minor field surgery, pediatrics and veterinary services. He was also skilled in land warfare weapons, explosives and communications devices. He was integral to the team and to the success of the overall mission.

Ryan received his mother's letters and they nearly drove him into a panic. He sent letters home and wrote emails, but Debbie seldom wrote back. A few of her letters did arrive and they were filled with misery and blame. How could he have left her so alone when he'd promised so much?

For days, Ryan had agonized whether he should request to be relieved from the mission to return home to his sick wife. But in the end, he couldn't bring himself to leave. He was there. The mission had been planned. His country and his buddies were depending on him. He was torn and in agony.

Didn't Debbie depend on him too? Hadn't he promised to love and protect her? Ryan was crazy with worry, at a time when he needed to focus on the mission and on his duty.

The mission went forward and, despite an intense firefight where two of his buddies were wounded, the mission was accomplished and the military commander was rescued. The news about the rescue would never appear in the media. It was all top secret. No one— except the soldiers involved—would ever know what had happened.

None of his family or Debbie's family would know how important and how dangerous the mission had been.

When Ryan finally returned home, it was too late. Debbie had taken an overdose of sleeping pills and she was dead. She was only 24 years old.

Debbie, his beautiful tragic fawn, was dead. All his lofty, empty promises to her boomeranged back on him, mocking him, chiding him and wounding him. He hadn't helped or saved her, his love, but he had saved the life of a military commander he'd never met and would never know.

He had protected and saved the commander, but he had not protected or saved his own wife. He'd left her lonely and lost to die alone in some cheap motel room 10 miles out of town.

It was then that Ryan's dark days moved in, suffocating him with guilt and loss. All the love that had swelled his heart was gone. Vanished. He hated himself, and his romantic daydreams, and his silly words, and his silly empty promises and worthless dreams.

Ryan shook away the old, festering thoughts, reawakened by that girl's visit. What was her name? Keri? The late afternoon lay quiet and still, the sun slanting light across the waving thin fingers of dune grass.

Ryan pushed away from the saw horses, walking aimlessly. Why had Keri really come? What was the point?

Back inside the house, Ryan reached for the empty lemonade glasses that still sat on the dining room table, illuminated by rays of sun. He paused, noticing Keri's lipstick on the rim of her glass. It was a deep red. He stared at it, remembering those full sensual lips. Keri's lips. He recalled how nervous she'd seemed. He recalled her diamond-shaped pretty face and high cheek bones. She was attractive. Maybe she was in her late twenties. Maybe 30 years old, like him.

Ryan stood there, with half-hooded eyes, sinking deeper into recent memory and impression, a kind of debriefing, after a mission. He scanned the "lemonade group"—in every detail—revisiting place, sound, smell and quality of light.

In his mind, he saw Keri sitting there at the table. He sensed a quiet, restless woman, a contradiction of sorts. That often indicated impulsiveness and possible temper. He knew that from his military and psychology training, as well as his experience in combat, sizing up soldiers who were about to go into battle.

Keri had dressed with care: stylish linen pants, a well-designed blouse that accented her neck and breasts. Ryan liked the layered style of her long blonde hair and the way the wind had ruffled it. He liked the way the sun burnished it, lavished it with highlights of yellow and gold.

When she'd shined those crystal blue eyes on him, he was surprisingly taken into them. He saw strength and attraction there; he saw a careful intelligence and he sensed more—much more—behind those blue watery lenses, and he was intrigued. She held secrets. She held desire. She held mystery.

When she stood to leave, he noticed she wore heels. He hadn't noticed before that. Really? She came in heels? Vanity? She wanted to impress a man? Him? She would be about 5 foot 6 inches tall without them.

The tilting up of her chin denoted pride, or a shy woman feigning courage, with a desire to project confidence. Which was it?

Ryan wandered into the kitchen, still reviewing his first impressions of Keri as he placed the glasses in the dishwasher.

Keri had searched him out. Why? What specifically had Sophia told her about him that inclined Keri to want to find him, to meet him?

And why did Big Pete escort Keri up to the house? What was that all about? Ryan would ask him about that later. Ryan shut the door to the dishwasher and leaned back against the new Formica counter.

It was all very interesting. It had given him a few minutes of entertainment, a welcomed diversion. And now he needed to get back to work. He pushed out of the rear screen door and walked back to his outdoor workbench and the electric saw.

The afternoon lengthened, and the work didn't go so well. Ryan was distracted. His mind was busy and tangled with old memories, and with a resurgence of unwanted emotions. He finally packed it in for the day.

Thank God the next morning he'd be back on the Sally May, lobster fishing with Charlie Bates—and Charlie was a man of few words. He was a good man to be with after being with a pretty girl who'd given off perfume and the scent of mystery. Charlie wouldn't even notice that Ryan was distracted by the secrecy and allure of Keri. Ryan didn't even know her last name.

When Ryan's cell phone rang, he saw it was Big Pete. "Yeah, Pete."

"Is she still there? Keri?"

"No. She left a long time ago."

"Why?"

"I don't know."

"You didn't insult her, did you?"

"No..."

"She's a pretty one."

"Why did you bring her up here?" Ryan asked.

"Because she was looking for you. I was being a gentleman. Some of us are gentlemen, you know. And I wanted to know *why* she wanted to see you, and how you would respond."

Ryan sighed. "Satisfied?"

Big Pete's voice softened. "You gonna see her again?"

"No. Why?"

"Damn it, Ryan, you are one big blockhead, you know that? I could use others words, but blockhead works good right now. A pretty girl comes to see you and you just blow her off?"

"I didn't blow her off."

"Did you show her around the house?"

Ryan's voice dropped to a near whisper. "No."

"Did you show her around the place, the bluffs, the dunes?"

Ryan hesitated. "No."

"How long did she stay?"

"I don't know. Maybe thirty minutes."

"Blockhead!" Big Pete shouted, then hung up.

CHAPTER 12

"What was Ryan's response when you told him about your friend's death?" Burt asked.

Keri stared distractedly, picking at her grilled octopus appetizer. "He looked sad but he didn't react much one way or the other. I was only there for about thirty minutes. He has a gorgeous house on a bluff that looks out over the ocean. It's a really stunning place."

Keri and Burt were at Dayna's Grill, sitting on the outside patio in a cozy spot away from the crowds. The warm air was scented with honeysuckle from surrounding bushes, mixed with rose from the rose garden that enclosed a bubbling fountain.

Keri took in the Dayna Grill crowd: the chic martini drinkers, the sun-bleached blondes checking out the Polo dressed men, two with black hair lacquered to their skulls, one with wild hair like a flared match. Those same men were making lusty queries of the ladies with their up-and-down, straying eyes.

There were casual families with polite kids, and silver-haired couples from lavish beach houses, tasting a Bordeaux or Burgundy, viewing the big orange sun slip behind trees and gilded meringue clouds.

The patio area had a feeling of summer celebration, as the blue sterno candle lamps were lit, and Miles Davis's muted trumpet played *Summertime.*

"Does Ryan live alone?" Burt asked.

"Yes. Alone. He and a friend own a lobster boat."

Burt wore a blue blazer, light blue open shirt and green khaki pants. He sipped his cold vodka martini with relish, observing Keri with new interest. He'd noticed a change in her. She had a dreamy, far-away look, as if she weren't totally present in her skin.

"Will you see Ryan again?" Burt asked, casually.

Keri looked up, a bit startled. She seemed to truly focus on him for the first time. "See him again? Oh... no. I just went to give him the news about Sophia. That was it. No, I won't see him again."

Burt squeezed a wedge of lemon over his icy plate of six Wellfleet Oysters served on the half shell, his favorite summer appetizer. They were pink, glistening in their own liquor.

"Do you mind if I get personal?" Burt asked, not looking at her.

Keri chewed, thoughtfully. "I suppose that depends on how personal you get."

"You're a beautiful woman, Keri. Have you ever been close to getting married?"

Keri swallowed, not meeting his eyes. "I was asked once, but it didn't work out. There was another guy... recently, but I wasn't ready. I guess I haven't met the right person. I know that's a cliché, but..." she shrugged, leaving it hanging there.

"I liked being married," Burt said. "I really did. That probably sounds a bit old fashioned, but when I married Erika, I was happy and I thought it would last.

I really did. It didn't occur to me that we'd ever divorce. Don't I sound naïve and perhaps a bit too romantic for an attorney? Well, I was a romantic. I think I still am. I still believe that a man and a woman can truly love each other, get married, and live happily ever after. What do you think, Keri?"

Keri's eyes blurred as she reflected. She began remembering things—things she hadn't recalled in years. There was a winter, when she was about 12 years old. It was bitterly cold, and the wind was frigid and sharp, packed with little pieces of ice that nibbled at the night windows. Outside Keri's bedroom window, the trees were black and bare, and Keri watched them shake and creak, their branches reminding her of skeleton hands.

Keri's mother, Monica Lawton, was in her bedroom crying. Little sobs, a few moans and then more sobs. The sobs were loud in the quiet house. Keri's father wasn't there. Keri's brother, Dwight, had a private room downstairs, in the back of the house. Did he ever hear their mother crying? Oddly enough, they'd never discussed it.

Monica Lawton was a quiet, personable woman and, though not a beauty, she was blonde and fashionable. She loved wearing heels that brought her up to 5 feet 6 inches tall. If she could be imposing, and at times arrogant, given her high I.Q. and two master's degrees, she could also be exceptionally generous to her friends and colleagues.

Monica's and Keri's relationship was more intellectual and practical than demonstrative, with understated feelings of love and respect. Most of their private talks were held in cars or bookstores or coffee bars and cafes.

"I'm not so fond of Sophia, Keri," her mother had once said when Keri was 10 or 11. "She's a braggart and a show-off. Her manners are atrocious."

Keri went home to look up the word "braggart."

Monica dragged Keri to the Boston Lyric Opera to see sexy *Don Giovanni*; to recitals and concerts to hear sopranos floating delicate high tones; to oratorios to hear booming throaty baritones.

Keri and her mother also attended the Boston Conservatory whenever Beethoven was featured. Keri sat in wonder, hearing Beethoven's crashing melodies and thundering piano sonatas or string quartets.

Her mother once leaned over during such a concert and whispered. "Beethoven said 'She that divines the secret of my music is freed from the unhappiness that haunts the whole world of women.'"

Even then, Keri knew her mother had substituted the words "she" for he, and "women" for men.

Sipping hot chocolate in the coffee houses, Monica also espoused some philosophical concept or quote.

"Educate the children and it won't be necessary to punish the men."

"Who said that, Mother?" Keri had asked. She was 12 or 13.

"Pythagoras."

Monica taught high school history until she became disillusioned with the educational system. Edward suggested she didn't need to work. He made plenty of money.

Monica left teaching and began tutoring. To her surprise, five years later, she was making more as a tutor in English, math and history than she had been making as a full-time teacher.

Nearly every time Keri and her mother sat for a "mother/daughter talk," Keri sensed a cave-like emptiness inside the woman, as if she were constantly struggling to find a plan, a method, a solution to fill up an inner void. Within the proud, private woman, Keri sensed innate loneliness, something afraid and full of longing.

Once, in a tender moment as they worked in the flower garden at the back of the house, Monica suddenly stopped weeding. She slanted a somber glance up at her 12 year-old daughter, as if something urgent had struck her.

"I want so much for you, Keri. You're so pretty and smart. I'd do anything to make you happy." Her soft feathery voice was hypnotizing and haunting.

"I *am* happy, Mother."

Monica looked at her daughter, searchingly, as if trying to locate that happiness. "Are you, Keri? Are you really?"

And then she'd gone back to work, pruning the flowers, burrowing in the ground, as the light of the morning sun lit up her wintry face.

Keri's father, Edward Lawton, was a tall, straight-shouldered man, with dark, penetrating eyes, a thin worry of a mouth and a stable, procedural spirit. He liked routine. He liked watches and clocks, and he had an almighty respect for time.

"Being late for any appointment is a sign of rudeness and disrespect," he often said.

Edward worked for a major Boston insurance company as a senior actuarial analyst. He used statistical models to analyze data and calculate the probability of costs associated with product failure, accidents, property damage, injury and death. Edward was paid handsomely to estimate the likelihood of catastrophic events, such as hurricanes, earthquakes, pandemics and terrorists attacks, as well as to assess the risk exposure of insurance companies.

"Is God a God of chance, Keri, throwing dice in an earthly crap game, or is he a God of probabilities, allowing the human being to make his or her own choices, based on their DNA, economic background and past experience?"

Keri thought her father a gentle, gracious man, who often entertained her with trivia and statistics, because he loved them like a banker loves his investments.

Keri and Edward would sit together on the porch swing on warm summer nights, and he'd banter on about some piece of information that completely captured Keri's attention.

"Did you know that ants stretch when they wake up in the morning? Did you also know that Thomas Edison, the light bulb inventor, was afraid of the dark?"

As night descended and the fireflies magically appeared like sparkling gold dust, Edward kept up the never-ending spellbinding trivia, while the swing rocked and squeaked.

Keri would stare at her genius father in wonder, content and relaxed, smelling his musky scent, listening to his slow, measured voice. "Did you know, Keri, that dolphins sleep with one eye open?"

Keri had laughed at that. "No, I don't think so," she said. "No way."

"And did you know, Keri, that a sneeze travels out of your mouth at over 100 m.p.h.?"

Keri laughed again, pretending a sneeze and catching the big watery spray in both hands.

"And, Keri, did you know that you'll eat about 35,000 cookies in your lifetime?"

"I want more than that," she exclaimed, and her father laughed and kissed her on top of her head.

"And I'll make sure you get more than that," he said, lovingly.

Sometimes Monica would wander out to the porch, and the trivia would stop, abruptly. She sat in the rocker with a book, usually biographies or nonfiction about women of the American Revolution.

And then there was only the slow metronome squeak of the swing and the fireflies and the silence.

The next winter, when Keri was 13, she learned the reason for the silence, for the distances between her parents; for the voids. There was a shift in the quality of mood, from polite respect and dutiful pecks on the cheek, to strained affability. Edward traveled more frequently for work, and he worked longer hours.

"Work... always more work than I can handle, Monica, but they won't hire anyone else to help me," he'd often say.

Her father was having an affair with a much younger woman—a coworker. Keri heard the arguments through her parents' bedroom door. They did not shout. Keri never heard them shout—even when the atmosphere of treachery and anger was as thick as dark clouds, and heavy like humidity.

Their voices were strained with control, every word articulate and clearly enunciated.

"Bastard."

"It just happened. It wasn't planned."

"I should have divorced you, Edward, years ago. Why did I stay? What a great big fool I am. What a stupid woman."

"Mona, we haven't been happy for years. You know that. Were we ever happy?"

Keri shut her eyes. Those were the words that landed like arrows into the bull's-eye target of her heart. Before she left the house she called Sophia.

"Meet me. I've got to talk. The coffee bar."

Keri left the house and wandered the cold, icy streets. In the coffee bar where she and her mother often came for hot chocolate and coffee, Keri entered alone. She sat alone and hovered over the hot chocolate until it was cold and tasteless.

Sophia finally came. She took a seat across from Keri, without taking off her coat. When Keri told her what had happened, Sophia stared hard.

"Damn... Of all the people in the neighborhood, I thought they were happy."

"Well, they weren't happy!" Keri snapped. "I knew that. I could see that!"

Sophia backed away. "Okay, girl, down. Down. Cool down."

Keri angrily pushed the paper cup of hot chocolate away and folded her arms tightly across her chest. "Why do people even get married? I mean, I like Bobby Cook, but I certainly wouldn't marry him."

"Bobby Cook is a little shit, Keri. You're too good for him."

"Well I like him, but I wouldn't marry him! So why do people get married?"

"They shouldn't," Sophia said, straightening up, proud of her opinion. "It's a bullshit thing. I mean, look at my parents. If it wasn't for TV and the dogs, they wouldn't have anything in common. I tell you, I am not, not, not—I'm never getting married. No way."

Sophia left ten minutes later, already late for dinner.

Keri loved both of her parents. They loved her. She knew that. They loved Dwight, even though he was mostly off playing hockey and was oblivious to what was going on. He was more like his father. He lived in his head and he lived for sports.

Keri was on an island, isolated, lost and abandoned. She ordered another hot chocolate, even though her first lay untouched, the marshmallow melted, looking like a white smudge.

When Monica finally found her daughter sitting there in the coffee bar, she sat down opposite her. She took both Keri's hands, squeezed them, and looked deeply into her daughter's eyes.

"It's going to be okay, Keri. Everything is going to be okay."

Her parents divorced five months later.

"Keri?" Burt said. "Keri?"

Keri's eyes cleared and flickered. Her attention returned to Dayna's Grill.

"Yes… Burt. I'm sorry. I guess I just tuned out for a minute."

"Everything okay?" Burt asked, pushing his icy plate of empty clam shells away.

Keri's thoughts were scrambled. She attempted a smile. "It's been a tiring day." She rubbed her eyes.

It was dark when their entrees arrived. They ate slowly, the conversation aimless and flat. Burt saw his once promising connection with Keri grow tenuous.

Most women found him attractive and interesting. Keri just seemed bored. It was too bad, he thought. He slumped and felt the return of loneliness.

Burt drove Keri back to the beach house and parked in the driveway. He didn't lean to kiss her.

Keri forced a bright face. "That was fun, Burt. Thank you."

He shrugged. "Maybe we could do it again some-time?"

Burt saw the bland interest in Keri's eyes. He knew he'd never see her again.

"Yeah, sure," she said.

Later, after a shower, Keri entered the guest bed-room and packed her bag. It was time to get back to her life. The emails were piling up. The boss was waiting. Monday would be a busy, crazy day.

After she stored the suitcase near the door, Keri paced from the bed to the double glass doors several times, her slippers whispering across the wood floor. Her new diary lay on the turned-back bed, waiting, beckoning her to write something. Anything.

She flopped down on the bed and picked it up. She opened it to the first page and reached for her pen. The pen tip touched the page. Keri's breath moved in and out. Her eyes wandered the room, from floor to ceiling to walls. Time waited, as if standing over her shoulder, peering down with tremulous anticipation.

But the feelings beating inside her chest wouldn't form and translate into words. The pen felt heavy, the page, a vast arid desert. It was a daunting journey, too challenging and too perilous to take right now. After all, what if someone found her diary and read it? Now *that* was a good excuse not to write anything down.

As Keri drifted into sleep, she saw the image of Ryan standing high on the bluffs, his beach house to his back. He seemed to be searching for something. Perhaps it was a lost ship. A lost swimmer?

And then, there was sleep.

CHAPTER 13

It was a work nightmare. Keri returned to her job and was swiftly called into a meeting with one of the owners, Stan Ogden, several staff members and two irritate employees.

On the previous Friday, Keri's assistant, Carla Vasquez, had discovered a serious paycheck problem: the deductions in some employees' paychecks did not match the benefits they had signed up for and were receiving. Five of the fifty-one employees were either paying for benefits they weren't enrolled in, or they had signed up for benefits they weren't paying for.

"How did this happen?" Stan asked, his face pinched in irritation and concern. "I just don't understand how this could happen."

Keri could have become defensive. She could have told them the entire heath care benefit system was a mine field, and their own software system had glitches and issues, but the fact was, she was the one responsible, and she had made a big mistake.

The group was seated around a circular conference table, with all eyes fixed on Keri. She'd barely had time to glance over the pages Carla had placed in her hand only a half hour before.

Keri felt the familiar nauseating anxiety. She was taking on stress like a leaky, pitching rowboat takes on water in a storm.

She stared into the eyes around her, seeing consternation and hostility. Mitchell was seated across from her, a tight, pugnacious smile on his lips. Was he enjoying this moment of watching her being grilled, like a medium rare sirloin steak?

And then there sat Polly Conway, the tart-faced, tattooed girl with the feisty spiked red hair and constricted pout of a mouth. She was always probing the place, looking for the smallest infraction, the slightest flaw, the most tenuous inaccuracy, so she could point, blame and swell with moral indignation when it was discovered that she'd been right all along, while her offender had not only been wrong, but predictably wrong. And then she'd present a little yawn of bored, self-righteous satisfaction, and say something like "If only everyone had just listened to me in the first place we could have saved a lot of time and money."

Polly sat glaring at Keri with a new and improved hatred. Her standard line was "I don't come to this place to make friends—I come here to do my job and then go home."

Keri wished she'd been able to fire Polly three months ago, when she'd insulted several employees and alienated others, but Stan had said to wait. He believed Polly would come around.

Keri cleared her voice. "I don't know how this happened. As you know, I've been away and the situation has just come to my attention, so I haven't had time to drill down and get to the bottom of it. Here's what I'm going to do. I'll go over everything, meticulously, and then I'll meet with each employee involved and show them what their deductions were and what they should have been, and we'll figure out how to rectify the situation. I will apologize to them, as I am apologizing to all of you. I will work with accounting and keep you informed, Stan, until all this has been settled. Obviously, we'll have to refund the employees who were paying too much for their benefits, and figure out how to get retro-active payments for those who weren't paying enough."

Keri heard a police siren go by. She thought, *"That was synchronistic."*

"Again, I apologize for this," Keri said.

The room fell into an icy silence. Every one was staring down at the table except, predictably, Polly Conway.

"Didn't I say two months ago that something was wrong with my deductions?" Polly said, with heat. "Why has it taken until now for this to be discovered? I just don't understand it. No one ever listens to me."

Later that week, Keri worked 13-hour days, repairing the damage, speaking with employees and accounting and documenting everything that had happened. She also went to work on creating a new, clear and concise HR policy/employee benefit booklet.

On Friday morning, she was near exhaustion. She was finishing up the last of her emails, when she reached for her half-drunk latte. Just as she brought it to her lips, her cell phone rang. Whoever it was, they weren't on her contact list. The area code was somewhere close by. Probably a sales call. She didn't answer it.

It was just after lunch when Keri left Sandy's Sandwich shop and started back to the office. The day was hot and sticky and she wished she was back on the beach, languishing in the silky cool wind, hearing the bark of seagulls. She wished she could lie on that beach and sleep for two days. Her eyes were sore and sandy and her body felt punished from overwork and lack of rest.

She paused by the glass entry doors of her red brick building to listen to her three missed calls. The first was from her mother. She wanted to know if Keri could meet her for dinner that night. Keri sighed. She was bone tired, but how could she say no? Her mother was seeing a man—the first in about two years—and she'd want to discuss every detail and get Keri's opinion. Keri quickly texted back that she would meet her. The second call was a hang up.

Keri was reaching for the chrome handle of the door when she heard a voice that froze her. It was soft and tentative.

"...Keri... Keri. Hi... Keri this is Ryan Carlson. Hope I'm not bothering you. I got your number from my mother. Hope you don't mind. You're probably at work. I'll make this short. I...ah.... Well, I didn't even show you around the house when you were here last week. I didn't show you around the place. Well, anyway, I just wanted to say that if you're ever back this way again, let me know. I'll show you around. Okay... bye. Oh, and Big Pete said to say hello."

Suddenly, Keri was wide awake. She stepped aside to let others enter the building, while she listened to Ryan's message a second, third and fourth time.

For the rest of the afternoon, Keri swung between ecstasy and nerves. Should she call him back or just text? What should she say? At her desk, she jotted down a couple of phrases, hoping to sound casual, projecting mild interest.

At 4pm, she snatched up her phone and began texting.

Hi, Ryan. Got your message. Yes, I was at work.

Keri paused, she watched two emails pop up on her laptop. One was from Stan and the SUBJECT was *Polly Conway.*

Keri groaned, swiveled away and stared at her texted words while nibbling on her thumbnail. What she texted next would be crucial. Should she jump at his invitation—an obvious request for a kind of date? Should she say she was busy and would get in touch at her next opportunity? Maybe make him sweat a little? Maybe he wouldn't sweat. Maybe he only called her because Sally told him to, or Big Pete.

A text appeared. It was from Mitchell.

Doing anything tomorrow? How about a movie or something?

Keri got up and strolled to her window. She was on the sixth floor, looking out over trees, rooftops and a parking lot. A plastic bag blew across the lot, driven by a burst of wind. It sailed, crashed, slid along the ground, hitched a ride on the next gust of breeze and flew away out of sight.

She shut her eyes in desperate concentration. When she opened them, her lips were tight, eyes narrow with determination. Her thumbs went to work on Ryan's text.

What about tomorrow?

Keri deleted it. Too direct.

Are your free tomorrow? I could come. Weather is supposed to be good.

Keri grimaced, as her thumb hovered over the send button. She inhaled a breath and tapped SEND.

She stood, waiting.

Carla knocked and Keri flinched and pivoted toward the door. Carla came in, shutting the door behind her. Carla was a full-figured, attractive and smart woman of 28 who had two kids and a husband who was a cop. Keri had hired her a year ago, even though Carla hadn't finished her Bachelor's degree in Human Resources. She'd proved to be invaluable—she'd found the benefit's package debacle and she'd worked as hard as Keri to figure out how it had happened and make changes so it wouldn't happen again.

"What's up?" Keri asked.

Carla leaned back against the door. "Polly Conway. She just left Stan's office. She told him he should fire you. She said you're incompetent and unprofessional."

Keri sat on the edge of the windowsill. "That woman!" Keri said, sharply. "What is her problem?"

"Stan wants to see you."

"What did Stan say?"

Carla shook her head. "He didn't say. He said he's sent you two emails."

Keri nodded. "Okay. I thought I could get out of here early today. Want to come with me, Carla?"

Carla shook her head again, slowly. "No way. Anyway, Stan just wants you."

Keri rolled her eyes. "Wonderful."

Stan's office was square, austere and practical, with one window and one withering plant on the window sill. There was an unremarkable-looking old brown fabric couch pushed against the far wall and one black and white photo above it, depicting a classic 1950s/1960s mainframe computer. There was a gray plastic chair positioned in front of Stan's gray, glass-top computer desk.

Keri entered, shut the door and stood by the gray plastic chair. Stan Ogden looked up from over his white rimmed glasses. He had a boy's smooth complexion and a boy's expression of wonder. His 45 year-old shoulders were stooped and his lips parted, as if he were always on the verge of comment. His slant gray eyes were small and nearly always in motion, as if they were directly connected to his humming-bird quick mind. Stan's once blond hair was thinning out and combed in cross currents, giving him the appearance of a distracted professor.

"Hey, Keri. Sit down. Sit down, please sit down."

Keri did so.

Stan spoke rapidly, and it was often difficult to get a word in once he got going. He also had the habit of drumming his fingers while he spoke, which made it difficult to focus.

"So how's it all going? How's all this benefit mess shaking out, Keri?"

"It's good. It's all been fixed. I sent you the PDF report and the updated policy booklet."

"Yeah, yeah, saw them. Haven't read them yet. Tomorrow or tonight or Sunday. But I'll read them. Good. Good. Good to have it all hammered down again. Good. Everybody seems happy again, and you know how much I love happy, Keri. I'm a happy guy who likes to run a happy ship."

Stan took a quick, hurried breath. "Now speaking about happy, I'm sure Carla told you all about Polly Conway. She's all stirred up, as usual. She's smart as hell and a great programmer, but she gets all worked up about people. She's not a people person, Keri, but, of course, you know that. I know that. Hell, everybody in the place knows that by now. Okay, so she comes in here and she demands that I fire you."

Keri started to speak, but Stan threw up his hand and kept going.

"I told her that she can't demand anything. I told her she needs to calm down, get a grip and focus on her work. She says, you've cost her money and she wants to be reimbursed immediately. Right now. She says we owe her six hundred dollars and she wants it right now."

"Stan, I did..."

Stan cut her off. "Now, I'm sure you spoke with her about this whole thing, because you are the best communicator I have ever known. So I tell Polly, she needs to get a big grip and calm down. She says, she's going to quit unless I fire you."

Keri sat on the edge of her seat, feeling reactive anger rise. She started to speak, and again Stan cut her off.

"So I said, Polly, I've got over 50 people working for this company. I said we all try to row up the river together. Notice I said up the river and not down the river, because that's what this business is, Keri. It's getting up every day, getting into our big boat together and rowing up the friggin' river together as a team. It's a challenge, every damn day to row, row, row up the river. So I said, Polly, if you don't want to row up that river with us, then it's okay to get out of the boat. Our boat. Go ahead and get in your own boat and row wherever the hell you want. Then she says, she'll sue us, because you have cost her six hundred dollars."

Keri just happened to glance down at her phone. She saw a text pop up. It was from Ryan! Keri's eyes expanded. She flitted a glance up at Stan and then back to her phone. She swayed between outrage and sexual excitement. It took all her willpower not to read Ryan's message.

"So I told Polly to settle down and take the weekend off to think about it. Then she called me something—hell, I don't remember—and walked out."

Stan lifted his hand, helplessly, then let it fall. "What are you gonna do with somebody like that, Keri? What?"

Keri spoke up quickly. "Stan, I told her we'd cut a check for the six hundred twenty-two dollars next week. What is her problem? She's going to be fully compensated. I apologized to the woman five times and it wasn't easy."

Stan shook his head. "Keri, I want her out of here. One way or the other. On Monday, regardless of what she says, I want you to call a meeting with her, and fire her. I'll make sure there is a security guard outside the room just in case. Now, if she wants to sue, she can. It's not going to go anywhere but, you know what? I've had it with her. Just get her out of here, away from this company and away from me, okay?"

Keri sighed. How she dreaded that. "Okay, Stan. I'll meet with her first thing on Monday morning."

Outside Stan's office, Keri hurried down the hallway to the stairwell. She pushed open the gray fire door and stood at the top of the stairs.

Her pulse was high as she tapped her message and read.

Tomorrow is good, Keri. Anytime. I'll be around. See you then.

Keri looked up, feeling a warm stirring inside her chest. She smiled, reading the text again. All the frustration and anger she'd felt in the meeting just melted away into sweet, sexy visions of strolling along the beach next to Ryan.

She texted back. *I'll be there about 10am.*

CHAPTER 14

At 9:45 the next morning, a glorious June Saturday, Keri was climbing the steep, two-lane asphalt road up and over the bluffs that led to Ryan's house. As she crested the hill, she glanced left and saw the morning air lying soft and blue over the glimmering ocean. Ryan's house loomed ahead. Her mind whirled as she imagined the day before her. It all seemed fantastic— like a forgotten dream suddenly remembered.

She felt that pit-of-the-stomach flutter as she approached, feeling vulnerable and powerful at the same time, like a 16 year-old on her first date. New and unexplored sensations quickened her pulse and made her jittery. When her tires popped across the gravel, Keri saw the front door open and Ryan appeared, tall and resplendent. Keri heard barking dogs coming from around the house, but she didn't see Brownie or Tippie Toe.

She parked and shut off the engine, taking him in as he descended the stairs and started toward her. She emerged from the car waiting, her heart thrumming. She noticed a new magic about him, the lithe body, the wide shoulders, the long legs and easy walk of a man who moved with the careful honesty and natural dignity of a big cat. He wore a royal blue T-shirt, khaki shorts, sandals and narrow sunglasses.

When he was there, before her, they stood in the full wattage of sunlight, him with his hands in his pockets, she erect, unsure, excited.

"Hello, Keri," he said, softly.

His voice fell away into the quiet anthem of the sea.

She lifted her sunglasses to the top of her head and squinted a look at him. Had they done this before? Stood in this same spot, under this same glare of sun, with the same sound of the sea striking the rocks below? Did that rowdy call of a blue jay sound just at that precise moment, as if cued by special effects? Did that single engine airplane pass over the sea and wink in the sun for just a few seconds?

"Hello, Ryan," Keri said. "What a beautiful day."

They stood awkwardly, two strangers searching for words, measuring feelings, hovering in expectation.

Finally, Ryan indicated toward the house. "Come in, Keri. I'll show you what I should have shown you the last time. It's a work in progress, so don't expect too much. I'm trying to restore it the way my grandmother had it years ago. The salt and the sea air are hard on it. It needs constant repairs."

They started for the house.

"The last hurricane that came through here really beat it up," Ryan said.

Keri noticed his voice seemed a little shaky from nerves. She wondered how many other people had visited the house, other than Big Pete.

Inside, Ryan gave her the grand tour. The downstairs rooms were comprised of a living room, dining room, kitchen and back bedroom, where Ryan slept. Though it was still being restored, it was immaculately clean and simply furnished, with a double bed and chest of drawers. To one side was a photo of Sally Carlson. On the other side sat photos of men in uniform, probably some of Ryan's service buddies. Ryan didn't linger. They left the room and he showed her the kitchen and the Butler's Pantry, where a back staircase led to the second floor.

The other rooms were decorated in rich Victorian colors of burgundy, plum, ruby and emerald. In the living room, there were a sofa and a loveseat with a subdued paisley pattern embossed in a rich, magenta fabric. Keri ran her hand along a settee, admiring it and the gentleman's armchair, lady's chair, and four side chairs.

The fireplace was empty, with a brass screen in three hinged panels. Over the fireplace was the original mantel with cupids at the corners, and above that, was an oil painting landscape of the bluffs and sea displayed in an ornate gilded frame.

"When did your grandmother purchase the house?" Keri asked.

Ryan turned to her. "She didn't. Her grandfather bought the land back in 1884 and he built the first part of the house. My grandfather added on to it. The house sat further back then and wasn't so close to the bluffs. Little by little the sea has been eating away at the land."

Keri turned to look out the window at the shining sea. "What will you do when the bluffs get too close?"

"I'll have to move the house back, or knock it down and build one further back. But I don't think that will happen in the next 20 or even 30 years."

Upstairs, the rooms were mostly empty of furniture, but they had the same general color scheme as the downstairs. There was a four-poster queen bed in one bedroom, covered by a white quilt, and a double bed in the other. The glossy wood floors had large throw rugs and the walls were newly plastered and painted in egg shell blue.

Ryan proudly showed her the two newly-remodeled bathrooms.

"You've done a lot of work," Keri said. She noticed a staircase that wound up tightly to the third floor.

"Does that lead to the attic?"

"Yes. There's lots of work to do up there. It's crowded with stuff, antiques, old clothes, and old photos. There are Christmas cards packed in boxes that date from the 1920s, 30s and 40s."

Keri lit up. "Oh, I'd love to rummage around up there."

"Not today," Ryan said, looking up into the shadowy darkness. "It's over a hundred degrees up there."

Keri ventured a look. "This is not like the beach houses you see today," she said. "It's so lovely and historic. How long have you been restoring it?"

He shrugged. "Oh... months now. I hated to see it falling apart. It didn't seem right somehow. My grandmother loved the place. We were close, she and I."

Keri ran her hand along the smooth plastered wall. "When I first saw the place, I thought that you could make a fortune if you rented it out for private events."

Ryan avoided her eyes. "Yeah, probably could but it's not my thing. It's the peace I like, and I want to preserve the land."

Keri folded her arms and nodded, wishing she hadn't spoken about it. It sounded so mercenary, so focused on profit.

They spent the next hour strolling across the property: up and down the dunes, across the front lawn to the small wooded area adjacent to the house, the rock garden and the remains of his grandmother's vegetable garden on the left of the house. In the back yard, they ventured to the edge of the bluffs overlooking the water, finally resting under a wide, spreading elm tree to the right of the back door. Keri sat cross-legged, taking in the far reaching views, the new lavish beach houses and condos off to the east.

"I'm sure you've been offered a lot of money for this land," Keri said.

Ryan had his back up against the tree, his knees drawn up to his chest. "Yes. The last time was a month ago. A large developer gave me an offer I couldn't refuse."

Keri looked over. "But you did refuse?"

"Yep. He wanted to build a big sprawling hotel and resort. Just before my grandmother passed away, I visited her. She told me I could do whatever I wanted with the house and the land. She advised me to sell to the highest bidder. She said it had had its day. She said it was a dinosaur, compared to the new beach houses and town houses."

"But you want to preserve it?"

"Yes, partly. It's so quiet up here and there are so few places these days where you can be quiet. After I left the service, I needed quiet... And I needed something to do. I needed a project. Something to work for. I guess I needed all that after my wife died."

Ryan picked at the grass. "I guess Mom told you all about my wife? About Debbie?"

"Yes, but not in a lot of detail."

They were quiet for awhile, as the morning fell into the lazy spell of yellow afternoon.

Keri looked at him. "Ryan... do you have plans after you've finished all the work on the house?"

He stared out to sea, watching surfers skim the waves, and the fishing boats on the horizon. A sailboat was leaning into the wind. "No. I don't have any plans. That's the way I wanted it and it's been good. I don't think I want any plans. I live. I fish. I work on the house. That's it."

Keri felt her sitting bones anchor her body into the ground. She shut her eyes and became fully conscious of the wind on her face, of the sun's warmth, of the caressing peace of the area. She was relaxed and at ease. As she breathed, she was gently surprised by how comfortable she was just being around Ryan. He was not difficult to talk to, as Big Pete had claimed. He was not the dark, imposing man she first thought he was. She sensed he had an unusual sensitivity to people and to the Earth. She sensed a powerful inner strength in the man. Was he still in conflict, still working to untangle complex emotions and to expel old demons? Was he hiding himself away from the world, up here in this glorious world of sparkling sea, wide blue sky, and a half-restored Victorian house?

She looked at him, her mind busy with giddy things, her feelings like bubbles rising, spinning. She liked being in his company. He seemed solid and grounded. He seemed like a good man.

Ryan allowed his eyes to settle on Keri and study her. He'd been watching her all morning, enjoying every gentle move and turn of her head. He loved her long, dreamy eyelashes, her glittering blue eyes that held wonder and uncertainty. He loved her body, the slim contours of her hips, her long legs, the fullness of her breasts, her blowing, scattering blonde hair, and the pleasing warm sound of her mellow, whispery voice.

She was easy to be with—easy to talk to—delightful to look at. What would she be like to touch? To kiss? It had been many long months since he'd had these radical and delicious thoughts. Since Debbie's tragic death, no other woman had stirred him, excited him or interested him. How strange it was that Sophia had told Keri about him.

Ryan leaned forward and his eyes met Keri's. They stared at each other boldly, freely exploring, feeling the rise of something intimate and pleasurable.

"What did Sophia tell you about me?" Ryan asked.

Keri lowered her eyes. "Well...actually, Ryan, she didn't tell me anything about you. You were her secret."

He looked at her, trying to understand. "I'm not sure I... Then how did you know about me?"

Keri climbed to her feet. Should she tell him? Would he be angry at her?

She laced her hands behind her back. "Ryan...after Sophia's death, her parents sent me some of her personal items to go through. They were still too upset and heart-broken to do it themselves. One of the items I found was a diary."

Ryan stiffened. "A diary?"

"Yes. Sophia kept a diary during the summer she met you. I read it. Most of it was about you."

Ryan glanced away, thinking, processing. He laughed a little, but it seemed a private laugh. He turned back to Keri. His face was again impassive, expressionless, like the first time she'd seen him.

"So you read it and then tracked me down?"

Keri didn't look at him. "Yes…"

"What did Sophia say about me?"

"She was very much in love with you. That's mostly what she said."

He nodded, but didn't speak.

"I wanted to be honest with you, Ryan. After I read the diary, I thought maybe you'd want to know how Sophia felt about you and what had happened to her. Then I thought, I wanted to see for myself what you were like. Sophia and I had been best friends since we were 8 years old. We told each other everything. We never kept secrets. But you were *her* secret. No one knew about you, not even me."

Keri let that settled before she continued. "While she was seeing you, she was engaged to be married."

Ryan looked up, surprised. "Married?"

"Yes…She didn't want you to know."

Ryan swept his hand through his hair. "She and the man she was engaged to—her husband—were killed in that plane crash?"

"Yes."

Ryan lowered his head and ran his hand across the grass. "Sophia was full of life…a little desperate somehow. She once told me she didn't think she'd live long and she wanted to experience as much of life as she could."

Keri eased back down on the grass, gently startled. "She told you that?"

"Yes. We met in June, on Brandy Beach. We used to jog together along the tide. She bought me little presents, shirts, a belt, aftershave lotion—always expensive stuff. I told her not to, but...she did it anyway."

Ryan adjusted his sunglasses and searched the sea, as if looking for something.

"By July, she wanted to get married. I was pretty surprised and I told her flat-out that I wasn't ready. I told her about Debbie, but that didn't stop her. She wanted us to run off together. I told her I couldn't run off. I had a mission coming up. A dangerous one. I shouldn't have told her that but I wasn't thinking too well in those days."

Ryan looked at Keri. "I guess she probably said all that in the diary...? Well, anyway, I liked Sophia. She was fun, and I guess I needed some fun after Debbie... but I wasn't in love with her and I told her that. She said I'd love her soon enough. She said boys always fell in love with her. That's when she'd get that desperate look in her eyes, like time was running out or something. I thought it was because I had to leave. I didn't know she was engaged."

Keri felt Ryan's attention on her. She removed her sunglasses, wanting him to see her eyes, uncovered, wanting him to see that she was holding nothing back.

"I thought I knew Sophia, but I don't think I did," Keri said. "But then maybe we only show pieces of ourselves to certain people and different pieces to others. I don't know..."

Ryan removed his sunglasses. "Sophia spoke about you, Keri."

Keri lifted her eyes. They shone with nervous interest.

"She said you were a true friend, a good friend. She said she loved you like a sister."

Ryan smiled. "Sophia said she'd never introduce me to you, because..."

Ryan stopped, suddenly timid.

Keri waited.

Ryan slipped his sunglasses back on. "She said we'd get along, you and me. Was that in the diary?"

Keri leaned back, bracing herself with her hands. "No... she didn't write that. Like I said, the diary was mostly about you."

Ryan watched Keri from an interior distance, amused by Sophia's insight. Ryan did believe that he and Keri would get along. He was sure they'd get along very well.

"So maybe you know me pretty good?" Ryan said. "I mean, because of the diary."

Keri looked at him, uneasily. "I'd like to get to know you."

Ryan canted his head left, like a robin listening.

"I could have stopped reading Sophia's diary, Ryan, but I didn't. Sophia never expected her private diary to be read. I shouldn't have read it."

Ryan stroked the end of his nose. He pushed up to his feet. "Well...it's a helluva thing, isn't it? I mean, here we are, thanks to Sophia."

Keri shrugged, loosely, evaluating his expression, his mood. "Yeah, here we are."

The wind blew in, circling them and tousling Keri's hair.

The moments lengthened as they stood in the extremity of thought, feeling and decision.

Ryan lifted his head, a decision made. "How about I go back to the house, make some sandwiches, grab a bottle of wine and we have a picnic?" Ryan said, amazed by his light mood. Amazed by the bright colors, the squealing cries of the gulls; amazed that he unexpectedly felt new life pumping in his veins.

Keri stood there, trying not to tremble, but she did. "Okay."

"Are you a vegetarian?"

"No."

Ryan grinned, a wonderfully boyish grin. "You never know these days. Okay, I'll surprise you."

"That sounds like fun."

Ryan started off, stopped and pivoted. He grinned. "Yeah, it does sound fun, doesn't it? Don't run away."

Keri wanted to reach out and grab this spectacular day and hold it gently in her hand, like a delicate yellow butterfly. She wanted to look at it, study it and never let it flutter away.

CHAPTER 15

On Monday morning, Keri met the dreaded Polly in the conference room. Keri was professional, efficient and polite. Polly, on the other hand, was rude, insulting, impossible and, in the end, she quit. When Keri entered Stan's office to give him the news, she was beaming.

Stan looked up from his computer with worried surprise. "What are you so happy about? I heard Polly quit. Wasn't that stressful? Being around Polly is always stressful. Hell, just having her in the damn building is stressful. Was it bad, that whole encounter with her? You were in there for over twenty minutes."

Keri grinned broadly, lifting her hands. "It wasn't so bad, Stan. It wasn't bad at all. In fact, it all went better than I thought. And it's such a beautiful day, Stan. How can anybody be unhappy on such a beautiful day?"

Stan stared at her, incredulous. "Keri...it's raining. It's cloudy, muggy and Bleh! You're a wonder, Keri. A real wonder. I never know what the hell you're going to say next. Is that good or bad? Hell, I don't know."

Keri was ecstatic. Ryan had invited her to spend the week-end with him. Both days! She would drive out Saturday morning and stay until Sunday evening. Of course, Ryan had made it a point to offer her a separate bedroom. "If you stay overnight, we can have two days together," he reasoned. Saturday would be spent on the beach, exploring the attic, heat or no heat, and cooking dinner together.

On Sunday, Ryan would take her sailing.

The first wonderful Saturday they'd spent together had been a perfect dream. They'd fallen into easy conversation and had had a wonderful picnic on the bluffs, getting buzzed on wine, sharing a few childhood stories, talking about the seagulls and the view, carefully bypassing any talk about Debbie or Ryan's tours of duty.

That evening, as they stood by her car before she drove away, they'd nearly kissed, but Ryan had hesitated. He withdrew, his eyes staring out into space, seeing nothing. Keri suspected he was remembering events from the past. Debbie? His missions?

Insects were whistling and scratching at the fading light, and a low, yellow, half-moon was rising over the trees. It had been so romantic.

Keri waited, wanting his kiss—a soft gentle kiss—a kiss to seal the perfect day, a kiss of promise for the days to come.

When Ryan looked at her, his eyes seemed distant, his voice rusty. "Can we do this again? Maybe next Saturday? Maybe you could stay the night... in your own room, of course. The finished one on the second floor?"

Keri again waited for the kiss, but Ryan didn't stir.

"Yes. I'd love to come, Ryan."

So all week Keri was high, floating on anticipation, imagining the weekend to come, barely able to contain her excitement at being with Ryan again.

On Friday afternoon, Keri shot out of the office at 4:04—not her usual 5:30. She went shopping for the weekend, buying a new aqua bikini, two tank tops, two pairs of shorts, new sandals, new deck shoes, a lacy bra and five pairs of Victoria Secret underwear. She packed enough clothes for a 10-day cruise.

At 8'clock on Saturday morning, she was on her way to Crandall Cove under a wet, metallic sky and the promise of rain. By the time she reached Ryan's house, rain was pelting down. Ryan met her at the car with an umbrella, took her overnight bag and ushered them both across the lawn and up on the porch.

Ryan shook out the umbrella, while Keri shook out her damp, frizzed hair. As she straightened, tossing her hair back, Ryan was looking at her. He smiled, shyly, a big man who'd fought battles and who'd faced death and loss, and yet here he stood, smiling at her so tenderly. It moved her.

"I'm glad you came back, Keri," he said, quietly, as rain drummed down around them.

On impulse, she reached out and touched his arm. "Me too."

He glanced down at her hand, his soft eyes lingering on it. He lowered the suitcase, leaned and kissed her. It was a soft brush of lips that awakened her, sending her spiraling into warm desire. There was a curving sweep of wind that came from the sea-scented beach, quickening their heartbeats and offering the riddle of attraction and the promise of love.

Keri heard the distant grumble of thunder as Ryan slowly backed away, holding her in his lovely eyes. Low rolling clouds came from the ocean, crawling across the dunes and the tops of trees, enclosing the couple in a private, ghost-like world. The hiss of rain made the moment intimate, isolating them, holding them suspended in breath and desire.

Inside the house, Ryan deposited Keri's overnight bag in the second floor bedroom. The room was spotlessly clean, the 4-poster queen bed covered by a white quilt, and throw rugs spread out across the polished wood floor, slightly damp from humidity. There was a refinished antique chest of drawers, a deep walk-in closet and blue curtains that billowed from open windows.

Keri's attention was seized by a roll top oak desk that hadn't been there on her last visit. She went to it, running her hand across its finish.

"I found it upstairs," Ryan said. "I thought you might like it. It was my great grandfather's, from the 1920s, I think."

The tambour was in good condition and it clattered up easily. Keri examined the fitted shelves, drawers and pen holders. The base had two pull-out shelves above the pedestal drawers, and each pedestal had four drawers with wooden handles and oak linings. Keri loved the slots, the worn varnish, the cracks and the dark spots, probably from coffee spills. She loved the old smell of it, slightly stuffy, slightly woody.

"It's wonderful. Thanks, Ryan. The room is lovely. So welcoming."

Pleased, Ryan left the room, stopping at the threshold. He turned. "Well, make yourself at home. Have you had breakfast?"

"Yes."

"Okay, well…" he placed his hands on his hips and looked seaward. "Well, I guess it isn't a beach day."

"I'd love to explore that attic," Keri said.

"Then we'll do it. I'll be downstairs. Let me know when you're ready."

A half hour later, they were in the steamy, stuffy attic that smelled of dry wood, mold and dust. Keri had piled her hair on her head, and put on jean shorts and a yellow tank top.

Within minutes of exploration, her T-shirt was clammy, clinging to her back and breasts. She smiled to herself, noticing that Ryan was deliberately averting his eyes from her chest as she carefully lifted items from boxes: 1920s style dresses with sequins, silk and rayon stockings, a bust bodice that was used to restrain a woman's chest when dancing, various colors of flapper's step-in panties, and 2-3 inch high-heeled shoes.

Holding one of the racy-looking dresses up for Ryan to see, Keri lifted an eyebrow.

"Your great-grandmother must have been a real party girl."

Ryan was stooped under the low beamed ceiling. "Oh yes, so the stories go. She was definitely the black sheep of the family. Her name was Lily. I think there's a picture of her somewhere in these boxes, and post cards she mailed from New York when she lived in Greenwich Village. I haven't been through them all yet."

"The dresses are so fragile," Keri said, running her finger over the pleats. "I'm almost afraid to touch them."

Rain slanted down across the windows, beating at the roof. A windy roar circled the house while Ryan opened more boxes for Keri to explore. He found an old oscillating fan and switched it on, surprised it worked. It stirred the warm, moist air across their bodies.

Keri found a vintage cut & polished crystal decanter, various beautifully carved smoking pipes, their deep bells still smelling of sweet tobacco, dolls from the 1930s and multicolored hair pins that Sophia would have loved.

Ryan showed Keri a milk crate full of 78 records in their original fragile brown sleeves, including records by Bing Crosby, The King Cole Trio, Eddy Arnold, and Hank Williams.

When Ryan produced an early 1960s record player, housed in a leather case, Keri's eyes brightened.

"Does it work?"

"Let's find out." He opened it, checked to see if it had a needle, and plugged it in.

The turntable began to spin. His eyes lit up. "What do you know? It does work."

Excited, Ryan reached in a second milk crate and retrieved an old 45 record in its original sleeve.

"I found this record a couple of weeks ago, but I hadn't seen the record player. It's Elvis Presley singing *Baby Let's Play House*. Let's see what happens."

Keri watched in wonder as Ryan carefully slid the record out of its protective case, grasping it by the edges. He gently lowered the record onto the turntable and lifted the tone arm.

"Ready?" he asked, enjoying the anticipation on her face.

Keri nodded.

He lowered the needle. It scratched across the vinyl—then popped. When Elvis' restlessly young, echo-laden hiccupping-voice broke through the little speaker, Keri sat up, applauding.

> *Oh, baby, baby, baby, baby, baby*
> *Baby, baby baby, b-b-baby baby, baby*
> *Baby baby baby*
> *Come back, baby, I wanna play house with you.*

A bass guitar thumped away under his voice; an electric guitar twanged.

Ryan snapped his fingers while Keri swayed, a big smile playing across her face. When the song finished, Ryan found another Elvis 45. *Are You Lonesome Tonight?*

Elvis' romantically haunting voice filled the low angled space of the attic, melting into the steady tap of the rain. Keri felt the impulse to stand. She did so, keeping her warm eyes on Ryan. She motioned to him with wiggling fingers. He came to her, his head and shoulders hunched under the low, sloping roof.

They hovered, meeting each other's eyes. Keri's were dreamy, her body aroused. Ryan was lost in personal memory, his mind in two worlds. Keri was shaking his heart loose, and he was confused by the impact of emotion.

He reached for Keri's hand. With his other hand he held her in the small of her back. Their dance was a simple wandering circle, with Ryan's head lowered into Keri's lush, perfumed hair. Keri shivered a little, her body alive with scent, sound and sensation, as she eeled into Ryan's wide chest. Elvis' breathy voice urged them closer, in a steady surprise of movement and attraction.

The record finished, but Keri and Ryan kept dancing, oblivious to the persistent skipping stylus on the vinyl.

Keri felt Ryan's body suddenly grow rigid. After they separated, his face was under tight control. Keri explored his eyes, looking for a confirmation of affection, but she saw only distance and confusion. His entire mood had shifted.

"The rain stopped," he said, flatly.

Keri stood staring, thinking, swelling with emotion. "Yeah... it stopped."

Ryan switched off the record player and replaced the records in the crates. Following his lead, Keri repacked the boxes and turned off the fan.

The attic smelled rainy, and it was eerily calm. Neither spoke for a time as they stood awkwardly, their eyes moving. Ryan searched for words, but none came. He seemed to be stuck in the glue of an aching memory.

In truth, he was afraid, and he didn't want Keri to see it, sense it or smell it. He wasn't afraid of bullets or battle. He wasn't afraid of the sea. He wasn't even afraid of death. He was afraid of love, of being in love, of giving oneself to love and then losing it again.

Debbie's lonely and awful death had nearly finished him. In the months that followed, Ryan had fought to keep the pain and guilt locked away. They had paced about inside him like wild breathing beasts, always waiting for the right moment to pounce.

So far, Ryan had succeeded in keeping the beasts away. He'd moved to a new town, begun restoration on the house, gone into partnership with a fishing boat and fished long hours—all in a heightened effort to keep those dual beasts locked in that cage. They had slept.

But Keri had awakened them. They were about to burst out of the cage and roam the dark regions of his mind. The first time he'd seen Keri, he'd felt a catch in his chest, as if the monsters were rattling the cage. It had all happened at that very first meeting, when he saw her standing there in bold yellow sunlight.

Opening his heart to Keri could cure him or it could take him back down into pain. Could he take that chance?

They left the attic, Keri first, Ryan behind, carefully navigating the narrow staircase.

Keri knew something had happened up there, but she didn't know what it was. Ryan had just suddenly and inexplicably disconnected from her. He had unplugged his feelings just like he had unplugged that record player. At the moment of supreme connection, he slammed the door on his heart.

With the absence of music, wind and rain, the house was alive with quiet. Ryan fell into a deep silence, Keri into confusion and doubt. Maybe she shouldn't stay the night. Maybe Ryan wasn't ready or even capable of having another relationship. Maybe he never would be. But what about her own feelings? Could she ignore them? Could she just walk away, now that she'd been startled by the possibility of true love?

In a matter of days, she had fallen hard for Ryan. Maybe she'd fallen for him as she'd read Sophia's diary, the power of her words and emotions so thrilling and intoxicating that it had stirred her into action.

Regardless of the reasons and the mystery of her feelings, she'd fallen for Ryan. She wanted to be with Ryan. She wanted this with all her heart.

CHAPTER 16

After they'd left the attic, Ryan excused himself, saying he needed to make a few phone calls. Keri closed herself off in her room with her diary, sitting hunched at the roll top desk. She was desperate to write something—anything to let the words pour out of her. But the frozen streams of emotion had not thawed. There was no melting, no coalescence between heart and head, no natural flow, just jumbled thoughts and words that lay barren in her frustrated heart.

Had she ever felt love? True love? Was that the problem? Had she lived her entire life in a kind of perpetual night, her eyes deluded by moving shadows, believing love to be mere attraction or sex or compatibility? After seeing Ryan, why did her life burn brighter, burn hotter, burn with desire and confusion? Why did she burn with the fear of love, and burn with the infinite possibility of love? She imagined herself as a medieval explorer about to sail her three-masted tall ship away from the Old world to the New one. The sea was vast. The voyage long. Success uncertain.

Inspired by these thoughts, Keri grabbed her pen, bringing the tip to the wide blank diary page. She pressed the point into the page. It formed a period. It would not move. Her little sailboat gathered no wind. She did not sail.

About a half-hour later, Keri was downstairs sipping a cup of tea when Ryan appeared, his hands resting in his pockets. His mood had shifted again. He was lighter and his moody expression had vanished, though his manner was apologetic and subdued.

Keri half-expected him to say that her visit had been a bad idea. Instead, he suggested they go to Dan's for lunch.

They climbed into Ryan's white Ford SuperCab and drove to town, both looking skyward, checking the agitated gray clouds, searching for signs of the sun. By the time they parked near Dan's, the sun had broken through fat rolling clouds and sparkled the day. Before they stepped into Dan's, Ryan checked the sky once more.

"How about we go to the beach after lunch?"

Keri tried to read his mood. He was still recessed, but his eyes had brightened.

"Sounds good," Keri said.

Dan's Drink & Eat was about half-full, but every pair of eyes in the place found the couple and stared with fascination. They had never seen Ryan, the perennial loner, enter with anyone, especially a female. It seemed to jar the room to full wakefulness, as though they struggled to recall some old sea story about a mermaid and a fisherman—something that would help them adjust to this new astounding image.

Keri saw Big Pete seated at the bar. He twisted around and she waved at him.

He lifted a hand, a big crooked grin on his face. Doc waved, too, his handlebar mustache lifting. Two attractive women in their early twenties lowered their smoldering eyes to half mast, chilly over Keri's presence. They'd been eyeing Ryan for months.

Ryan lowered his head, feeling all the eyes swinging around as they passed the tables to sit at an empty booth in the back of the room, near the kitchen door.

The room was poised with speculation and little mumbling whispers.

"Is that Ryan's sister?"

"Don't think so. Pretty, huh?"

"Yep."

"He looks nervous."

"Do you think she's Ryan's type?"

"What's his type? Never seen him with any woman."

"Think she's staying with him up at the house?"

"Why not?"

"How did they meet? Maybe somebody from his past?"

"What past? He never talks about the past."

"He ain't gonna fish all weekend with that girl in the house."

"So why should he? If I was with that girl, I wouldn't go fishin' either."

Ryan inhaled a little nervous breath and reached for the paper menus propped between the sugar dispenser and the salt and pepper shakers.

"Are most of these people fishermen?" Keri asked, glancing about out of the corner of her eyes.

Ryan nodded. "Yeah, most. Not all. Some own the shops, some work in the shops, some do landscaping here and west of here, where you saw those new corporate beach houses and townhouses."

They contemplated the menu over two beers, as the juke-box thumped, as the room hummed with conversation. A thin, toothy waitress in her early 40s came over, acknowledging Ryan with a sharp nod of her dyed blonde, Little Orphan Annie hairstyle.

"How's fishing, Ryan?" she asked.

"Not bad, Bette. How's Lucky Dan?"

"Lazy. Playing cards. Makin' money. Makes more money at poker than he makes off this place. That's why I stay with him. He's a polecat with a lot of good luck."

Bette didn't look at Keri.

"This is Keri, Bette."

Bette's cool glance looked her over. "How are ya?"

"Fine. Good," Keri said.

Bette's eyes shot back to Ryan. "Big Pete said the house is coming along."

"Yeah. Getting there."

"How are the boys?" Ryan asked.

"Getting' into trouble. There's too much stuff out there in the world, Ryan. I want Dan Jr. to go into the Army or something. Guess what? He don't want to go. B.J. hates school and won't go."

"What's Dan say?"

"Dan's playin' cards. The boys want to learn, but Dan says they don't have the luck. Don't ask me how Dan knows, but he knows about luck or, maybe he's just the luckiest son of a bitch I've ever known. Anyway, welcome to my world."

Bette flipped off her chatty switch and turned on all business. "What's it going to be, Ryan?"

Keri ordered the fish and chips and Ryan the lobster roll. Bette whisked away through the swinging door, into the kitchen.

Ryan leaned forward. "That's Dan Wilson's wife. She basically runs the place."

"Dan gambles?" Keri asked.

"Yeah... and he's lucky. That's how this place became Dan's. It used to be *The Seafood Hut*. He won it in a poker game from a guy named Wayne Huber. Wayne now captains a fishing and cruising boat off Keyport, New Jersey."

Keri took a sip of her beer. "When do you fish?"

"I was out three of the last five days. I took the weekend off."

"Your partner doesn't mind?"

"Charlie? Yeah, he probably does. I sent him a sub. The guy needs the money. He and Charlie get along okay, as good as anybody can get along with Charlie."

"You get along with him?"

"We don't talk much. We work. That suits us both."

"And you fish for lobsters?"

"Yep."

"Do you supply restaurants in Boston?"

"Yeah, some. It's competitive. Almost 90 percent of all American lobster is trapped in Maine."

Keri smiled. "So that's why you ordered the lobster roll?"

"Yes, and because I really like Dan's lobster roll."

"You supply him?"

"Of course."

Keri looked toward the kitchen. "Have you ever met Bette's sons?"

"Yeah, a couple of times."

"What did you think?"

Ryan eyed her, questioningly. "They're...how should I put it? A little wild. Basically good kids, as far as I know. Never hung around them that much."

"Maybe you should."

"Should what?" Ryan asked.

"Hang around them."

"What do you mean?"

Keri took a sip of water. "I just had a thought. Maybe you could help them."

Ryan lifted his beer mug and leaned back, waiting.

"I'm a human resources manager, Ryan. It's the way my head works. Why don't you ask the boys to help you work on your house?"

Ryan narrowed his eyes on her. He took a long, slow drink of beer. "Why?"

Keri folded her arms. "Because it would be good for them and it would be a win for you. I'm sure you could use some help with that big house."

Ryan looked out across the room. He and Keri were no longer a source of interest. The diners had drifted back to their own conversations.

"Human Resources," Ryan said, thoughtfully. "I should have asked what you did. My social skills are kind of rusty. You work in Boston?"

"Yeah, a tech company."

"You like it?"

"Well enough."

"I like working alone," Ryan said.

Keri stared into her foamy beer. She traced the rim of her mug with her index finger. "Just a suggestion."

Ryan studied her lean neck, her hair shining under the light in gradations of blonde, caramel and honey; her creamy skin and soft, delicate, blue eyes. Keri's lips were red and ripe and slightly open, as if waiting for a kiss.

Ryan swallowed away desire and the last of his beer, feeling the birth of a new attraction. Keri came to him in waves—high curling waves from a warm Caribbean sea, breaking near shore, splashing, sliding, covering him, rinsing him clean.

They ate, mostly in silence.

To reach the beach, Ryan had built a steep wooden staircase with sturdy railings on either side. It led from his front yard down the side of the bluffs. An old one had rotted away and collapsed in a heap after the last raging storm, forcing him to build a new one.

Ryan escorted her down the stairs, pausing to ensure Keri was close behind, her flip-flops solid on the steps. She wore her new aqua bikini, a white cover-up and a floppy hat. He wore baggy orange trunks and a loose fitting T-shirt that rippled in the wind.

It was a private beach. Keri spread out two bright beach towels while Ryan jammed the pole of a beach umbrella deep into sand, anchoring it. The afternoon sun glared off the sea, baking their shoulders and dazzling their eyes.

Ryan offered Keri his hand, indicating toward the ocean. "Ready?"

"Ready," Keri said, with a firm nod.

She felt his fingers close around hers. It was heaven.

They ventured toward the tide line. Cool water rushed in, splashed and ran across their feet like cold silk. The sand shifted. Pebbles and polished stones rattled and sucked at their toes.

"Let's go for it," Ryan said.

They sprinted into the sea, their legs kicking high, bodies arched forward in playful attack. At the last moment, before the wall of wave engulfed them, they released hands. Ryan charged, dived, disappeared, then surfaced. He broke into a forward crawl, then glanced about, looking for Keri. She was right behind him, dropping under waves, surfacing, bobbing. They swam further out together, growing small. They swam past a windsurfer with a red sail, and continued on, retreating further until they were only specks in the vast undulating sea.

Toward late afternoon, they strolled across the unwrinkled sand, close to the tide, cool on the bottoms of their feet, Keri in her broad, wide-rimmed floppy hat, Ryan in a Boston Red Socks cap. They walked and drifted, sometimes moving in close so that their hips touched.

They watched three surfers gliding under a charging wave, arms outstretched, feet dancing across the surface of their boards. Keri said she wanted to learn to surf and he promised he'd teach her the next time she visited.

One surfer dropped to a knee, jaw jutted out, struggling, as the ocean chased him; a second coaxed the board right, seeking balance and strategy. The third shot across the surface, his board spraying water like white smoke. Keri mimicked them, her arms raised in mock balance, her narrowed eyes measuring the curving waves and the wind.

Later, they lay close under the umbrella and dozed and spoke in whispers about the sea, about the day and the beauty of the place. Their lips were often close, but Ryan did not kiss her, beating back desire, fear and anger at himself. He had not passionately kissed a woman since Debbie. Yes, he had kissed Keri gently, but not passionately.

He had not been with a woman since Debbie. He had not expected to feel the gathering desire he was feeling now, lying there next to Keri. Beautiful Keri. Intelligent Keri—startling him with her warm, blue eyes.

For dinner, Ryan sautéed fresh sole with lemon, white wine and garlic. He steamed broccoli, mashed potatoes with lots of butter, and opened a bottle of Sauvignon Blanc.

They sat at a picnic table outside, on the newly completed mahogany deck, gazing out at the dying red sun and the indigo sea, hearing the night sounds all around them. They ate in candlelight, and Keri made little delicious sounds, lost in the romance of taste and sensation. No man had ever cooked dinner for her. No man had ever instructed her to sit and relax while he served her. No man had ever entranced her in so many unexpected ways.

As darkness settled, it was a night of magic. The half-moon tossed shimmering platinum petals across the water, shapes slowly fell into silhouette, and a soft wind circled, trembling the candle flames. Keri heard a different kind of hooty bird call, and the moan of a distant train. Glancing skyward, she saw the darting shadows of bats, looping nervously over the lawn.

The wine added lightness, and a gentle flush of longing that stirred across her skin, completing the magical spell. Would Ryan come to her bedroom during the night?

"This is as close to heaven as I've ever been," she said, seeing Ryan's handsome face in flickering candlelight, his eyes glistening, watching her.

Ryan had a kind of epiphany. It occurred to him that restoring the house just for the sake of restoration made no sense at all, unless he could share it—share it like this—with Keri. Had he somehow known she'd come into his life? Is that why he didn't sell the land? Is that why he felt compelled to restore it to its elegant, original state?

"We'll go sailing tomorrow," Ryan said. "It's Big Pete's boat. It's not the classiest boat, but it'll do."

While they cleaned up, Keri was quiet. Whenever she spoke Ryan's name, her voice was low and breathy. Ryan watched her, blinking slowly, his expression tender. He found ways to touch her and brush against her, as they stacked the dishes, as they passed from outside to inside, with dishes and candles. Ryan allowed his fingers to find a bare spot on her arm, or he touched her shoulder. Keri yielded to his touch, wanting more.

As the humid, romantic mood crescendoed, Ryan's phone rang. It was 10 o'clock. Sally, Ryan's mother, was on the line. Ryan hesitated before answering it.

Sally's voice was low and conspiratorial. "Is Keri there?"

Keri had returned to the deck with a cup of tea, to give him privacy.

Ryan stayed in the kitchen. "Yes."

"And?"

"Mom...This isn't like you."

"So sue me. How's it going?

Ryan waited. "It's been a good day. A very good day."

"I haven't heard you say that in a long time, Ryan. A very long time."

After the call, he and Keri returned to the beach, playing in a sudden, drenching rain.

Keri showered, towel-dried her hair, and sat on the bed, listening to the quiet noises of the house. Would Ryan find an excuse to come upstairs? After the rain storm, they'd said good-night quickly, both cold, heading for showers. Ryan had simply run his hands over her hair and thanked her for a great day. Should she pretend she'd left something downstairs? No. Ryan must know how she felt. He obviously needed more time. She finally got into bed at eleven, switched off the bedside lamp and pulled the sheet on top of her. The moon was covered now by clouds, and in the darkness, she couldn't see her hand in front of her face. She heard the scratch and sing of insects, and a lovely breeze whispering in from the windows. She felt the sudden gnawing of desire. Would Ryan ever wrap his arms around her and kiss her freely, completely? Press his body next to hers and lose himself in passion?

She slept fitfully. At some point, deep into the night, Keri heard a terrified voice shatter the stillness, echoing through the house. She sat up bolt erect, her eyes wide, the hair standing up on her neck. All she could make out was,

"I can't get out! Don't shoot! God! Don't shoot them!"

CHAPTER 17

At breakfast the next morning, neither spoke about the nightmare, but Ryan was quiet and preoccupied. He made some phone calls while Keri checked her messages. There were two from her mother, one from Mitchell asking her out for that night, and more from friends. She answered her mother and Mitchell and ignored the others.

They arrived at the marina at 9:30, under generous sunlight. They parked and carried the cooler and beach bags along the marina until they arrived at Slip D-18, where Big Pete's sailboat was docked.

Keri studied it, hearing the slap of water against the bow, and the call of the gulls overhead. It had a white hull with blue stripes, a white painted mast and boom, and a lot of room on the foredeck for storage or sunbathing.

"It's bigger than I thought," Keri said.

Ryan turned to her. "It's an Irwin 43, built in 1986, I think. Not the most beautiful boat to look at but a good sea boat. She's a bit stiff, but very stable. Big Pete says she hobby-horses in rough seas, but we won't have to worry about that today. Seas are calm, with just a little wind."

Ryan stepped aboard, set the cooler down and extended his hand to help Keri aboard.

"The galley is to starboard, beside the companionway."

"And starboard means?"

"Oh, yes, sorry." He pointed. "Starboard is right."

Ryan took her on a quick tour. There was a large cockpit, with new bimini top, a pedestal helm and stainless steel wheel. They stepped onto the open foredeck and along the wide side decks, as Ryan noticed a few stress marks and the refinished teak that Big Pete had finished a month or so ago.

As an afterthought, Ryan looked at her, the bill of his cap pulled low across his forehead. "I forgot to ask. Have you ever been sailing?"

Keri held up one finger. "Once, off Nantucket a few years ago. I was just a passenger. I don't know anything about sailing."

Ryan nodded. "No problem. We're just going out a little ways. Just an easy day of sailing."

Below, they explored the upscale interior, the shutter blinds over the windows, the bathroom (called *the head*), the over/under berths, and the two private staterooms. Keri stored their supplies in the galley refrigerator while Ryan climbed back on deck and re-familiarized himself with the color radar, the color sonar, the color GPS and the two autopilots. He checked the fuel. The tank held 105 gallons, and Big Pete had said there were 85 gallons remaining. He was right. That would be enough. Next, Ryan examined the high-aspect cutter rig with twin headstays, and then checked the triple battery banks. All were good.

When Keri came up, he handed her a life jacket, helped her into it and then swung into his.

Twenty minutes later, they were motoring out toward the open sea, the shadows of clouds dragging across the water, a persistent gull following them, dipping, swinging left, gliding right. Very white clouds decorated a very blue sky, with patches of sunlight falling on the distant white line of beach.

Keri sat in the cockpit, the warm salty air blowing over her, the world wide with sky and sea, a dazzling blue world that opened out to infinity. She breathed it in, feeling renewed, feeling charged and free.

There was perfection in that moment—that one and only moment—that moment without a pendulum to measure time and place. There was just a NOW. She was with Ryan, she was bathed in sunlight, kissed by wind and blessed by earth, sea and sky.

Ryan guided the boat to where the wind was blowing directly over the bow. Before he released the mainsail, he checked to ensure the wind indicator on the boat's mainmast was pointing forward. He told Keri that by doing this, raising the sail would be easier, since the boat's movement would be minimized.

A soft wind puffed the sails, and they bloomed and swelled. The boat shuddered and leaned and seemed to glide above the water, like a cloud. With the engine quiet, the wind whooshed across their ears, ruffling the water. Keri clapped a hand on the crown of her floppy hat, then tied the neck cord, as she looked skyward at the iceberg of a white cloud riding off to the west. She saw spectacular views of rolling green hills, lavish beach homes and a weather-beaten rocky coastline. After Ryan handed her a pair of binoculars, she focused the lenses and grew animated with excitement when she saw Ryan's house appear in the hazy distance, like some rising mythical landmark.

"How fast are we going?" Keri asked.

"About 3 knots. I'm going to take her a little farther out so we can catch more wind."

Once Ryan was comfortable with position and direction, he sat down next to her, his right hand resting on the top of the wheel. She'd watched him handle the boat with gentle grace and patience, working with easy assurance. It was attractive and admirable.

"Having fun?" he asked.

She nodded, smiling. "Yes. I'm having a lot of fun."

"About 70 percent of the world is covered by ocean. Did you know that?" Ryan asked.

"No... I didn't."

"We've explored less than 5 percent of the ocean. We have better maps of Mars than we do of the ocean floor. And about 94 percent of life on Earth is aquatic. Land-dwellers are a very small minority."

Keri laughed a little.

"What's funny?"

"When I was a little girl, my father used to tell me things like that. He loved trivia and knew so many facts about the world."

"I'd like to meet him."

Keri stared out into remoteness. "Maybe someday. How did you learn to sail?"

"From my father, when I was about 8 years old. He loved the sea. He said a boy who lives near the sea should know how to sail, so he bought a Daysailer just so he could teach me. It was a sleek little thing—a traditional sloop with a main and genoa, and a pivoting mast. It could carry up to 4 people, but most of the time it was just Dad and me. Mom didn't like sailing. It always made her nervous and seasick."

"Why didn't you go into the Navy?"

Ryan squinted into the light as he checked the sails. "I thought about it. A buddy of mine wanted to go into the Army Special Forces. He wanted to wear that green beret cap, so I went with him. And I guess I liked the idea of unconventional warfare—fighting in teams…working in small teams to train and lead guerrilla forces. Well, anyway, it appealed to me then."

Keri watched Ryan gently adjust the wheel.

"Your mother said you became a medic."

He nodded. "Yeah… I took to it. I liked it. The training was good. I learned minor field surgery, basic pediatric medicine, and some veterinary skills. They came in handy when we went into a small village to win over the hearts and minds. I could help a sick kid, deliver a baby and set a dog's broken leg. Sometimes I visited a village Medical Outreach clinic and helped out there."

"What kinds of illnesses did they have?" Keri asked.

"Most patients came with headaches, pains in the stomach, eye complaints, skin complaints. A lot of the children had worms and got diarrhea in the hot weather. I did some minor surgery."

Keri stared at him, the sharp lines of his jaw, the thick forearms, his T-shirt billowing in the steady wind. She let out a long sigh.

"That must have been satisfying," Keri said. "You were making a difference."

Ryan turned to look at her. "Maybe on good days. On a bad day, those clinics were attacked. Kids were killed...people I'd just patched up, killed. Then I had to fight. Then it was time to kill."

Ryan's face sealed shut.

The boat skimmed across the water in silence. The bright morning turned hazy and cool when the sun slipped behind a mountain of a cloud.

"What were you like as a little girl?" he asked, obviously changing the subject.

"Shy, curious, a good student. Don't I sound boring?"

"No. You sound normal. How nice."

"One thing, though. I had a very difficult time learning how to tie my shoes. I just couldn't seem to figure it out. It made no sense to me. My father spent so many patient hours trying to teach me."

"Are you close to your father?"

She shut her eyes and ran a finger tip across one eyebrow. "No...not in a long time."

Ryan waited.

Keri opened her eyes, watching the play of wind in the sails.

"He used to light up whenever he saw me. That was such a wonderful thing for a little girl to notice. To know that you were adored by your father. And I was so proud of him... he was intelligent and kind."

Keri shook her head. "Well, anyway, he and my mother divorced when I was 13. He met a younger woman. Everything changed after that...well, of course it would change, wouldn't it?"

Ryan glanced away at the sea, watching the spray as the boat rose and fell.

Keri continued. "A couple of years ago, I saw my father. I hadn't seen him in a year or so. Anyway, there's this local outside market, where night fishermen unload their catch. There are fruit and vegetable stands, and dessert stands, with pies, cookies and taffy, all locally produced. So I was there, shopping for fresh fish. I looked up and there was my father. He lit up just like he always did when he saw me. I could have been 8 years old or 10 or... I was 28."

Ryan adjusted the wheel, steering left. "Did you talk to him?"

"We tried. We said 'How are you?' and 'Nice market,' you know, things like that. He and his second wife divorced last year. He's alone now and he's never really been the loner type. He didn't look so good. He looked a lot older."

"Have you stayed in touch with him?"

Keri sniffed, pursing her lips. "No. I haven't seen him since. We talked last Christmas. That's it."

Ryan turned his face to hers. "It's hard to let go of hurtful things, I guess."

"I saw a therapist for awhile, because I couldn't get over that he had betrayed us. It seemed personal. Selfish. Thoughtless. He just left us all hanging there. I think I took the divorce harder than my mother did."

Keri laughed a little. "Do you know what Sophia said about it? She said, 'That divorce was the best thing that ever happened to your father and mother. They didn't have anything in common.'"

Keri smiled. "I was so mad at her for saying that. I didn't talk to her for over a week. But Sophia was a good, persistent friend. She'd never let me stay mad at her for long. She bought me a present—she once bought me a kitten. My parents freaked, but I loved that kitten—Lancelot—that was his name. Why I named him that I don't know, but I had him for 13 years."

Keri took a breath. "Well listen to me blah, blah on. I don't usually talk so much."

As Ryan listened to her, he grew warm with feeling, imagining her as a little blonde girl, tagging along after aggressive Sophia. Sophia was no doubt the outer strength, but Keri was surely the inner strength. The solid ground, the anchor and more. She could be a soft rain, a charging ocean wave, a bright sun, a string of wispy fog. She was a mystery, and yet she was revealed, like moonlight throwing a path of light across the sea.

Ryan was not a poetic man, but Keri made him poetic, made him think, made him feel when he didn't want to feel. Made him believe that things were possible. Good things. Loving things. The static that had crackled in his brain for so many months often cleared when he heard Keri's low, soothing voice, when he thought of her, when she stared into his eyes with those blue, wondering eyes of hers, as if she could see into him and, by seeing into him, heal the hurts, the sounds of guns, the sting of guilt, the ringing pain of loss.

Keri leaned into Ryan, and at the touch of their bodies, she took a breath, feeling as if she had been under the sea for a long time, starving for air, reaching up for life with straining fingers, seeing the world from blurring, watery eyes.

With Ryan beside her, she had surfaced. She could breathe.

They sat there under good sunlight, under a high blue sky, under high rippling sails, and they drifted into the golden heart of the day.

At 6:30 that evening, they stood by Keri's car. They could hear the soft murmur of the ocean. They saw swallows swoop, lift and dart away over the trees. Ryan's hands were restless.

"I had a great time," Keri said.

Ryan's eyes came to hers. "Can you come next weekend?"

She combed her hair with her red fingernails. Her voice was soft, but her shining blue eyes were loud with delight. She looked into the breeze when she spoke.

"Yes, I can come."

Ryan smiled. "Well, that's good then."

CHAPTER 18

The following week, Keri felt the fire of want and desire so keenly that she couldn't concentrate on anything. There were new hires to interview; new health care requirements for small businesses to address; meetings about the number of consultants per shift; new team assignments (now that Polly was gone); and then the issue of motivational offers, such as bonuses Stan was complaining about because of his bottom line, even though he was the one who had suggested them in the first place.

Keri and Ryan texted often. After Sunday night, their relationship had seemed to be moving forward into wonderful possibilities. Keri felt suspended, waiting, hungry for Ryan—starving for him. Her temper flared at the slightest irritation.

Isn't love supposed to make you happier? she thought. Shouldn't she be high on life, the way she'd felt when they were sailing? Then why was she feeling so agitated?

She had no time to think about it. Her apartment needed cleaning, she had to do laundry, she had to buy a wedding present for a colleague who was getting married in a couple weeks, and she had to have dinner with her mother, because her mother was agonizing over a new relationship with some minor political figure.

All Keri wanted to do was be with Ryan. Her body longed for the medication of him. Memories of his touch came crashing in during every meeting, every lunch and coffee break, every busy thought. Did Ryan feel the same way? Would their relationship grow or would Ryan's past throw up a wall between them and any possible future? Was that the source of her new anxiety? Is that why she was edgy?

Her brain became a traffic jam of horn-blowing questions.

After work she went with friends to a local hangout and drank two glasses of wine. Most of her friends thought Keri was edgy and distant because of Sophia's death. They tried to console her with kind words and laughter. Mitchell sat on a barstool beside her, sliding bowls of mixed nuts and olives her way.

Mitchell's black hair had grown long. He parted it on one side and moussed the top back, making him look a little Latin. His steady dark eyes circled her, his thin face and bushy eyebrows were set in curiosity.

"Did you find your soldier, Keri?"

The bar was bustling, the music loud.

Keri held the stem of her wine glass up so she could stare into it. "Yeah, I found him."

"Ah," Mitchell said, with a knowing nod of his head.

"Ah, what?" Keri said, sharply defensive. "What does that mean? Ah?"

"I don't know what it means, Keri, only *you* know that, but from the way you've been acting at work, I'd say you're moving through some early version of love."

Keri turned to face him. "Mitchell, that is so intellectual. Some early version of love. It's so cold and sterile... So..."

He cut her off. "So, right?"

Keri opened her mouth to speak, then thought better of it. She didn't have to explain anything to Mitchell, especially her feelings for Ryan.

The days had a slow-motion pace to them. The meetings seemed meaningless, the paperwork and documentation pointless. When Ryan texted that he'd be fishing the next day, Keri got rattled. She texted him back, *Be careful.*

On Friday night, Keri had dinner with her mother. They ate at Roxy's Café, a small, narrow trendy restaurant near Boston. It had polished chrome, parquet floors, white table cloths, a white marble bar with a swirling black vein, and deep leather couches and chairs in the lounge. The music was jazz, the menu known for its pasta and fish.

Monica Lawton wore light brown slacks, a navy jacket, and a flattering cream colored top that helped hide her thickening waist. She had just turned 59. Keri thought her mother's new chocolate brown hairstyle—a cropped bob—erased some years from her round face, but added weight to her overall appearance.

Monica sipped a cold gin martini, while Keri had her usual white wine. They ordered dinner and, while waiting, bantered casually about the place, politics and the hot weather. They were lingering, holding, their feet shifting, like thoroughbreds behind the starter gates waiting for the bell. Mother and daughter had always done this. It was the unspoken protocol, the ritual.

They shared the common trait of control and delay. The expression of the personal put them on a precarious path of thorns and thistles.

"I suppose we're meeting tonight because you'll be with your new boyfriend tomorrow," Monica said, circling the rim of her glass with a giant olive.

Keri hesitated. Ryan didn't fit the boyfriend label. Man friend didn't work either. Lover seemed odd and too new a word to fit. So what should she call him? Companion? Guy friend?

"Yes... I'm seeing Ryan tomorrow."

Monica had always been a buxom, full-figured, sexy woman that tanned easily. Kim's father was the opposite: tall and thin, with a sallow, narrow face. They were physical opposites and they had mostly been mental opposites, and maybe every-other-thing opposites, Keri thought. Opposites attracted, and opposites bounced off each other and struggled to find ways to connect. In the end, they didn't connect, except they'd birthed Keri and her brother.

"Do you like him?" Monica asked, her deep brown eyes avoiding her daughter's face.

Like? Keri thought.

"Well, I suppose you must like him, if you're spending so much time with him," Monica said, answering her own question. "Did you say he'd been in the military?"

"Yes."

"A soldier. I never thought of you dating a soldier."

"He's not a soldier anymore. He's a fisherman."

Monica blinked, her eyes focusing on Keri's face, waiting for more.

Keri saw her mother's disbelieving expression, and she glanced away toward the bloated lounge, where chic women held frosty glasses of mojitos, pink cosmos and cloudy dirty martinis. Men in suits hovered, displaying smiling, white teeth, clutching beer necks or old fashioned glasses of gleaming, brown whiskey.

Keri wished she was with Ryan, seated on the patio, listening to the wash of the sea.

"What does he fish for?" Monica asked.

Keri gave her a look. "Lobster."

"Really? A lobsterman."

"He also owns a beautiful house that overlooks the ocean. The land is worth a fortune. It's been in his family for years."

Monica chewed on the olive. "You sound defensive."

"You sound supercilious."

"That's a big word."

"Don't try and label him, Mom. He's more than any label. Everybody is more than what they do. More than a label. He was in the Special Forces. He went on many dangerous missions. He has a B.S. degree and he's a trained medic. He did more good and worthy things in 10 years than most people will do in a lifetime."

"I see fire in your eyes, Keri. You must like him a lot. I'm not sure I've ever seen that before."

"Mom, why are you trying to provoke me? Why do you have to create an argument every time we have a simple conversation? It's not pleasant. It's not the kind of relationship a mother and daughter ought to have."

Monica stared at her daughter, and then she drained her martini. She looked about for the waiter. "I want a glass of Merlot with my dinner."

Minutes later, their dinners arrived. Monica had sea bass and Keri had gnocchi with mushrooms, peas and pancetta.

"Your father called me," Monica said, abruptly, not looking up.

Keri stopped chewing, dread filling her gut. "When? Why?"

"He sounded like he'd been drinking. He wanted to meet. Get together."

"Why? After all this time? Why?"

Monica lifted her head, her eyes fixed and hard. "I don't know. I told him I have no desire to meet. I told him I was dating someone else and I was happy."

They both went back to eating, picking at their food, locked in silent, troubled thought.

"He called me...I don't know, maybe a week ago," Keri said.

"Did you talk to him?"

"No. I let it go into voicemail. He didn't leave a message."

Keri lifted her head. "Maybe he's sick or something."

"I don't know," Monica said. "After all this time I can't stand the thought of even thinking about him."

Keri laid her fork down. She toyed with the ends of her hair as she worked to form a thought. "Did you ever love him, Mom?"

Monica reached for her glass of wine and lifted it, but it never arrived to her lips. Her fingers tightened around the stem and she slowly lowered the glass back to the table.

"I don't know. I must have. Maybe when we were in college. Maybe when he told funny stories and we laughed. Maybe when I thought he'd be a good father because he was so practical and was so good with his hands. Maybe when he talked about how much he wanted children—especially a little girl. A little blonde girl."

Keri lowered her head.

"Yes, maybe then I loved him... or thought I loved him."

They sat in heavy silence, neither eating.

Finally, Monica took a drink of wine. "I'm feeling a little bit high. There must be a lot of alcohol in this wine. It's from California, I think."

"I think I love Ryan," Keri blurted out, and as soon as it left her lips, she wanted it back.

Monica didn't stir. She waited, intrigued.

Now that it was out, Keri let it all go. "I feel it in my body—this kind of ache for him. I know we've just met, but I feel it. It doesn't matter what anyone thinks about it or how ridiculous or impractical it may seem. He makes me happy. When I look at him I come alive. I wake up and I think, why haven't I seen the world with such hope and happiness before? I'm ecstatic and I'm terrified. I'm edgy, anxious and perplexed, mostly, all at once."

Keri exhaled an audible breath and pushed her half-eaten dinner away. "And now I'm starting to sound crazy."

Monica licked her lips and swallowed the last of the wine. "Well, I guess I should say something wise or supportive, but I don't know what to say. I've never seen you gush about any man before. Of course, I'm happy for you, Keri. I want you to be happy."

The busboy cleared the table and when the waiter returned, they both ordered cappuccinos.

Monica reached and took her daughter's hand. "It's too bad Sophia isn't here. You could have shared all this with her. She could have met...I'm sorry, what is his name?"

"Ryan..."

"Yes, Sophia could have met Ryan and you all would have had such fun together. Sophia was a bit volatile and unpredictable, but she was always fun to have around."

Keri considered telling her mother the whole truth—the truth about Sophia's diary—but then she decided against it. She still felt she was on emotional, shaky ground.

"Yes, it's too bad," was all Keri said.

Outside, mother and daughter strolled in the warm summer air, finally stopping at an ice cream shop. They pointed, tasted and were conflicted, just like they'd always been, even when Keri was a child. Keri stood by the display case and watched her mother agonize over her choice, knowing that, in the end, she'd wish she'd ordered the other thing, the better flavor, or the newer flavor. Anyway, the one she hadn't chosen.

Back outside, licking ice cream cones, they passed a big white house displaying an American flag on a porch post. Keri paused for a minute, thinking of Ryan, thinking of all the soldiers and veterans. Ryan had sacrificed so much for his country. They passed a gift shop and window-shopped, ambled by a closed barbershop and stepped across a railroad track, all in silence.

Monica turned to Keri, the mound of pistachio ice cream a melting mess, streaming down her sugar cone. She looked at her daughter with tender eyes.

"No, Keri. I've never been in love. I've played at it and puzzled about it. Maybe I even circled it when I was married to your father, but I've never felt what you seem to feel. Does Ryan feel the same way?"

Keri shrugged. "I don't know, Mom. I hope so."

Keri leaned over and kissed her mother on her cheek.

"What was that for?" Monica asked, touched by it, but holding back.

"For nothing. Because...I love you."

Monica smiled. "My dearest Keri, I have loved you from the day you were born. I remember I held you in my arms and your father oohed and ahhhed and we both made fools of ourselves. Your father said, 'What a beauty, isn't she, Monica?' And I said, 'We did good, Edward, didn't we? Look what we did, and it's so good.'"

Keri and her mother never did discuss her mother's new boyfriend. Keri knew her mother well enough to know that she'd avoided the subject intentionally, not ready to open up about the relationship, which probably meant it wouldn't last.

CHAPTER 19

On Friday afternoon, weather forecasters were predicting a severe storm to hit the Massachusetts coastline on Saturday afternoon. Ryan texted Keri to see if she still wanted to make the trip. She did, replying that she'd leave early Saturday morning and arrive at the house sometime around 9am.

As she left Boston, Keri noticed the sun had lost its luster and was drifting into a mass of gray, stringy clouds. A half hour from Crandall Cove, muscular dark clouds slid ominously across the sky, darkening the mood of the day. The rumor of thunder traveled with her as she approached Crandall Cove, and she felt the first fists of wind punching at the car.

She was excited by the prospect of being cocooned in the great beach house during a storm with Ryan, huddled near the fireplace, sipping wine. Maybe they'd throw on slickers and hats and venture out to the cliffs to watch the turgid sea toss itself about under a rolling, angry sky, and taste the salt rain on their lips. It would be frightening and invigorating, especially with Ryan next to her.

Keri arrived at the house to the sounds of electric saws, roaring power tools and a nail gun. Tippie Toe and Brownie were rambling across the lawn, their noses sniffing the ground, playful and barking at all the activity.

On Friday, Ryan had taken Keri's suggestion and invited Dan Jr. and B.J., Dan and Bette Wilson's two teenage sons, to help him with the house. But they'd refused his offer.

Early Saturday morning, Big Pete dragged them out of bed at 5:30am, took them to breakfast and then drove them up to Ryan's house at 7:00. He pushed them out of his truck and pointed to the house.

"Work or walk," he said. "And if you walk, you're gonna run into me, because I'm everywhere and I'll be watching you. And when you do run into me, I'm gonna throw you right back into my truck and haul your sorry asses right back up to Ryan's place. Then I'm going to kick your lazy asses out. Do you understand me, boys?"

The boys were useless for the first hour or so, slouching about with bored attitude, but when Ryan climbed the roof with his nail gun and started shooting roofing nails, Dan Jr. took a sharp interest. As soon as Dan Jr., a tall and lanky 19-year-old, took an interest, so did 15-year-old, stocky B.J.

By the time Keri arrived, around 9:30, Dan Jr. was on the roof, shooting a nail gun, and B.J. was helping Ryan reinforce the windows with storm shutters. Already the busy wind surrounded them, shaking the trees, bringing an urgency to the morning. She heard a recital of birds as they skimmed the roof and the tops of trees and sailed away on blustery currents. Keri saw the sway of sea and heard it tumble and crash into the cliffs below.

Ryan descended a ladder and met Keri near the front porch. He was all energy and purpose, but his eyes lit up when he saw her. He kissed her lightly on the lips.

"Glad you came. Good trip?"

"Yes. It's busy around here."

Ryan looked skyward and then out into the darkening sea, noticing surfers already taking advantage of the higher swells and waves. They were gliding over the water, catching the curls, dancing across their boards.

"The storm's coming faster than they predicted. Winds could gust up to 60 miles per hour. Big Pete brought the boys up to help me secure the house."

"Is there anything I can do?" Keri asked.

Ryan glanced over to the deck. "Anything you see on the deck needs to go inside: the grill and folding chairs. Also, any plants you see. Don't lift anything heavy. I'll do that."

They all worked until after 11am. By 11:20, Big Pete had come back for the boys.

He stood on the front lawn with Ryan and Keri, taking in the restless sea and close purple clouds. "It's going to be a big storm," he said. "It's an ugly looking thing on the weather radar. Hope the wind doesn't rip off that roof you just put up, Ryan."

Ryan stood there, looking, nodding, speculating into the sky.

After Big Pete and the boys left, Ryan and Keri were out on the deck, gazing out at sea. Their uneasy eyes scanned the lowering horizon, their bodies close. The wind gusted and rattled the windows and moved through Ryan's T-shirt, shaking it, puffing him into a balloon. Leaves blew everywhere, in sailing chaos.

They heard the tide slip away and climb back up, growing louder as the minutes crawled toward afternoon.

Keri laced her hands behind her back. "Where are the dogs?"

"In the basement. Brownie is scared to death of thunder and Tippie Toe doesn't like rain. I built them two houses down there so they can hide."

When it started to rain, Keri and Ryan locked eyes. They stood motionless as rain pearled on the eves, waited for the extreme moment, then fell, splashing around them.

"Here it comes," Ryan said. "We'd better get inside."

Inside, Ryan lit a fire while Keri made coffee and ham and cheese sandwiches. They spread out a blanket on the floor and sat back from the fire, away from the stretching heat, listening to the storm build; listening to the rain strike the shutters and wind whistle around the house. Their conversation was ordinary, self-conscious and wandering. At times, it faltered. Both felt emotion, and their hearts were beating with hope and desire, but their words were unsure, exploring and shy.

Ryan stared into gleaming fire, the mug of coffee posed at his lips.

"A dollar for your thoughts," Keri said.

He looked at her in mock astonishment. "A dollar? That's a little high, isn't it?"

"Inflation. And surely your thoughts must be worth more than just a penny."

Ryan smiled. "I was remembering being in this house during a storm when I was a boy, about 10 years old. I spent a week or two here every summer with my grandparents."

"What were they like?" Keri asked.

"My grandfather was a sturdy, cranky old man, who didn't like many people. He used to say that his neighbors were his enemies."

"He sounds like a guy to stay away from," Keri said.

"He wasn't so bad, really. Fortunately, he liked me. We got along real good. I used to help him fix things around the house. He took me fishing and beach combing. My grandmother was quiet and, I guess you'd say, thoughtful. They were definitely opposites. All the neighbors loved her and hated him. Talk about opposites attracting."

"What did you do when it stormed?"

"My grandmother read to me."

"Do you remember the books?" Keri asked, listening to the hiss and pop of the fire.

Ryan sat up cross-legged. "Well now, let's see. *Lad, a Dog* was probably my favorite. It had a brown cover and an illustration of a Collie on it. She read it to me three or four times over the course of a couple of years. The pages were dog-eared and the cover all faded, but I loved it. That's what I was remembering when you asked me what I was thinking. The last time Grandmother Ollie read it to me was during a storm like this. I sat here by the fire and she was in a rocker, of course. Every grandmother has to be sitting in a rocker. She read very slowly and clearly and she would perform all the voices. And she was good. She really brought the story to life. I never wanted the story to end."

Keri fixed her warm eyes on him and, in that instant, she was struck by a kind of crisis. It was a sudden and astonishing moment. She felt that darkness was encircling her, like a fog. It wasn't smothering or frightening. Oddly enough, it helped her awaken to a startling realization: she had spent most of her life cut off from love, or even the possibility of love. She stood aside from it, like a witness, watching others fall in love, but keeping herself at a distance from it, afraid of it. Afraid to enter love and immerse herself in it fully, afraid of the pain and loss. Afraid that she'd wind up like her parents, bitter, disillusioned and alone. Keri saw that the encompassing darkness gathered around her had been a kind of cautious self-protection that kept out the light of love. Had Sophia seen that?

While Keri sat there listening to Ryan, the darkness slowly began to dissipate. She was struck by a flash of illuminating light. It came from some inexpressible place, deep in her beating chest. It expanded out around her, replacing the darkness. Her body seemed to awaken to the realization that she was lit up from within.

All at once, she was alive with love, pulsing with love, awakened by love. Awakened by her love for Ryan. Now, she was eager for it. She longed for it and she wanted all of it. She wanted a new life with Ryan, a long, growing relationship. She wanted to be a wife and a mother. She wanted to have a family with Ryan! For the first time in her life, she wanted to have a baby.

It was a new and a ridiculous thought—a thrilling thought—and an alarming one. Her breath deepened as she listened to him speak about Lad, a dog who fought off a burglar, rescued an invalid child from a poisonous snake and won ribbons in a dog show.

This man, Ryan, this ex-soldier, who'd experienced war, personal loss and unspeakable violence, was also incredibly gentle and playful. He was kind, quiet and generous. He was a riddle to be solved: a sexy, powerful warrior, and a lovely, sensitive man.

Ryan laughed and grew animated as he recounted the story of *Lad*, even as the storm darkened the room and the dancing firelight played across his masculine face, his boyish face. Masculine when he stared at her, and boyish as he recounted the book with such simple pleasure; as he recalled being a boy of 10, lost in the wonder of the story and in his grandmother's enchanting voice.

Keri wanted to make love to him right then, to feel the intimacy of his body and breathe his breaths, the breaths of love. She wanted to be a woman for him. She wanted to be a mother, and have his baby. The moments lengthened, softened and then fell into silence.

Ryan's face changed. Keri watched him. He was listening, like an animal in the wild, aware of a threat. The experienced hunter-warrior in him seemed to take over.

"Is something wrong?" Keri asked, the glory of her feelings ebbing.

Ryan opened his mouth, without uttering words. He listened.

Keri listened. The pitch of the storm changed sharply. It rose to a throaty kind of moan. The house trembled.

"This isn't just any storm," Ryan said, with concern.

He unraveled his legs and pushed up, traveling fast to the nearest bay window. He peeled back a curtain and peered out.

The storm was roaring in, throwing high winds and driving rains. A sharp crack of lightning ripped open the silence and Keri flinched, as thunder cannon-balled across the sky. Ryan pulled his phone and checked the latest weather report.

Keri got up, folding her arms. "It sounds wild out there."

Ryan's words were quiet, his lips almost motionless. "We're getting a direct hit from a super cell."

Even in the big house, there was a feeling of being trapped in a war zone. Ryan gazed up at the ceiling and then down at the walls, his eyes calculating. Lightning shattered the sky and the house vibrated to the crashing of thunder.

Keri shivered a little. "It sounds like there's a war going on out there," she said, and then wished she hadn't as she viewed Ryan's troubled face. Ryan would know what the true sound of battle was.

He was standing rigid, eyes moving.

"Is the house safe?" Keri asked.

"Yes... It's the town. The wind must be coming in at 70 miles per hour or more. Some of those old buildings may not survive this."

Ryan went to the front door, snatched a rain slicker and hat with a chin strap. He turned back to Keri.

"I'll be right back. I'm just going to take a look," he said, struggling into the slicker and securing the hat.

Keri looked on, nervously. She heard herself say, "Don't, Ryan. It's not safe out there."

"I won't go far. Just want to have a look around."

Keri sucked in a troubled breath.

Ryan pulled open the door and stepped out into the battering tempest. A hard, slanting rain attacked him, curtains of it sliding across the world. The looping, briny wind was strong and gusting stronger. It kept driving him back. Each time, he redoubled his strength, hand clamped down on his hat, standing his ground. Clouds hurtled across the sky like charging armies, obscuring the jet-roaring sea. Ryan saw flying branches and leaves, and he imagined the high watery walls of the sea tumbling into the marinas and into the little town of Crandall Cove. Was the town prepared for this? No weather person had predicted this ferocious storm.

Ryan leaned back against the house, glancing about at a boiling mass of blinding wind, clouds and punishing rain. This was not a summer thunderstorm. Ryan suspected the winds were at near hurricane force.

CHAPTER 20

Back inside, Ryan texted Big Pete, Doc and Lucky Dan. Minutes later, he received a text from Big Pete.

Tree fell on nursing home. Need help. Some injuries. Dr. Mason at hospital. Will come soon. EMS out on calls. U come now!

Ryan faced Keri. "I've got to go into town. A tree fell on the nursing home. There are injuries."

The storm's whistling breath nearly covered Ryan's soft voice.

"I'll go with you."

"No. Stay here. It's crazy out there."

"I'm going," Keri said, in defiance.

Ryan studied her for a quick minute, saw her resolute eyes, and nodded. He left for a moment, soon returning with a black medical bag.

Keri looked at it.

"I keep it for emergencies," Ryan said.

They swung into raincoats and hats and left the house through the side patio door, Ryan sliding it closed behind them.

They bent into the pushing wind, feeling hard chips of rain strike their tucked faces. At the truck, Ryan yanked open the driver's side door for Keri and she piled in, sliding to the passenger's side. He handed her his medical bag, slid behind the steering wheel and slammed the door.

Keri stared out in dazed wonder at the black storm's fury. "I've never seen anything like this."

Ryan started the truck, staring grim-faced. He cranked the wipers to max, watching as they struggled to slap away the exploding splotches of water. "Yeah, this is a bad one."

They drove in a brawl of flying leaves, sticks and slinging rain, all driven by a huffing wind that shoved the truck and tilted the world. They splashed across pot holes, pooling streams and muddy, rutted roads. Keri had a hand on the dashboard, bracing herself, as the truck bucked and bounced its way down the side of the broken asphalt road to the two lane highway that led to the nursing home.

They passed through the edge of town and Keri strained her eyes to see a smattering of people, peeking from sheltered garages and doorways, their frightened, dismal faces watching the wide arms of the chaotic storm engulf them.

"How much farther?" Keri asked.

"About a mile," Ryan said, straining to see ahead, his high beams shining in the fog and rain. He swung the truck about several times to avoid hitting falling branches and debris scattered along the road. A police car passed on the opposite side of the road, its blue dome light flashing, its siren screaming.

Just ahead, Ryan saw a tree, uprooted, lying across the road. Keri went ridged, her mouth opened to scream. Ryan whipped the truck right. It skidded across the narrow shoulder of the road, and jumped over broken branches. Ryan floored the accelerator and the tires screeched, found traction and shot away.

Keri's heart pounded in her ears. She glanced at Ryan, whose face was set and determined.

"Almost there," he said.

Crandall Nursing Home was just off the highway. It was a long, rectangular brick building, nestled in close to a grove of trees and an unfinished housing project, where Big Pete had been working. As soon as Ryan bounced into the parking lot, they saw the felled tree lying treacherously across the right side of the building.

Ryan braked, threw the truck in park and killed the engine. Ryan took Keri's hand and shoved the door open. Keri clutched Ryan's medical bag as they ducked into the wind, and rushed inside.

Ryan was met by Big Pete and the nursing home's manager, Sara Boggs, a tall, middle-aged woman with beauty-shop sculpted black hair and alert, worried eyes. Her hands were in motion, pointing, twisting and adjusting her tight red sweater.

"They're in the Rec room," she said, pointing. "We normally have a nurse on duty, but she couldn't make it in. We moved all but the injured into other rooms."

Big Pete was standing by. "Trees knocked down the power lines, Ryan. There's no electricity," he said.

Keri heard the sound of scared human voices and feet. She heard the rushing sound of wind, and she felt a funnel of humid currents whipping through the place, blowing papers about.

"Show me the way," Ryan said.

"Over here!" Sara said, pointing left off the main hallway, taking the lead. "The tree crashed through the

Rec room. There were 15 in there when the tree came down. I heard a loud pop and then the awful crushing sound, and screams when the tree fell."

The group hurried down the dim, carpeted hallway, past a circular lobby desk, a wheelchair and a cleaning cart.

They burst into the recreation room and found five people huddled in a dry corner of the dripping room, cramped and shivering. Two employees were there, comforting the injured, frightened and dazed residents. They'd covered them with shawls and blankets.

It was a smashed room, with scattered books, magazines and pieces of glass. The TV had been bashed and tossed away, tables upturned. Amazingly, a couch and an armchair remained untouched and undamaged. A wizened man, dressed in overalls and a fading white shirt, sat crouched and weary in an armchair, shards of glass from the shattered window scattered about his feet.

"Sounded like a pencil just broke in half," he said, blandly. "It was louder than a pencil though. Scared the hell out of me."

Ryan hurried over and checked him out. He had a shallow cut on his cheek and a small bump on his head.

"A book or something hit me," he said.

Ryan felt the bump. He didn't think it was serious. He opened his medical bag, pulled on gloves, and reached for a sterile bandage and antiseptic. He quickly cleaned the cut and put a Band-Aid on it.

"I'm okay, young man," he said. "See to Helen over there. She's hurt bad. We was sitting together. The tree just missed her, thank God."

Ryan went to Helen. She lay on the couch, covered by a blanket, her frail body shaking. There was a gash across her face and several cuts on her neck and right arm. A small drop of blood rolled crookedly down her cheek. She tried to speak but Ryan whispered to her.

"It's okay, just rest, Helen. Just take it easy. You're going to be fine."

Ryan felt her skin. It was cool and clammy. She was pale. He took her pulse. It was weak and rapid. Her eyes lacked luster; she was just staring.

Ryan glanced at Keri. "She's in shock. Get a pillow and raise her legs."

Keri did so.

Ryan checked her breathing. It was a little strained, but he didn't see any chest wound or deep wound to her neck.

Ryan reached into his medical bag and rummaged through the items. He pulled a package of gauze from his bag, and popped the plastic open. He cleaned the face wound and then applied pressure to it.

Big Pete had gone for soap and water. When he returned, Keri took over applying pressure, and Ryan washed the scrapes and wounds, applied antiseptic cream and covered the affected areas with sterile bandages.

Big Pete towered above them. "EMS will be here as soon as they can. With the power lines down and so many people calling in for help, it may take awhile."

While Ryan worked on other injured residents, Keri stayed with the woman, keeping a soft hand on her shoulder.

"You're going to be fine," she said. "Just rest now. You'll be in the hospital soon."

The woman smiled faintly and her trembling mouth formed a "Thank you."

Ryan treated a sprained wrist for an 88-year-old man, and dressed more wounds caused by flying glass and debris.

Big Pete left to assist the nursing home employees usher the able residents out the back door into a waiting school bus. It was to drive them to the high school gymnasium, where cots, hot food and fresh water were waiting.

An ambulance and EMS arrived 20 minutes later—Dr. Mason five minutes after that. By then, Ryan had stabilized the 5 injured residents. He and Big Pete had moved them to the infirmary and they were resting comfortably.

Dr. Mason and the EMS compared notes and called the ER. Minutes later, the injured residents were evacuated to the hospital. On the way out of the nursing home, Dr. Mason stopped to thank Ryan. He was a small man, who looked like a sci-fi Hollywood movie scientist, with black rimmed glasses and small probing eyes.

"You do good work, Ryan."

"Glad to be of assistance."

Once everyone had been moved to safety, Ryan, Keri and Big Pete said their goodbyes to Sara Boggs and started back down the quiet hallway. The wind had subsided, although rain still drummed the roof and windows. The trio paused at the double glass doors and ventured a look outside.

"Over 70 mile an-hour gusts," Big Pete said. "One helluva storm. The Deerfield River is over 10 feet. That's a lot of water."

"You heard from Lucky Dan?" Ryan asked.

"Yeah. He's got some water damage. So do the bait shop and diner. I think they'll be okay. There was a helluva surge up through the marina. Some boats got smacked around."

"Did yours?" Keri asked.

"No, I tied her down real good. I don't take no chances these days with these storms. They're a lot worse than they used to be. Okay, you two. Be careful getting back home. I'm going to Dan's for a couple of beers and to look around."

"Call me if you need me," Ryan said.

The drive back to the house was not as dramatic as the trip in. Ryan switched on the radio to the local station and heard that nearly 300,000 residents were without power.

"That's going to include us," Ryan said.

"Will all your food spoil?"

"I turned the refrigerator to the coldest setting, just in case. Should be all right. I have a gas stove, so we'll be able to cook. But we'll be using flashlights, lanterns and candles for lighting."

Keri liked the sound of that.

By 6 o'clock that evening, the storm had fled, roaring off east and out to sea. Ryan removed the storm shutters from the front and side windows, while Keri chopped garlic and onions, broccoli and cauliflower. She roasted them with salt and pepper and olive oil, and steamed some potatoes. After Ryan retrieved the grill, Keri stepped out on the patio and grilled chicken breasts, taking in the quick, fresh, salty breeze and listening to the high surf hurl itself against the rocky cliffs.

They ate on the back patio with candlelight from a hurricane lamp. It was difficult to believe that only a few hours earlier, a major storm had gone ripping through the area, causing massive damage.

The wind was cool. Keri wore a white sweatshirt and jeans and Ryan a hooded burgundy sweat shirt and cutoffs. He complimented Keri on the menu, tasting the chicken and roasted veggies with particular focus.

"You're a great cook."

"Not really. I just learned a few tricks from an old boyfriend. He was a chef at a local restaurant in Boston."

Ryan lifted his glass of white wine and they toasted. "To good local chefs and to excellent students."

Their conversation was mostly about the day, the storm and the nursing home. Keri had things she wanted to say, but it didn't seem like the right time. Ryan was distant and tired. A little preoccupied. Perhaps it was the tension of the day, she thought.

Ryan *was* tired. The day had been stressful. His emotions had run high and loud—the raging storm and broken nursing home brought back the urgency and pumping adrenalin of battle. No, it wasn't the same, but there had been the hot nerves, the taut straining muscles and the fluttering stomach. The sweats were the same. Would he ever forget the sound of guns, the cries for help, the last sighing breaths of the mortally wounded?

Keri had been beside him all day, and Ryan had found that both thrilling and disorienting. Keri was blurring his memories of Debbie; his feelings for her, his stabbing guilt for leaving her to die. Debbie had once been the truest fact of his world. Debbie had been his reason to come back home. Debbie had been his first love.

Ryan stared at Keri, allowing his eyes to roam her soft face, the moist lips, the lush blowing hair. Was he ready to let go of the past? Could he let go of what had been true and good? Was he ready to gamble on another love? Could he really give himself completely to Keri, or would he always be holding something back?

"Is everything all right, Ryan?" Keri asked, observing his somber eyes.

Ryan lowered his eyes. "Yes... Yes... everything is fine."

Keri shifted, uneasily.

As night descended, Ryan stared out on the lawn, littered with branches, broken limbs and leaves.

"There'll be a lot of cleanup out there."

"I'll help. It'll be fun."

Ryan took her hand, squeezed it and smiled at her. "Thanks for your help today."

Keri returned the squeeze and held him in her eyes. Longing gripped her, stirring desire. "Of course," she whispered, rubbing his hand with her thumb, hoping to rekindle their physical intimacy. But Ryan didn't respond. He stood, gathered the plates and took them into the kitchen.

Taking her cues from Ryan, Keri followed him into the house. He found a jazz station on the battery-run radio, but while they listened and cleaned up, they were mostly quiet, moving like shadows around candlelight. The relationship seemed to be struggling to find a new foothold, as the brand new relationship was falling away and a new one was evolving in slow, cautious steps. Neither quite knew how to move it forward, what words to use or what actions to take. Neither seemed able to take the first step.

"I think I'll go up and shower," Keri finally said, moving toward the staircase.

"Wait," Ryan said quickly. He moved toward her. He gently took her shoulders. She hovered, waiting. He leaned forward and kissed her on the forehead. Keri quivered at his touch, waiting for more, wanting more. But they stood in the darkness like two frightened teenagers, suddenly aware of the depth of their feelings. Ryan was not quite ready to leap into love.

"Good night," Ryan said softly, running his fingers down her arms and loosely holding her hands.

"Good night," Keri answered, again electrified by his touch.

"See you in the morning, then," Ryan said, kissing her hand, such a splendid, old fashioned thing to do. And in that moment, she knew he loved her but was waiting, to make certain. Their lovemaking could never be a casual thing. Their emotions and desires for each other weren't casual, so how could the private and wonderful gift of lovemaking be casual?

"Yes, see you in the morning," Keri whispered.

And then she slowly mounted the stairs, gripping the banister for balance.

Upstairs, Keri moved slowly, as if stunned, as if she'd just been told about a miracle that would change her life forever. She heard Ryan let the dogs out, heard them bark and romp, and suddenly she knew. She was home. This was where she belonged.

She showered and slipped into bed, lying still for a long time. The night breeze was cool, her bed soft with contentment. She fell asleep and slept deeply until she heard Ryan's terrified, screaming voice.

"Don't shoot them. No! Stop! Don't shoot... Over there. Run. Run!"

CHAPTER 21

Morning brought singing birds, bright sun and an infinite deep blue sky. Keri awoke to the sound of barking dogs, hammers and electric saws. She tossed back the covers, bounced up and searched the back window. Seeing nothing, she hurried to the side window. There she found B.J. toting fallen branches and Dan Jr. raking leaves into neat little piles. She saw Brownie cutting in and out of her vision as he chased Tippie Toe back into the wall of trees. She couldn't see Ryan.

She glanced at her watch. It was only 8:03! She knew from the blinking digital clock that the electricity was back on. She quickly dressed in jeans and a T-shirt and hurried downstairs, grabbing her sandals on the way. The aroma of coffee drew her to the kitchen. She found donuts and a cheese Danish and helped herself, munching a chocolate donut as she exited the sliding doors to the patio. The morning air was cool, glorious and clean. She inhaled a breath and saw Ryan approaching from the cliffs, wearing jeans, an orange shirt and a ball cap. A wave of his hand sent her off to meet him, coffee cup and donut in hand.

"Good morning," he said, as she drew up to him. "I see you found the coffee."

"And a donut. You're all up early."

Ryan removed his sunglasses. "Yeah, well, Big Pete brought the boys and the donuts at 7am to help me with the clean-up. I held them off until a little before eight. Sorry if they woke you."

"I feel like a slacker," Keri said.

"Don't. There's still plenty to do, or you can just relax and do nothing."

Keri made a little face. "Do nothing around here? I don't think so. Were you checking out the cliffs?"

"Yeah, there's a lot of erosion. That was one brutal storm. It chewed away some of the beach too."

He glanced about. "I wish the house was further back. If we keep getting storms like that, we'll have to move the thing in 10 years."

"Did Big Pete say how the residents at the nursing home are doing?" Keri asked.

"Yeah... they're all okay. They'll be moved to temporary housing until the roof and walls can be repaired. The residents in the hospital are doing fine. No serious injuries." He turned to her. "Hey, is that all you've had for breakfast? A chocolate donut?"

Keri took a bite and chewed vigorously. "Yes, and I love it."

Ryan leaned down and kissed her closed chewing mouth. She stopped chewing, taking the kiss with new pleasure, feeling the heat of the sun on her face, feeling the heat of passion for Ryan.

When he straightened, she looked at him pointedly. "That was nice. Very nice."

He smiled at her. "I'm so glad you came."

Keri began chewing again, still tasting his kiss, wondering how much longer she could stand being so close to him, living with him, and yet not making love to him.

The day was an arduous one. She sprayed and washed the decks and patios, returned the deck chairs, tables and flowers, and helped Dan Jr. and B.J. clean the lawn of debris. She even took a stint on the power mower, cutting the grass.

In the afternoon, she followed Ryan into the wooded area adjacent to the house. He told her to keep an eye out for falling trees, hanging limbs, and snakes that could be in swollen streams.

Tippie Toe and Brownie galloped, searched and sniffed the ground, taking in the new, fresh smells. Brownie chased a rabbit, darting and fleeing through the trees. Tippie Toe struggled to keep up, barking out her encouragement. When the rabbit disappeared into thick undergrowth, Brownie growled, barked and circled. Defeated, he searched Ryan for help.

"Don't look at me, Brownie Boy. You let the rabbit out-run you."

Keri saw deer springing away in high elegance, smelled the sweet honeysuckle vines, and allowed the baking sun on her face, as she stared into the clean blue sky. She and Ryan held hands and wandered to the edge of the cliffs, taking in the distant marinas of Crandall Cove, sparkling in the afternoon sunlight.

"It's so beautiful here," Keri said, entranced. "So perfect."

Ryan smiled down at her. "It is, isn't it? It is perfect."

Big Pete came for B.J. and Dan Jr. at 5pm. They slouched into his truck, fatigued and sweaty from all the hard work. Ryan stepped over and handed them both cash, thanking them. Their faces lit up with gratitude.

Big Pete made a sour face. "Too much for these two lazy knuckleheads, Ryan. You'll spoil them."

Keri and Ryan watched Big Pete's truck retreat down the road, a trail of gray exhaust puffing from his tail pipe.

"Big Pete needs a new truck," Ryan said. "That thing belongs in a junk yard."

After showering, Keri and Ryan grilled hamburgers and potatoes, and shared a tomato salad and a bottle of beer. Since Keri had to drive home, she declined a glass of wine.

At seven, they rambled down to the beach. It was strewn with seaweed, shells and blotches of sea-foam. They stepped along the tide line, shining, their faces turned toward the perfect golden sun. Ryan reached for Keri's hand. Hers felt warm. His big and gentle.

The surf was surprisingly quiet, with only the occasional wave thudding in close, spreading out before them.

"Do you have nightmares every night?" Keri asked, not looking at him.

"I don't know. Maybe. Sometimes they wake me up. Sometimes not. Sorry if I woke you."

"Don't be sorry. Don't be sorry about that. Do you remember them?"

"Sometimes."

"Do you think they'll ever go away?"

He looked toward the sea. "I saw an Army shrink for awhile. He said they should gradually fade away. He also said, sometimes it takes years. I've talked to old vets from World War II. One guy said his never have gone away. He still gets them every few months."

"I'm sorry," Keri said, squeezing his hand. "It's so peaceful here. Maybe the sound of the sea will eventually wash them away. I hope so."

He turned to face her. "Did I tell you how happy I am that you're here?"

Keri laughed. "Yes, Ryan. You did, but don't stop saying it."

And then he stopped, gently took her shoulders and pulled her into him. He kissed her long and deep. Waves rolled in and splashed around their feet. Still they kissed. And then he held her and kissed her hair, and she pressed her face into his shoulder and breathed and felt wonderfully alive.

"Can you come next weekend too?" Ryan asked.

"I'm supposed to go to a co-worker's wedding on the Cape."

Ryan backed away and nodded, disappointed. "Well then, maybe Sunday?"

"The wedding is early and I'm not going to the reception. I could probably get here by four or five Saturday afternoon, if that's okay?"

A smile formed at the corners of Ryan's mouth. "Well, that's good then, isn't it? Okay."

Keri looked at him, somberly. "The ocean looked so scary yesterday. You're always careful when you're out there fishing, aren't you?"

"Of course. I'm always careful. It's not so dangerous. I'd never go out in a storm like that."

Keri shifted her weight. "It's just that, sometimes you hear stories. You hear stories about how treacherous the ocean can be."

"That it can." He smiled, warmly. "Thanks for being concerned."

Ryan looked at her. Her lips were glistening, her chin lifted toward him. Her hair was up, with wispy strands falling over her ears. The sun dress she was wearing was soft and flowing in the slight wind. He leaned and his mouth touched hers.

Keri shut her eyes, feeling a spiral of desire curl up her spine. They licked, nibbled and then parted, breath heating their faces. Just as Keri opened her eyes, Ryan moved back for another kiss. It was an open kiss, gentle and wet.

After they separated, Keri backed away, taking in air, feeling warm and ready for more of him. "Do you really want me to leave now, Ryan?" she asked, her voice low, eyes beseeching.

He touched her warm cheek with his hand. "I don't ever want you to leave."

As night surrounded them and moonlight leaked into the room, Ryan and Keri made love in Keri's bed. There was breath, heat and whispers. Their bodies joined and arched, lips explored and found secrets. Curtains billowed, the sea was close at high tide, and candle flames danced and threw trembling shadows across the walls.

There was low laughter from an owl, a sigh of wind, and an airplane making a tearing sound across the sky. The two lovers tangled, and fell, and slept for awhile. Ryan awoke first and he kissed her cheek and brushed a strand of hair from her eyes. Keri awoke and felt for his face, tracing his jaw line with two fingers.

"I've never done anything particularly well," Keri said. "I've never done anything extraordinary, like you have, Ryan."

"Nothing I've done was extraordinary, Keri. Far from it. Sometimes, I did more harm than good...most of the time in fact."

"You're too modest."

"Honest," Ryan said, kissing her forehead. "One has to be honest with oneself. Otherwise, life will tear you apart."

Keri stared up at him. "I've never thought of myself as special or talented or particularly gifted at anything. Why do I feel so extraordinary now?" Keri asked.

In dying candlelight, she navigated his face with her eyes: the well-formed nose, the sensitive mouth, the smooth skin and the cool, probing eyes, at times as warm as candle flames.

Ryan took her hand. "Connection," he whispered.

"Connection? What do you mean?"

"When you connect with someone—truly connect— maybe it makes a person feel extraordinary."

Keri snuggled her head next to his shoulder. "Why did it take so long, Ryan? I feel like I've been waiting for you my entire life."

Keri awakened in the velvety darkness, shifting gently to one elbow to see Ryan's silhouette lying beside her. The candles were out, the crickets calling. For a few heartbeats Keri watched him sleep.

She was a bright glowing jewel, radiating a rainbow of fire and color, each shade sparkling, dazzling, radiating with love for him. If he were awake, could he see it?

And then—at that sterling throbbing moment—life seemed so precious to her. So very rare and so very precious. Tears leaked from her eyes.

In her mind, she imagined that she had wrapped her hand around a doorknob and was about to nudge a door open—a door that had been closed and locked her whole life. Now, she was about to open it. She hesitated. What was on the other side?

She quietly left the bed and padded over to the roll top desk. She opened an inside drawer, felt and retrieved her diary. She found a pen. After drawing a little breath, she sat and opened the diary to the first page. She could not see the diary. She could not see a thing in this blackest of nights, where, ironically, she pulsed with light. The page was blank infinite darkness, a night sky void of moon and stars, her pen a shooting star about to streak across that black sky.

Keri put the pen to the page and wrote just one word. Happiness!

CHAPTER 22

The following week was a blur, as Keri worked in a haze of anticipation and happiness. Everyone in the office noticed she was high, happy and hovering somewhere between anxiety and ecstasy. Each day looped into the next, bringing problems and issues that Keri struggled to focus on. Still, she busied herself with anything she could get her hands on to distract her mind, as she waited for the clock to wind down and she could return to the beach house and to Ryan.

She was so tired at night that she instantly fell asleep, but then she'd awaken sometime around 3am, and was unable to fall back to sleep. Consequently, she felt a low dragging energy by the afternoon that was only cured by copious amounts of coffee.

She and Ryan texted often, mostly about simple things: work, food and the weather. He tempted her with beach scenes and sunsets and warm night breezes. She could hardly contain her excitement.

On Saturday morning, Keri attended her colleague's wedding on the Cape, staying just long enough to wish the bride and groom every happiness. Then she hurried across the spreading lawn to the parking lot.

She pushed through beach traffic and crawling lines of cars, angling around road work, finally reaching Ryan's house on Saturday afternoon at a little after 3pm.

When Ryan saw Keri's car approach, he descended the ladder, told B.J. and Dan Jr. to wait for him and then started toward the car.

Keri exited the car jittery, overflowing with anticipation, feeling her heart rate soar. As she walked briskly across the grass toward Ryan, it was soon apparent that something was wrong. He seemed to be dragging himself across the lawn. His face seemed pulled tight, and there was darkness in his expression, weariness in his eyes.

They closed the distance in a kind of slow motion, and with each step, instead of drawing closer, they seemed to be moving away.

Keri's high mood fell into rigid concern. Though the sun glowed hot on her face and shoulders, inside, she felt chilly.

They met. Ryan did not embrace her. His eyes slid away.

"Good trip?" he asked, numbly.

Keri couldn't avoid the panting rise of dread. "What's happened, Ryan?"

He pocketed his hands. Keri felt the calcification of his feelings.

He looked through her and beyond her, as if he were searching for something far out at sea or dancing in the trees.

Keri lowered her voice. "Ryan...are you okay?"

There was a long silence, only the sound of the thudding nail gun. "It's not going to work, Keri. I'm sorry."

Keri stared at him without comprehension, as if she hadn't heard him.

"Ryan..." was all she could squeeze out. It was a low, rusty sound. A hurtful sound. His body was a block of stone.

She stared into his face, and it seemed to occupy multiple worlds, layer upon layer, his eyes searching for the real world, the stable world.

"Ryan, is it something I've done?"

Still, he didn't look at her. "No. Nothing you've done."

"Then I don't understand. Why can't you tell me what has happened? Please, Ryan."

Keri saw Tippie Toe and Brownie dart off into the trees. She saw a dragonfly sail, hover and jerk across the lawn.

Ryan glanced back over his shoulder. "They're waiting for me. The boys. I don't want to leave them alone unsupervised. I should go."

He gave her a brief smile. "Sorry, Keri. I'm sorry about the whole thing. I can't explain anything right now. I thought we could... I thought I could..." His voice was swallowed by the heated breeze. "I can't."

And then he was gone, receding into the shimmering heat. Keri was motionless, pinned to the ground by shock, by the impossibility of the event.

With effort, with as much dignity as she could muster, Keri found herself climbing the stairs to the house. She'd left some things in the bedroom, some underwear, a pair of sandals, two tops, the diary. She stopped on the porch and gazed out at the sea, feeling utterly defeated and exhausted. After a few deep breaths, she went inside.

As she passed the dining room table on the way to the kitchen for a glass of water, she saw an opened 8 ½ x 11 manila envelope with six letter-sized envelopes scattered around it, accented by beams of sunlight. She stopped. All the envelopes had been opened, but their letters had not been removed, except for one. One 2-page letter lay partially folded, some words clearly visible.

Keri's breathing was shallow. She stared hard at the open letter, her face conflicted. For a difficult moment, she waited. Finally, she reached across the letter and cautiously shifted through the envelopes. Every envelope but one was addressed to SF Medical Sergeant Ryan Carlson. The address included his Company, the APO AE and the country, Afghanistan. The return address was from Debbie Carlson, 2417 Clifton Street, Springfield, Massachusetts. The date stamped on the envelopes revealed that they were over two years old. March and April. The last letter was dated April 2nd, the month and year Debbie committed suicide.

Debbie Carlson was Ryan's first wife, of course…of course she was. Keri hesitated. The other envelope had no address and the open letter lay next to it. Keri's heart thudded in her ears. Her mind whirled. She lifted her eyes, straining to make sense of it all. Slowly, her eyes returned to the manila envelope. She reached for it and read the date/stamp. It had been mailed only three days ago from Vicky Mathers in Springfield, Mass. Debbie's mother? But why?

Keri knew she shouldn't read the open letter, but she felt compelled to do so. She couldn't walk away. It was clear that Ryan had received the manila envelope that morning. It was clear that he'd read the letters and they'd brought all the pain and loss back. Keri felt anger and frustration. That damned envelope had killed their relationship. No matter what, she was going to read that letter.

Isn't that what Sophia would have done? What would Sophia have said if she was standing there with Keri?

"Read the damn letter, Keri. If it bothers you that much, just read the lines that are visible. Hell, I'd read everything in front of me."

Keri glanced about, as if being watched by invisible eyes. She stepped closer to the open letter. She tilted her head, slanting her eyes down on it, still tentative. The readable sentence was printed in bold pen.

Today is Debbie's birthday, Ryan. Remember!? You're the one who killed her! YOU! Remember the letters? Read them again and see how you killed her!

Keri stood frozen, shocked, holding her breath. She felt a presence and her head snapped up.

Ryan stood in the doorway, watching her, hands on his hips. There was rage burning in his eyes, humiliation on his face.

Keri looked down and away, in guilt and embarrassment.

They stood suspended, the day building toward late afternoon.

"Now you know," Ryan said, his voice under straining control. "Read the others if you want."

Keri stared down at the floor, contrite. "No..."

"Go ahead, read them all. What the hell? You've read that much. Read them all. Go ahead."

Keri stared into the floor, deadened by his cold voice.

"Debbie wrote more than one suicide letter, Keri. Sometimes she wrote one a month."

She heard the thud of the nail gun. She heard the high whiz of the electric saw.

Ryan crossed to the table, snatched up Debbie's last letter and presented it to Keri. She didn't take it. She trembled.

Ryan held it there. "Go ahead, take it."

Keri closed her eyes.

"I carried these letters home from Afghanistan. They were in our apartment—the apartment that Debbie had loved so much, but wouldn't stay in after I left. The letters went missing one day after Vicky, Debbie's mother, came over to accuse me of killing her daughter, for the fourth or fifth time. I lost count after awhile. Anyway, after we argued the last time, I left, leaving her standing there. I discovered later that Vicky went through my desk and took the letters Debbie had sent me... the ones there on the table. I knew she'd taken them but I didn't care. I figured she needed them more than I did."

Regret and memory seemed to be smothering him. His breath came deep and strong. "Vicky mailed the envelope so that I'd get it today. Debbie's birthday. Debbie would have been 27 years old today."

Keri smeared away tears.

"I can tell you what most of them say, word for word. I have a near photographic memory. *Dear Ryan: I'm sinking again. I need you. Where are you?"*

Keri stared into Ryan's face. His eyes were barren holes of misery. He continued to recite, without reading.

"I'm so alone. I'm scared. You promised me life would be good, Ryan. Where are you? I can't take this life, Ryan. I'm not strong like you. I hate it. It hurts too much. Goodbye."

Ryan lowered his head, defeated, deflated.

They both stood in sunlight for a very long moment.

Ryan stared down at the spilled letters. "I'm sorry, Keri," he said, his voice useless and beaten.

He indicated to the letters. "These things... these words never leave me. They're all part of the war I fought, and I'm still fighting inside. The nightmares come, the day sweats come, the shakes, the killing and death all come rushing back. Debbie's stupid, senseless death is always there, waiting for me every morning. It never leaves me, despite the medication...despite therapy. Despite everything."

Keri's face slipped. She wanted to say something— the perfect selection of healing words. No words came. How could she compete with a living ghost? With a parade of marching nightmares? She'd heard Ryan's screaming in the night. She'd seen his anguished face.

After Keri had gathered her things, she left the house, pausing on the porch. Ryan was far off on the bluffs, a small speck, staring out at the mighty sea. What were his thoughts? What would he do?

Keri loaded the car, slid in behind the wheel and cranked the engine. She rolled down her window and a hot afternoon breeze blew in, tossing her hair. After a final look at the house, Keri drove away, feeling listless and lost.

As she drove under pine and sycamores, past a feathery waterfall, she had the odd sensation that her insides were coming apart. She'd heard that love and loss can have that effect on a person. When her father left them for his new wife, Keri's mother had said something similar. All Keri had felt was betrayal and anger.

The impact of her love for Ryan was astonishing, and finally, in the end, maybe it wasn't really love at all. Don't authentic love and respect come after years of living and struggling together? After trials, tests and tribulations? Surely, it doesn't come so cheaply—so effortlessly—as it had come to her.

So she would be okay. It would all pass like summer clouds in the sky. A new season would come. The leaves would fall, the snows would come and life would go on just as relentlessly and impersonally as it always had.

Keri's and Ryan's relationship was merely a few days of conversation, some food and wine, some laughter, some sailing, some dreaming. Only one night of love making.

But they had been good days—a few long, good days that held an ineffable sweetness of longing and hope.

She would be okay. She prayed that Ryan would. She prayed that he'd find a foothold to climb up and over the mountain of guilt and loss that seemed to rise up, and block him from moving forward with his life.

What would Sophia have said?

"Dear starry-eyed Keri, you should have never read my damned diary."

It was the last day of June.

CHAPTER 23

It was August the 2nd, and Keri was propped up alone in bed in her comfortable one-bedroom apartment, tablet on her lap, surfing the web. She'd perused emails, searched for a movie and tapped through several fashion sites, all in an effort to distract her unsteady mind.

She glanced up from the screen, recalling a phrase she'd once read or heard that kept circumnavigating her brain, like a toy train circling a track. It went something like "The heart once expanded by love must continue to flower, like spring expands into summer, or it will die."

Why had she remembered that? It was over-the-top romantic, and excessively flowery, not something she'd normally remember. What did it mean, anyway? Yes, of course she knew what it meant. She hadn't seen or talked to Ryan in over a month. She thought he might call or text, but he hadn't. One time, she'd began a text to him.

Ryan: Hope you're well. I was just thinking about you and...

She deleted it.

The week after they broke up, Keri came down with some ugly bug and was out of work for three days. Her mother brought teas, soup and pills. They sat and watched old movies on Keri's new gray sofa, with soft coral pillows. Yes, Keri had agonized over purchasing the $1,200 couch, but after two weeks, she decided she needed it to help her recover from her breakup with Ryan.

Keri wrestled with ways to tell her mother about her breakup but, in the end, she couldn't. She felt too foolish. After all, she and Ryan had just met and yet, Keri had gone on and on about how much she loved him. Now it was over. She'd sound like a fool.

Her mother knew, though. Keri saw it in her compassionate eyes. Her mother knew it was all over. Monica knew the tale-tell clues of heartbreak.

So far, Keri had willed herself to stay calm. She'd fought to control her emotions and, for the most part, she'd won. She'd managed to run through all her options with logical and clear thinking. But the threat of stark terror and chaos was always waiting just outside the door, ready to burst in and consume her.

Keri laid the tablet aside, crossed her arms and stared at the bare wall.

"Okay, Keri, now what?" she said aloud.

Of course it had been a possibility, but it had seemed so remote as to not warrant any serious consideration. Certainly not after things had heated up.

She reran the memories of that night hundreds of times in her head—every detail—she and Ryan making their way through the house, shedding clothes and kicking them away as they kissed, touched and entered the bedroom. She recalled the love-making with an aching smile. It had been tender, ecstatic, liberating.

Ryan's weight and strength, his clever touch, brought her to swift climax. They had made love more than once that night, and she had been completely immersed in the wild magic of sensation, desire and love.

Keri knew her body well. She knew her monthly cycles—not that she was all that sexually active, but she'd lived 30 years in a body that she listened to and took care of.

When her period was late, she'd ignored it, denied it, pushed it away, even when she felt her body subtly shift and change. Her period was never late, at least seldom late.

On one particular day, as she sat behind her desk at work, her body suddenly felt fragile and alert, as if some intruder had pierced her skin. She heated up with memory, reliving her exploring hand on the smooth curve of Ryan's damp back, her grip of his muscled arms. And then, as she sat at her desk, she was again startled to rapture by his full wet kiss.

All at once, as if punched in the gut, she broke down into tears, her face in her hands, flat on her desktop. Her emotions beat away at her. Regret and confusion sapped her strength.

Later, as she left for lunch, colleagues passed in the hallway, their faces taut with concern, their mouths moving in little gossipy whispers. She must have looked terrible.

Keri slouched into her doctor's office, snatched two tissues at reception to blot her wet, frightened eyes and slipped inside to see the young but kind nurse practitioner. Keri had a pregnancy test.

Yep, she was pregnant.

She was surprisingly calm. Voices in her head said "What's the big deal? It happens all the time and it has been happening since the beginning of the Big Bang. What was the Big Bang, anyway, if not some giant orgasmic ejaculation where all creatures, great and small, were conceived and born to Mother Earth?"

But now in her bed, alone, Keri felt small and vulnerable. She felt low and desperate. She felt stupid, irresponsible and, surprisingly, she also felt the slow and gradual rise of a new kind of wonder.

As that wonder washed over her and swelled, she reached for her diary, which she now kept on the nightstand next to her bed. She flipped to the first page to see the only entry she'd written, written on that night, that startling night when she and Ryan had conceived the child that was now growing inside her.

Keri's eyes expanded on the word *Happiness!*

She tilted her head, keeping her eyes fixed on that one single and magical word.

Happiness!

For in truth, she had been ecstatically happy when she and Ryan were making love. It was in his touch, his breath, his intimate loving whispers. Their joining had struck her heart, opening secret doors, revealing all the beautiful and marvelous things that a man and woman can experience together, and that so few ever experience together, from what she'd heard.

Keri shrugged down, leaned her head back into the soft pillow and shut her eyes. She'd read the material, the information about the first month of pregnancy and what was going on inside her. She lay there, reviewing it in her mind, and while doing so, she focused on her abdomen, where her baby lay, nesting and growing.

The fertilized egg grows. A water-tight sac forms around it, gradually filling with fluid, the amniotic sac. The placenta develops. It is a round, flat organ that transfers nutrients from the mother to the baby and transfers the baby's wastes.

A primitive face takes form with large dark circles for eyes. The mouth, lower jaw, and throat are developing. Blood cells take shape. Circulation begins.

Now, after the first month, Keri's baby is about 1/4 inch long—smaller than a grain of rice.

Happiness!

At 4am, Keri awoke and sat up, blinking into the dark. What day was it? Was it a work day? An image of Ryan still clung to her eyes. A dream. He had reached for her. They were on the beach and he had reached for her, his smile warm and inviting.

"Don't hide from me," he'd said. "Don't run from me."

Keri got up, went to the kitchen, opened the fridge and took out a bottle of water. She twisted off the cap and took a swallow. What day was it? It was Friday, August 3rd. It was a work day. She felt tired. So tired.

Back in bed, she was nearly asleep when she heard Sophia's lilting voice.

"You wanted to get pregnant, Keri. You know you did. Maybe you can kid yourself but you can't kid me, darlin'. You knew what you were doing. When did you stop taking the pill, girl? Three months ago? Two months ago? You weren't dating anyone special, were you? You'd all but given up on meeting the right guy.

Guess what, sister girl, you wanted to have Ryan's baby. Okay, darlin' girl, now you've got your wish and you've got to tell him. It's his kid too. So, when are you going to tell him? The sooner the better."

Keri was lost in a shadowy world of half-dream and half-consciousness. She worked hard to move her lips, to respond to Sophia, but those heavy lips became rubbery, fat inner tubes rolling off down some hazy country road, where Keri was bicycling with Ryan. He was standing up on the pedals and she rode cradled on the handle bars, her legs flared out. They went flying through the warm buttery sunshine, him kissing her neck and she leaning back against him, giggling like a teenager, lost in bliss.

Keri looked left and saw Sophia standing in a vast, sun-drenched field, shimmering with red poppies. Sophia cupped her hands to her mouth for amplification and she was calling to Keri. Sophia looked troubled, upset. She was shouting out something as Ryan and Keri raced by on the dirt path.

"What?" Keri shouted, cupping her hand over her ear. "What are you saying, Sophia?"

When her alarm buzzed, Keri jumped up, slapped the thing off and toppled back down. She rolled over, covered her head and dozed a few more minutes before forcing herself awake.

CHAPTER 24

At 7pm on Friday, August 3rd, Ryan parked by the curb at 2317 Clifton Avenue in Springfield, Massachusetts, and killed the engine. It was an unfortunate neighborhood, with dusty or dinged up old cars, the occasional tree offering meager shade, and a boarded up house overrun with weeds and shrubs. Ryan saw rickety sheds and green 55 gallon garbage cans spilling out paper and plastic onto driveways and backyards.

Two prancing teens moved across an unsteady sidewalk that rose, cracked and fell away into clumps of concrete, sturdy grass and dandelions, down to a path that led to a basketball court enclosed by a high, chainlink fence. Inside, more teens were doing battle across a heat-shimmering asphalt court, shouting and huffing out effort, passing, dribbling and faking. One tall, graceful kid spiraled up out of the pack, and made a splendid hook shot.

Ryan looked on with a slender smile. It had been years since he'd played basketball, and he would have liked to join them. But he'd be intruding. They'd probably all grown up together, gone to school together and fought together, and they knew each others' girl-friends. That's the way it had been with him and his friends. That's the good thing about staying in the same house for years, growing up in the neighborhood alongside other kids. You played sports together, studied together, double-dated and, after high school or college, you got married and started a family.

Ryan slid down in his seat, postponing what he'd come to do. Instead, he allowed his thoughts to wander. After he'd joined the service, he'd lost track of high school friends, although he'd heard of the occasional marriage, divorce or death. So went life. It was fast and fluid, always in flux.

Ryan had hoped to have a child with Debbie. It might have saved her to be responsible for a small life. She might have grown stronger and happier at the same time. But it wasn't meant to be.

Ryan sat still, recalling Debbie's death and Keri's departure. He heard the slapping bounce of the basketball on the asphalt and heard the boys' cries. He became lost in longing and imagination.

What fun it would be to have son—to teach him sailing and sports and how to frame a house. What a crazy adventure it would be to have a little girl, all pretty and bright with new life. She'd be close to her mother, of course, but he would take her shopping and buy her things. What things? It didn't matter. He'd figure it out. He could teach her sailing, too, and how to swim and how to cook pancakes. That would be fun. They'd find fresh peaches at the Farmers Market and have peach pancakes. How nice that would be, to share simple everyday things with a woman you love, and with kids who'd shake you and wake you up to things you'd never otherwise experience.

These thoughts had come to him much more keenly after he'd met Keri. Keri had awakened him from his long, isolated dream, from his forced exile.

His face darkened. He narrowed his eyes, assessing his thoughts, probing his feelings.

How many millions of fathers had thought the same thoughts, dreamed the same dreams, and yet it was always a new and vibrant impulse in each man—the need to connect, to share life and love. To offer the best parts of himself to his kids so they could live happy lives and try to make a better world.

His head slowly turned toward Vicky Mathers' gray house. It was surrounded by a leaning chain-link fence, a worn out brown lawn, and a struggling flowerbed. Ryan's spirits sank as he looked at the place. It brought back bad, unwanted memories. When he and Debbie were dating, he came by to get her. The neighborhood had never been appealing, but it seemed to have gone from bad times to worse times.

Ryan kept both hands on the top of the steering wheel, staring at the house in a strange way, remembering both the sad and hopeful days.

Debbie's father was around then, a well-meaning, quiet man, who always seemed distracted by something. He'd been ignored and bullied by his wife, a woman of many parts, mostly parts of frustration because she'd once been pretty, popular and smart.

She'd made the mistake of marrying a man who'd inherited money—a good thing, so she thought—but then she watched him lose it all and more to gambling—a bad thing. Clay Mathers was no Lucky Dan Wilson of Dan's Drink & Eat. Clay spent most of his time running from creditors and thick-necked men who wanted the money he owed them.

After Debbie's death, Clay left Vicky. Ryan didn't know all the details and he didn't care to know. Ryan had tried to avoid Vicky since Debbie's death, and he'd never asked about the breakup of their marriage.

Ryan swung his attention away from the house with a deep sigh, dreading the encounter he was about to have, but determined to have it. It had to be done. It must be done.

Ryan thought of Keri. Lovely and fun Keri. Where was she? How was she? He missed her watchful, clever blue eyes, her smooth creamy skin, her small contagious laugh. Keri was wistful and classy, in her tight stylish jeans, loose tops and heels. She was tall and lithe, her gleaming blonde hair scattering playfully in the wind, her full lips often pursed in thought. He'd loved kissing those lips, licking at them, exploring them. There was magic in their love making, and an exciting intimacy.

In the month since he asked her to leave, the nightmares got worse and he shook awake, swimming in his sheets, swinging and slapping away bad guys and charging ghosts. Keri had opened him up in some bizarre way, releasing all the dark, hiding things. She'd disturbed him. She'd awakened him to the possibility of new love and a new life.

But he had to exorcise the old demons, once and for all, or he and Keri would never make it. He'd never make it. Vicky's envelope containing Debbie's letters had showed him that. When he opened the envelope and read those letters, all the devils had returned, all the self-hatred, confusion and regret had returned. He heard mortar shells exploding all around him, machine-gun fire tearing into bodies. He saw Debbie's sad smile and her petite, withered body lying so alone on a motel bed.

How could he have any kind of relationship with Keri until he reconciled all the past demons? Until he slammed the door on the past; until he healed the open wounds; until he allowed himself to fall in love again... and he had fallen in love again. He'd fallen in love with Keri.

Ryan left his truck, unlatched the chain gate and strolled up the walkway onto the porch. The front door was closed, the curtains drawn. He had noticed the light blue 1999 Ford Escort poking out of the garage. Vicky was home.

Ryan stared at the heavy brown door with its tarnished brass knocker, and then found the doorbell and pressed it. He heard a soft electric buzz. He waited with restless, turbulent eyes.

The door creaked open. When Vicky saw him, she made a blurred noise of irritation. She did not open the screen door. It was a barrier, a psychological mesh that separated the past and the present, that kept out threats and kept in ghosts and hovering shadows.

Vicky was stooped, her chaotic hair a thin, wiry gray. She'd lost weight since Ryan had seen her last. Her faded cotton dress hung loosely on her skinny frame, her face was pinched with wrinkles, and her dull, ice-cold eyes were glazed with fatigue. Those hard eyes looked back at Ryan, alive with new and old nightmares.

"What are you doing here?" she asked, sourly.

"I want to talk to you," Ryan said, his voice soft.

Hanging from the porch ceiling, wind chimes caught the breeze. The silver tubes touched and shimmered music. Ryan glanced at them, remembering that they were a birthday present from Debbie to her mother over three years ago.

Vicky looked sallow and a little spooked, not expecting to see Ryan framed in her doorway.

"I've got nothing to say to you," she said. Her voice filled with haughty strength and pride. "I'm finished with you. I was finished with you a long time ago."

"Then why did you send that envelope, Vicky?"

Ryan waited, staring into Vicky's accusing eyes. She grinned, sinisterly.

"Because you need to be reminded about what you did to my daughter."

Ryan felt a twinge of anger in his stomach. He controlled it. "I don't need you to remind me about Debbie, Vicky. I think of her every day."

"Well, you should have thought of her when she was alive. You should have been there for her, like you said you would. I told her not to marry you. I told her she'd regret it. She had other boys—better than you—who wanted to marry her."

Ryan's face clinched into red anger. "Yes, Vicky, and those were the same boys she went back to when I had to leave. The same boys who gave her the drugs. The same boys who killed her. So don't put that on me."

Vicky shook at memory and indignation. "You bastard! You don't know anything. You don't know what it was like to see her like that. To find her with some awful man in her bed using her, and then beating her. You don't know."

"Of course I know, Vicky. I tried to take her away from all that!"

"Then why did you leave her to die?"

"I didn't leave her to die. I left her because I had to! Because I was a soldier. Because I had a job to do and lots of people depended on me."

"Debbie depended on you. She was your wife, for God's sake! You should have come back to her when you knew she was on the drugs again. When she was sick and depressed."

"She came back to you, didn't she, Vicky? She came home to you and you'd thrown her out because she'd gotten pregnant in high school. Where were *you*, after I left? Why didn't *you* help her? You *were* here. You were her mother. Where were you, Vicky? Maybe it's time you stop blaming everyone else for Debbie's death and start being honest with yourself. Where were you? Why did *you* let her die, Vicky? Why?"

The hot words shot out of his mouth before he could stop them. They were terrible words—killing words—and he knew they'd struck her like bullets to the heart.

Vicky seemed to wilt. Her head lowered, as tears swelled her eyes. She trembled, her face sagged. A breathing, blowing wind rippled the wind chimes, as if Debbie were trying to speak, trying to console or blame or rage in the only way she could.

The ragged sound of a motorcycle tore by, like a threat. The basketball kept tapping the ground, the teenage voices ringing out.

Ryan resettled his shoulders, stung by his own harsh and accusing words. He worked to get control of himself. "Vicky... Vicky I didn't mean that. I shouldn't have said that."

Vicky's mouth went slack. Her chin trembled and she choked out some words Ryan couldn't understand. There were more mumbles and more tears.

Ryan shoved his hands into his jean pockets and looked away. "Vicky... I'm sorry. We have to stop this. We both have to stop all this and try to move on."

Vicky threw a look upwards, as if searching for God. "Move on?" she said, sharply, the wet metal of her eyes wide with indignation. Her eyes leveled on Ryan. "Move on to what? My baby is dead! Maybe you can move on but I will never move on. Never! Okay? Now get away from me and don't ever come here again or I'll call the cops on you."

Ryan stood resolute. "Vicky, I'm burning all of Debbie's letters. Every single one of them. If you have more and send more, I will burn those too. Debbie is dead and there's nothing anyone of us can do about it now. I have the rest of my life to live and I'm going to live it. I'm going to move on. You do as you like."

Ryan didn't want to leave her there like that, standing small in late evening shadow, with a punctured heart from the bullet-words he'd shot her with. But he couldn't take them back. They'd been fired. They'd deeply wounded her, and he was sickened by it.

He was tired of war, tired of fighting and tired of death. He wanted life, and he wanted more from life than to simply survive until the next battle, the next conflict, the next nightmare that left him panting, screaming and searching in the darkness for light. For the first time in his life, Ryan wanted to live without trying to save a country, a village or a Debbie. It was too heavy a burden to try to save the entire world.

Ryan hadn't worked it all out in his head yet, but after Keri left that last time, he'd spent hours thinking about it as he worked on the house, with Dan Jr. and B.J., as he swam at sunset, as he climbed back to the attic and played the Elvis songs that he and Keri had listened to. And then when Big Pete had come by, he'd had to listen to him tell Ryan what a big mistake he'd made in letting Keri go.

"What a stupid blockhead you are," Big Pete had said. "Such a pretty, classy girl and you send her away. Blockhead!"

After Keri had left, Ryan had paced the house, deep into the night, straining to think things through; struggling to get at his feelings and to connect all the dots. He recalled again what the military therapist had once told him. "Finally, you have to save yourself, Ryan, before you're capable of loving another. That isn't being selfish, it just means that if you feel good inside your own skin, others will feel good being around you. That's the best way to rescue the world."

Maybe that's what Ryan had learned from his marriage with Debbie. He'd wanted to save her from her own demons. He'd wanted to rescue her from her nightmares, from her addictions. But in the end, he couldn't. Maybe all he'd been trying to do was save himself.

Ryan felt the weight of the moment. He gave Vicky a final glance. She was staring down in defeat.

"Take care of yourself, Vicky," he said, in a low, tender voice.

He turned, descended the wooden stairs and walked briskly to his truck. He slid in behind the wheel and cranked the engine. Vicky was still standing behind the screen, a quiet shadow, when he drove away, past the basketball players who'd left the court. They were scattering, blotting their faces with their T-shirts, tipping back water bottles, punching and slapping arms and shoulders.

At home that night, he rummaged through his drawers until he found all of Debbie's letters, and all of Vicky's letters. He crammed them into the manila envelope and took them out to the highest buffs.

Under a swirl of stars, he lit two corners of the envelope with a lighter. The wind swiftly blew out each dancing flame. He lit the envelope again, and again the sturdy wind blew out the flames. Old pain and memory did not want to die without a fight.

Ryan grabbed the envelope and went back to the house. He gathered up an armful of wood and trudged to the staircase that led down to the beach.

Within 10 minutes he'd dug a fire pit. He placed the stuffed envelope at the base of the wood and used it to start the fire. The edges caught, flamed, leaped and browned. Ryan looked on in final despair as the flames engulfed the envelope, their orange greedy fingers reaching up, coiling around the wood, finally devouring all the letters.

Ryan stood under the glory of starlight, his eyes wet, his body shaking, the sea loud in his ears as he watched sparks rise to the stars.

CHAPTER 25

The next morning, Ryan was awake at 6am. After a shower, he went to the kitchen and made coffee. He sat hunched in early morning light, staring down at his phone. He'd slept pretty well. No nightmares.

He got up and made scrambled eggs and toast. As he ate them, dull gray light introduced a quiet, sleepy day. An occasional burst of wind wheezed through the windows.

Charlie Bates had called the night before, requesting Ryan join him on the boat the following night. Ryan suggested Charlie call Pete Halprin, because Ryan wanted to drive to Boston to see Keri, but Charlie said Pete's kid was in the hospital. In the end, Ryan said he'd be there.

Ryan stared down at his phone with bright, eager eyes. It was after seven. He'd take a chance. He drained the last of his coffee and reached for his phone.

He thumbed out a message:

Hi Keri. Can I come and see you? I'd like to explain some things.

He sent the message and waited, drumming his fingers into the table top. No return message. She probably wasn't up yet. It was Saturday, after all, and she was probably sleeping in.

Ryan got up and stepped outside on the patio, listening to the screech of birds, seeing fog hang in the trees.

At nine o'clock, Keri had still not responded. Uneasy, Ryan decided to cut the grass. He pushed the riding mower out of the garage, leaving Brownie and Tippie Toe shuttered away in their dog houses.

He filled the 3-gallon fuel tank to capacity and cranked the 16 horse engine. It growled to life. He climbed aboard and levered forward, bumping along out to the edge of the woods. On the slopes and hills, Ryan mowed up and down the incline, occasionally pausing to tug his phone from his jeans to check for messages. None from Keri. Maybe she wouldn't answer. Maybe she'd moved on. He couldn't blame her.

He continued on across flat ground, the smell of freshly cut grass assailing his nose. He sneezed a couple of times, feeling drowsy under the gray clouds, the droning spell of the motor, and the warm humid air.

At 10:30, Ryan shut off the engine and leaped off the mower.

Keri had responded. *I'm on my way to Portland, to see a friend. Surprised to hear from you.*

Ryan quickly texted back. *Can I see you when you get back?* He waited, nervously.

Keri responded. *I can come there. Sunday. Okay?*

Ryan straightened up, fully awake. *Yes. Good. I will be fishing till about 11am. Come early if you want. I'll leave the back door open.*

Ryan's thumbs were poised, waiting. He typed. *I've missed you.*

He was standing in the middle of the lawn, glancing about, suddenly remembering Keri's idea about renting out the house and the grounds to private events.

A few weeks ago, he would never have even considered it, dismissing it out of hand as ridiculous and intrusive. Now, as he waited for her response, he could picture Keri's enthusiastic energy infusing the place and bringing it to life again, using the property that had been dormant for so many years, in new ways.

Keri's text came through. *I've missed you too. So good to hear from you. See you soon.*

On Saturday night, Ryan was aboard the Sally May with Charlie Bates. They were 35 miles off Crandall Cove in a rising, choppy sea. Charlie Bates was at the helm, a stocky, 43 year-old solid man, with a blunt, indifferent face and pleased alertness. He talked little, drank little, didn't smoke and had a wife and two teen-aged daughters.

He was the son of a fisherman, and he'd been fishing for almost two decades. He and Ryan had built a good business over the months, with over 700 traps sitting on the bottom of the Atlantic Ocean. Two times a week, they'd take the Sally May out overnight and spend a 16-hour day hauling in lobster and crab, then they'd return the next morning loaded down with their catch. It was physically hard and demanding work, and there were times when Charlie's legs and hips ached so bad he didn't know how much longer he could keep at it. But he loved the sea; he loved the tilt and pitch of ocean and sky, the fishy smells and the hard rush of sea air. He loved the freedom and the silence and he loved the physical work. On land, there was so much noise, so much static and so much talk, so many beeps from cell phones, so many alarms assaulting you at every turn.

And Charlie like working with Ryan, who loved the sea and the silence as much as he did. Sometimes, they wouldn't say more than five words to each other for hours at a time. They knew the work and how to do it. That was all. That was art. That was perfection. That was friendship.

At around 3am Sunday morning, Charlie put the Sally May on autopilot. They were moving due south at six knots. He told Ryan he was going to catch some sleep and he'd be back up by dawn.

Ryan waved him off and went to work, pumping water into Sally May's holding tanks to chill, so that when they reached their first string of traps a few miles farther south, the water would be cold enough to keep the lobsters alive for the return trip.

Ryan looked up into the close sky, swarming with stars, and he was content to be in the cool beautiful night with a gentle rolling sea. Inevitably, he thought of Keri and he felt the high beat of his pulse.

After he and Charlie unloaded their catch, he'd see her again. Maybe she'd meet him at the dock. Maybe she'd come smiling at him, her lips waiting for a kiss, ready to forgive him for his stupidity for sending her away. He would ask her then, as he swam in the blue glory of her eyes and touched the shining luster of her hair. He would ask her to marry him. If it was too soon—if she wasn't ready—that would be okay, but at least she'd know how he felt. She'd know that he loved her, and that he wanted to build on that love every day, for the rest of his life.

Ryan took a breath and tottered over to open a metal hatch on the deck. It was covered by two 35-gallon Coleman coolers, enormous plastic insulated ice chests that he and Charlie had filled before leaving the dock six hours earlier. They weighed about 200 pounds, and Ryan had to move them to get to the hatch. He'd done it before. He snagged a box hook onto the plastic handle of the bottom ice chest, braced his legs, leaned back and yanked with all his strength.

The handle snapped.

Ryan stumbled backwards, losing his balance, tumbling across the deck toward the back of the boat. It was wide open, a flat, slick ramp leading into the sea. Ryan's body was in helpless flight. He reached and grabbed for anything as he flew past, his fingers just missing. He plunged into the cold dark sea, stunned, taking in a mouthful of water as he went under. He surfaced, spitting water, alarmed, searching, slapping at the sea.

It took panicked seconds to realize his dilemma.

He yelled for Charlie, but Charlie was asleep on a bunk below the front deck. And the diesel engine was loud, and the 45-foot boat was moving away from him at six knots on autopilot. The navigation lights were retreating into the black, endless night.

Ryan shouted for Charlie, repeatedly, until his throat tightened from fear, and from the gulps of salty water.

Then the boat was gone. The lights faded to black. There was silence. Dead silence.

Ryan had been in life-threatening situations many times in his life. He'd been shot at; been in many fire fights; been attacked head-on; been knifed once in the leg; been pinned down by mortar attack; but he'd never felt so utterly and completely alone as he did now. He felt as though he were the last man living on earth. Except, he was floating in the black Atlantic Ocean 35 miles from any land.

CHAPTER 26

Saturday night, Keri was in Portland at her friend Roxie's apartment, sleeping in her spare bedroom. At 3:13am, on Sunday morning, Keri jerked awake. She sat up, a sense of urgency brewing in her chest. She was just able to recall the fleeting tail of a dream that was fast receding into the murky black water of her mind.

She shut her eyes, straining for recall.

Creeks were smoking in the cold. Frost dusted the land, glistening like jewels, as the sun rose. Ryan was standing off in the distance under a grove of trees, white vapor rolling from his mouth. He was smiling at her, waving. Then he pointed to a path and started walking away from her.

She called out to him to wait for her, but he was gone, disappearing in a flash of shining light.

"Wait!" she shouted, suddenly feeling the air, cold and strong.

Sophia came running, bursting out from the trees where Ryan had vanished. Her mischievous, daring eyes were large, her voice high and strident.

"Go get him! Go now!"

Keri opened her eyes, fully awake. She kicked off the blankets, swung out of the double bed and stood in the darkness of the small room.

The dream was familiar only to her imagination— yet it seemed intuitively real and elusive, hovering between reality and fantasy. She was not attracted to, nor had she ever been interested in, the occult. But the dream held her in a kind of threatening fascination. It was something delicate and flimsy, yet vital and authentic.

Her breath came fast and her heart beat hard against her chest. She could taste danger. A thick metallic taste, a sickening coppery taste.

Keri took several breaths to ease the agitation of her mind, and then she rolled back onto the bed, covering herself. She lowered her head into the thick, soft pillow, closed her eyes and tried to sleep. Sleep wouldn't come. Images of Ryan came cutting in and out of her inner vision. She sensed danger. Something was wrong.

At 6am, she pushed up, grabbed her phone and texted Ryan. Nothing. Minutes later, she sent a second text, and then a third. She knew he was normally up by 5:30 or 6. At 6:30, she called him. It rang and dropped into voicemail. She left a message, asking him to call her as soon as he received her message.

At 7am, when she hadn't heard from him, she paced the room, feeling each minute push against her with new anxiety. Finally, she looked up the phone number for Dan's Drink & Eat. Seven rings later, she heard a sleepy, male voice.

"Dan's..."

"Hi, is Big Pete there?"

"Big Pete? No. He don't come in this early. He's out anyway."

"Is Bette there?"

"No. Who is this?"

"Is this Doc?"

"No, it's Hack."

"My name's Keri. Is Ryan Carlson there?"

Silence.

"Hello? Hack, are you there?"

"Keri who?"

"Keri Lawton. I'm a friend of Ryan's... and Big Pete's."

More silence.

"Is Ryan there? Hack, please, I need to speak with him."

"No, he ain't here. You ain't heard?" the voice said, now awake.

"Heard what?"

"Ryan's missing. He was lost on the Sally May early this morning. The Coast Guard's out searching for him."

Keri felt a slap of terror. "What do you mean he's lost?"

"Charlie woke up and couldn't find him. Said he must have fallen overboard."

Keri tried to swallow. "He couldn't just fall overboard," Keri said, refusing to take in the truth. "I mean, he's experienced. He wouldn't just fall overboard. Why would Charlie be asleep? Why can't they find Ryan?!"

"Well, I'm just telling you what they told me."

Keri's breath came in short, staccato gasps. She struggled to reign in her panic. "He can't be missing. I mean, how can he be missing?" Keri said, her mind hot and spinning.

"I'm just telling you, that's all. We heard about it this morning. About 6:30. There are a bunch of boats out there looking for him."

Keri struggled with images and words and impossibilities. "Do you mean he is out in the ocean all by himself? Out there floating in the ocean?"

"Yep... that's where he is. Well, at least that's where we hope he is."

Keri couldn't speak. She closed her eyes and massaged her forehead. When she spoke, her voice was small and pinched. "They'll find him, right?"

Hack cleared his throat. "I don't know. I mean, we hope so, don't we?"

Keri was dressed, packed and on the road by eight. When she told her friend Roxie what had happened, she was understanding.

"Call to let me know how you are," Roxie said, her sleepy brown eyes narrow with concern.

Keri piled into her car and shot away. She drove much too fast, searching the sky with dread, seeing gray clouds moving in. The weather report said it was going to rain, but only light showers, thank God.

It would take her about two hours to reach Boston and another hour or so to reach Crandall Cove. Surely they'd find Ryan before she arrived.

Just outside Boston, she pulled over and called Dan's again. This time she got Doc.

"Nothing yet, Keri. The Coast Guard's out there with boats and a helicopter. About a dozen locals are out looking for him, too."

"How could he have fallen out of the boat, Doc? It doesn't make sense."

"I don't know many of the details, Keri. I just hear bits and pieces of things."

"Has anybody called Ryan's mother, Sally?"

"Don't know about that, Keri. Maybe Big Pete did. He's out there in the Coast Guard helicopter looking for Ryan. Lucky Dan and his two boys are out on the sea too. Hell, half the town wants to get out there, and I'm afraid they're all going to mess up the Coast Guard's search. Too many damned boats getting into everybody else's way."

Before Keri got back on the road, she called Sally Carlson. Sally picked up on the third ring.

"That you, Keri?"

"Yes, and I can tell from your voice that you've heard about Ryan."

"Yes. I shouldn't talk long. I'm in the car, on my way to Crandall Cove."

"I'll be there in less than an hour," Keri said.

"Ryan called me last night," Sally said. "He said you were going to the house today. He sounded good, Keri. He sounded so good about it. He told me he was in love with you."

Keri could tell Sally was holding back tears. Keri was doing the same.

"I love him, Sally. I love him very much."

"Well, then, we'll pray real hard for him."

"I'm sure they'll find him," Keri said, struggling with her own emotion. "They've got a lot of people out there searching for him."

"Well, Ryan's tough, Keri. He won't give up. The Special Forces taught him how to survive in tough situations. And he's a good swimmer. We'll just pray, won't we?"

Keri drove on, determined, struggling to calm her emotions. She whispered encouragement to herself. She whispered prayers for Ryan. She talked to Ryan. She told him he had a lot to live for. He had everything to live for. Their lives were just beginning.

A half hour away from Crandall Cove, it sprinkled rain.

CHAPTER 27

Don't panic, Ryan. Stay focused, keep it simple and stay positive.

Those were Ryan's first thoughts, after the initial shock of water and the near panic that struck him when he realized he was completely alone in the middle of the night in the Atlantic Ocean.

Ryan knew that the first thing he needed to do was kick off his boots, so that their dead weight wouldn't drag him down. While he treaded water, he reached down and pulled off his left boot. Struggling for balance, he turned it upside down, raised it up over the waves, then plunged it back into the water, trapping a boot-size bubble of air inside. He tucked the inverted boot under his left armpit. Then he did the same thing with the right boot. They would help him stay afloat.

Ryan bobbed in the water, letting his mind settle, letting ideas and contingency plans bubble up to the surface. He was not in a good situation. He was not wearing a life vest. Stupid. He was at least 35 miles off the coast of the nearest land. Not good. When would Charlie wake up and find out he was missing? Would

Charlie even have a clue as to what time Ryan had fallen into the ocean?

How cold was the water? About 72 degrees. It was chilly, but not unbearable. When was dawn? About two hours away. Once light came, Ryan knew the Coast Guard would come looking for him. Charlie would discover Ryan had fallen overboard, and he'd scamper over to the VHF radio that was bolted to the ceiling in the wheelhouse and snatch for the microphone. He'd switch to channel 16, the distress channel, and call the Coast Guard. He'd tell them there was a man overboard.

Ryan faced the sky, seeing a half moon swimming in and out of wispy dark clouds. There was a five-foot swell, and Ryan rose and fell with it, feeling like a piece of driftwood, floating aimlessly.

Ryan knew that Charlie would feel terrible and guilty about the whole thing. He knew what he'd think. I should have stayed up. I should have woken up earlier. I should have told Ryan not to work alone in the middle of the night. Ryan pictured Charlie at dawn, his tired, desolate face trying to focus all his energy on directing the commercial boats in north-south tracking lines. Charlie would never give up the search, and Ryan worried about Charlie's bad knees and his nagging right hip.

Ryan's only goal at this point was to stay afloat until dawn and then check the horizon for boats, search the sky for a helicopter and scan the water for the fin of a 350 pound blue shark. One or two might come by for a visit. Not a happy thought, but one he had to consider. Ryan made sure he had his buck knife in his pocket.

He did. He could snap it open and slash or stab if the sharks decided to move in on him.

But now, all he could do was stay positive, stay afloat and wait for dawn. It was not easy beating back panic. It's easier when you're engaged in a firefight or an operation. All your energy is focused on the task. Skill and experience take over and you perform without awareness.

Here, now, he was just an infinitesimal speck bobbing in the Atlantic Ocean, at the mercy of the elements, his endurance, his luck and his control of his mind and thoughts.

He shut his eyes for a moment and he saw Keri— Keri was looking at him with pleading eyes. She toyed with the ends of her hair, as she did when she was nervous; she closed her long eyelashes just before a kiss; she reached for his cheek with her long, slim fingers, and touched him.

"It feels so good to be with you, Ryan. It feels so right."

He recalled the Saturday evening after dinner, when they burst from the house and descended the staircase, returning to the beach. A sudden squall blew in, spitting rain. Keri presented her face to the sky and stuck out her tongue. He'd laughed at her. It was such a girlish thing—a wonderfully spontaneous thing. Her hair got wet and he'd raked strands of it from her face.

Then the tide rushed across the hard sand, spreading, foaming and bubbling. It encircled him. Ryan stood frozen in the center of an instant lake, perplexed. He felt childish and silly. Being with Keri did that to him. He lifted his right foot and slapped the water flatfooted, like something a kid would do. Water exploded from his foot, splashing Keri in the body and face. She threw a hand up for protection, laughing, ducking, running away. Ryan kept at it. Great geysers shot up around him, and he jumped and stamped his feet in a kind of weird, splashing, circular dance. Fountains jetted up and drenched him.

Keri howled with laughter. Then, on an impulse, she ran at him in full gallop. He gathered her up in his arms and swung her about, loving the feel and the weight of her, loving the way she laughed, breathless and high.

After he eased her down, they kissed, long and deep. The swirling water circled their legs and foamed at their feet. Rain pelted their heads and washed their faces.

Ryan felt chilled. The first real chill. Ryan knew, based on his height and weight, plus the weather and the water temperature, he had about 17 to 18 hours before hypothermia took over and his muscles gave out. The whole, blunt truth was even more sobering: very few people survived more than three or four hours in the Atlantic, especially without a raft or some flotation device.

Ryan forced those thoughts from his mind. He needed to keep his mind active, thinking, planning, anticipating. Okay, once Charlie called the Coast Guard, what action would they take?

The Coast Guard Station near Crandall Cove would issue instructions to launch whatever boats were available. Perhaps they'd approve the use of a helicopter or two, and possibly even a search plane.

A Coast Guard cutter, an 87-footer, would get into it, while someone would man the computer, using computer simulations. They'd use the newest search and rescue program, called Sarops, which can generate as many as 10,000 points to represent how far and in what direction a "search object" might have drifted.

From the last known location of a lost seaman, operators input a variety of data to calculate the ocean currents and wind direction. Sarops then creates a map of a search area.

Of course, the problem was that no one would know precisely when or where Ryan had dropped into the sea. It could turn out to be a 1,600-square-mile search area. That would be impossible to cover.

Ryan was a needle in a very big haystack, with time running out.

Okay, fine. These Coast Guard guys are smart. Charlie's smart. Big Pete is smart. They'd have to find a way to narrow the search.

"Think, boys," Ryan said to himself. "Check the hatch cover. It will be upside down on the deck. Every mariner knows that is bad luck. I would not have left it there. The pumps were on, sluicing cool ocean water through the lobster tanks. What does that mean, boys? It means I had been getting them ready for the day's catch. It's summer. We wait to start filling the tanks until we reach the 40-fathom curve or 240 feet. That's when the water temperature begins to drop. The 40-fathom curve is about 10 miles east of the Sally May's first trawl. How are you doing, boys? Now Charlie, you will find the broken handle on the ice chest. Got it? You'll be able to figure out about when I splashed into the Atlantic. Narrow the search, boys. Narrow the search and find me."

CHAPTER 28

Sally met Keri on the lawn at Ryan's house. It had stopped raining and a breeze sprang up and scattered their hair. They hugged and went inside, as Sally brought her up to date on what she knew, which wasn't much. The Coast Guard was out in force. Both a helicopter and a search plane had been dispatched. So far, nothing.

They sat in the kitchen, sipping coffee, their phones near. At times they were elaborately conversational, at other times, quiet and anxious. Both presented brave faces, but inside they were clinched with fear and dread.

Keri wanted to tell Sally about the baby, but with the world tilted in anxiety and expectation, it was simply not the right time. Keri wished now that she'd told Ryan she was pregnant. Maybe it would have helped galvanize him—give him one more reason to fight for life.

Why hadn't she texted him that she loved him? All she'd said was that she'd missed him. A damned text. She hadn't even called. Her mind was cranking out thoughts and words, spinning off in all directions.

A stupid, cheap text was all she'd sent Ryan. She'd spoken no words of love. There'd been no face-to-face kiss, no telling him that he was going to be a father. She'd sent a text, just like thousands of smartphone owners do every day, texts about TV shows, or junk food choices or which videogame they should play.

Why didn't she call him back as soon as she'd received his text, telling her he wanted to come and see her? Simple. She was angry at him. She was hurt. She wanted to make him wait and worry that she might have moved on. She wanted to play hard to get. How adolescent was that? But then he hadn't contacted her for over a month.

Keri took a deep breath and thought of him. She could almost feel his presence, the calm strength of him. So often the quiet was all around him; when he moved, worked or cooked, he didn't seem to stir the air, as if he were in complete harmony with the moment.

She stood staring out the kitchen window, watching seagulls course the darkening sky, braying like donkeys. She felt the deep, fresh excitement that stirred within her grow. It was the baby—their baby. Their future. He had to come back.

At 11:20, Keri and Sally were out on the deck, gazing out to the rolling sea. Their uneasy eyes scanned the horizon, their bodies close and tight with tension. They heard the tide slip away and climb back up, as the minutes crawled toward afternoon.

Keri laced her hands behind her back, her eyes filling up with the sea. She recalled what Ryan had told her when they were sailing on that glorious, sun-blessed day. "About 70 percent of the world is covered by ocean."

Keri shivered. Ryan was out there, alone, in that vast watery world.

"Will they give up the search if they don't find him by sunset?" Keri asked.

Sally twisted her hands. "I don't know, Keri. I hope not, but I just don't know."

At that moment, Big Pete was whistling his usual tuneless melody. He sat figuring and concentrating in the backseat of the Coast Guard's Jayhawk helicopter, as it went rumbling over the metallic gray ocean. He wasn't supposed to be in the helicopter, and there were strict regulations against such things, but that didn't stop Big Pete. Actually, nothing and no one stopped Big Pete if he set his mind and mountain of a body to it. He knew both pilots, because Big Pete knew most everybody, and they knew him. Most everybody did. So in early morning light, Big Pete insinuated his big body into the helicopter and shouted.

"LET'S GO!"

Big Pete and pilots Bill Coster and Tommy Pine had been staring down at the water since about 7am. By late morning, they were growing discouraged. They had a few false alarms— sea turtles and mylar balloons—and with each sighting, they'd followed the same protocol: the man who saw the object called out: "Mark. Mark. Mark."

Bill Coster would push a button in the cockpit that would mark the location, and he'd swing the Jayhawk back around and check it out.

Bill had been in the Coast Guard for six years, flying a Jayhawk for two, and he had never once pulled anyone alive from the water. He'd trained for it countless times, plucked dummies out of the ocean, run through checklists and drills, and he knew his job inside and out. But the cold hard truth was that nearly every time someone fell overboard in the North Atlantic, they drowned.

At 11:19 a.m., the helicopter completed another parallel search pattern—their third of the day.

"How much fuel you got, Bill?" Big Pete bellowed over the whack of the engine.

Bill shouted back over his shoulder, ignoring the head mic. "We're about an hour from bingo fuel."

"What the hell's bingo fuel mean?" Big Pete shouted.

"When we only have enough gas to make it back home."

Big Pete cursed. He was not going to let Ryan perish.

Big Pete started his breathy whistling, pointing his eyes down on the shaking sea.

"Come on, Ryan, where the hell are you?" Big Pete whispered.

Big Pete shut his eyes and concentrated. He thought strategy, and in his mind, he pictured a blackboard just as he'd always done before a football game. He mentally drew out numbers and coordinates. He thought about it. He scrambled it, changed it, moved things around. He pictured the map in his head. The map of the entire search area.

An idea struck. His eyes popped open. "Hey, Bill."

He leaned forward. "Let's do a simple track-line search: let's go south-southeast for about 10 miles, straight through the main search area, then turn north for another 10 miles and then veer north-northwest. If

my sense of direction is right, that'll take us back toward Air Station Crandall. Yes?"

"That's gonna push our fuel, Big Pete."

"So push the damn fuel! I've got a feeling, based on
something Charlie Bates told me. I've been trying to
figure it out. Traps are always laid out along an east-
west line and there are buoys. If I know Ryan, he will
try to reach a buoy. He'll grab a rope and hang on.
That's what I'd do, and I'm betting that's what Ryan
did."

They went thundering off south, as Big Pete whistled and did something he hadn't done in years. He sent
up a silent prayer.

CHAPTER 29

Ryan had been awake for over 24 hours. He was cold, thirsty and near exhaustion. Lazy gray clouds rolled in above him, obscuring the sun. Ryan had a good idea where he'd fallen overboard. He knew this wide expanse of endless sea. He knew that several lobster fishermen had trawls close by. Each lobster trawl is a string of 30 to 50 traps, spaced 150 feet apart at the bottom of the ocean. At the end of each string, a rope extends up from the last trap to the surface, where it is tied to a big round vinyl buoy.

Ryan speculated that if he could float, swim and drift his way to a buoy, he'd be more visible to the searchers, and it would be easier to stay afloat.

Now he had to find one. Every few seconds a swell would lift him a few feet and when he crested a wave, he'd search the horizon for a buoy.

He'd crawled through waves, the current against him. For awhile, it seemed like he was drifting aimlessly out into oblivion. He wiped his blurry eyes and moved on, swimming, resting and, rising with the swells, searching.

Sunlight broke through, and warmed him for a time. Then it vanished again under gray haze. How much more strength did he have? His legs were cramping and his fingers felt like little stubs of ice. He could hardly move them.

Time melted into timelessness. When he finally spotted a buoy, his strength was nearly gone. Was he finished? Did he have the strength to swim to it? The ocean seemed to want him, to swallow him, to suck him down to its infinite, mysterious depths.

How strange, he thought. Just when he'd felt a new birth of life—a new beginning—his life was so very close to ending. A sudden burst of rain pimpled the water around him. He stuck out his tongue and drank. It tasted good.

The sea pitched him about like a toy, and he wondered if the sea gods were laughing at him. Look at Ryan Carlson, the tough guy, the Special Forces tough guy. You don't look so tough now, do you, son? The great big sea is going to eat you up and swallow you. You'll never be heard from again. How does that make you feel, tough guy?

Then Ryan heard a voice. It seemed to come from far off, like wind through rustling leaves. He struggled to lift his head, to pick up the voice, but it seemed to come from inside his head.

"I have secrets, Ryan. Secrets to tell."

Ryan blinked, sank beneath a swell, bobbed up and spit out water. That's when he saw it. So close to him. Very close. A buoy with a flag on top of it. He was almost there. He could almost reach for it.

Finally, he released the boots under his arm, took in a deep breath and started a slow crawl. He reached, sank, came up and used the current to angle himself directly into the buoy. It was so close now. So damned close. It was a melting mirage, then it was real, then it blurred, disappeared and flashed back into his vision.

He reached out and grabbed the rope. He missed, went under, shot up and reached again. He seized the rope, gripping it with his icy fingers, and hung on.

"I have secrets, Ryan. Secrets for you. Come back to me, Ryan."

Ryan sucked in air, listening to the voice. Listening to Keri's calling, soft voice.

"I have secrets, Ryan. Secrets. Come to me."

The Jayhawk was tearing across the water, all eyes inside on the sea. Nothing.

Finally, Bill yelled. "That's it, Big Pete. We've got to head back home. We're almost out of fuel."

"Wait!"

"We can't wait, Big Pete. It's over."

Big Pete pointed in a desperate reflex. "Over there! There!! Mark! Mark! Mark!"

Bill hit the mark button in the cockpit and swept the helicopter around.

Big Pete pointed, jabbing his index finger down at the sea. "He's there! The son-of-a-bitch is there! Look! Look!"

Bill, Tom and Big Pete lit up. There he was. Ryan was sitting on the rope between two buoys, waving frantically.

Marvin Banks, the rescue swimmer, clipped his harness onto the helicopter's hoist cable, and Tom lowered him into the water. As Banks swam to Ryan, Tom lowered a rescue basket, and Banks helped Ryan climb in.

Slowly, the basket twisted up toward the side of the helicopter.

When Ryan was helped inside, Big Pete gazed at him, whistling his tuneless song.

"Hello, you big blockhead. What are you trying to do, prove you're a tough guy?"

After Ryan was huddled under blankets, Bill Coster flipped the radio to channel 21 and called Charlie Bates, who was somewhere below them, staring out at the water, breaching the rolling waves, wiping his tired and bloodshot eyes.

"Hey, Charlie boy. Guess what? We've got your man. Believe it or not. He's alive!"

Ryan was rushed to the county hospital and treated for hypothermia, dehydration and exposure. He lay there waiting for Sally, Keri and Big Pete to come by, grateful for the Coast Guard and all the searchers who'd gone out looking for him. Once again, he felt connected and part of something, like he had when he was part of a team in the Special Forces. He didn't want to live alone anymore. He didn't want to feel isolated and at sea. He was happy and grateful to have friends. To have his mother. To have Keri, with whom he wanted to spend the rest of his life.

As Ryan closed his eyes and drifted off to sleep, he knew what Charlie Bates would be doing the very next evening, after the storm had passed. He'd get Chuck Lauden or Pete Halprin. They'd load on bait and ice, steer the Sally May past the lighthouse and go back to work. They'd return to the infinite rolling sea because it was their economic livelihood. It's what Charlie had done his whole life and would do for as long as he possibly could.

Would Ryan be able to go back and face the sea that had nearly swallowed him? Would he ever be able to work the sea again? He didn't know. Right now, he wanted to sleep. When he woke up, he wanted to see Keri, smiling down at him. He wanted to take her hand and kiss her.

One thing he knew for sure, the sea had washed him clean of his past. He'd had a rebirth. He'd been given a second chance and he was going to take it. He was going to ask Keri to marry him.

When Sally got the news that Ryan had been found, she collapsed into the kitchen chair and fell into tears.

Keri was out on the cliffs, praying for Ryan. She was telling him that she had a big secret to tell him. She kept mentally repeating it over and over. As the sun broke through the clouds and bathed her in gathering sunlight, she shouted it, tears running down her face.

"Come home, Ryan. I have a secret to tell you. Come home, Ryan. I love you. We're going to have a baby."

When Sally touched her shoulder, Keri jumped. She whirled around and saw the joy on Sally's face. She saw Sally's grateful tears. Keri screamed out with relief and happiness.

"They've got him, Keri," Sally shouted over the sea and wind. "They've got Ryan and he's alive!"

They fell into each other's arms.

CHAPTER 30

It was a sun-heavy morning, with a deep blue sky, calm seas and a cooling breeze that carried an early scent of autumn. It was September 1st, Keri's and Ryan's wedding day.

The high-spirited morning was already hectic with bustling caterers, a four piece band, 4 grills, 10 folding tables with wooden chairs, 10 picnic tables and way too many friends trying to help, getting in each others' way.

There were balloons, hanging lanterns, a badminton net, horseshoe spikes, and a big white tent with a long table that held meats, salads, bread, fruit, dessert, a keg of beer and a cooler packed with soda. Brownie and Tippie Toe were barking out confusion, rolling in the grass and sprinting off to catch a Frisbee that Big Pete kept slinging at them.

Two weeks before the wedding, Big Pete, Dan Jr. and B.J. helped Ryan build a trestle, with red and peach climbing roses. Keri had designed it and bought the roses.

At 11am, Ryan was under that trestle, next to his Best Man, Big Pete. Both were wearing dark suits, white shirts and ties, standing with their backs to the glistening sea. They faced a standing room only crowd, waiting for the music to cue Keri and her father, Edward.

When the four-piece band began playing the *Wedding March*, Keri and Edward linked arms and slowly advanced, strolling past guests who sat on white folding chairs, set up on either side of a grassy aisle.

When they arrived at the trestle, Edward Lawton kissed his daughter on the cheek and drifted away as Ryan took her hand. They faced the minister, Reverend Morris Gaines, a frosty-haired man with soft, blue-green eyes.

Ryan held Keri in his worshiping eyes, lost in longing and imagination. Keri's eyes held adoration, joy and love. Her honey-blonde hair shone, done up in a voluminous wrapped bun, finished with long fringy bangs. Her wedding dress was made of a crepe satin with beautiful silk thread topstitching. The neckline had a slight V, just enough to reveal the collarbones and show off Keri's long, elegant neck.

"You are a beautiful princess," Ryan whispered.

She squeezed his hand.

When the ceremony concluded, the couple swept out into the brazen sun across the expanding lawn, kissing, twirling and presenting themselves proudly to the applauding guests, who cheered, flung rice and toasted with flutes of champagne, beer and soda.

During the day, all sorts of people came by: Keri's former colleagues, fishermen, the Coast Guard, the regulars from Dan's Drink & Eat, and Ryan's Special Forces buddies, many wearing their crisp uniforms.

There was music, the clink of horse shoes, badminton battles, kids playing tag, more dogs barking, laughter and lively conversation. There were gathering lines by the white tent, taking seconds and thirds of fried chicken, steaks, hamburgers and roast beef.

After dinner, toasts were made—the shortest from Ryan, who still looked a bit dazed by the number of guests, and by his extravagant emotions.

"To my beautiful wife, Keri, the best thing that ever happened to me."

He leaned and gave her a long, tender kiss.

As the sun drifted over the sky, boys and men played catch, women wandered down to the beach for a swim, and Keri and Ryan mingled with their guests.

Keri had that strange feeling of unreality, that dreamy, out-of-focus happiness that isn't anchored in reality—at least not in any reality she'd ever experienced. How had all of it happened? How had she just suddenly appeared in this fairy tale—this romantic movie? How had she been so lucky? How could she be any happier and more in love than she was at that moment?

It had all happened because of Sophia. Sophia, whether she'd meant to or not, had made it all possible. It had happened because of Sophia's summer diary.

An orange September sun inched down to the sea, and as the light softened, the air turned refreshingly cool. Hanging amber lamps blinked on, lighting up the patio and the brick walkway that skirted the garden and newly constructed gazebo. The world became gentle and romantic.

Ryan took Keri's hand and they left the crowds. They descended the staircase to the beach and wandered along the edge of the tide, barefoot, Keri still in her wedding dress and Ryan with his suit pants rolled up to his knees.

The sun descended into the ocean like a benediction, bathing them in final golden light. Keri stopped and faced Ryan. She stood on tiptoes and kissed him.

"Let's live happily ever after, okay?"

EPILOGUE

I never seem to find much time to write in this thing. My life is hectic but wonderful. Today is a special day. David Patrick is asleep under the beach umbrella, all snuggled up in a cotton blanket and white cap. He's 2 months old today, but he doesn't seem to care. He's such a quiet, peaceful baby, more like Ryan that way. He does have my mouth and smile though, and my restlessness.

It's a gorgeous spring day with lots of sun. I came down to the beach because Ryan, Big Pete and Dan Jr. are remodeling the kitchen, installing new maple cabinets.

Our first major Crandall Cove Manor event is tomorrow, a wedding, with 200 guests arriving between 9 and 10am. Ryan and I will be meeting the event planner at 11am today, and two tents will be pitched by late afternoon. We're providing the property, the scenery and the beach, and the wedding parties are to provide everything else. It's easier and less complicated that way, and we still make a handsome profit, without a lot of the headaches.

Since I left my job, I've spent the last seven months creating a website, writing and distributing brochures and doing PR to promote the place. It's been an easy sell. Once people see the photos of the house and the property on the website, they want to come for a visit or book it on the spot. We're booked three days a week right through until October.

Ryan's been a great help, despite all he's been doing. He's in school studying to be a veterinarian. With his science degree from the military and his medical training, he should graduate in a little over three years. He's very excited about it, and plans to open a practice in town.

We have so many friends who come by to see David Patrick and help us get the word out about the place: new friends who helped to search for Ryan, and old friends who came to the wedding. Ryan and I are very lucky and very blessed.

David Patrick was born on April 3rd. He weighed 8 pounds 4 ounces and he took Ryan and me by surprise. At first, we didn't know what to do with him. We didn't get much sleep the first two months, but now we've fallen into a rhythm. Ryan often gets up with me at feeding time and hums little songs to David Patrick. Our lives have changed so drastically over the last few months that we've barely been able to catch a breath.

But I couldn't be happier. Ryan and I grow closer everyday. He wants another baby (2 max) and I'd love to have a little sister for David Patrick. I'd love to have a daughter, and I know she'd be crazy in love with her *father. Ryan already has a name picked out for her: Mackenzie.*

Sally comes by often and baby-sits and Mom, too, has stayed over several weekends. She and David Patrick are best friends. He always lights up when he sees her, and she's happy in her relationship with her new man, a lawyer in Boston.

My father has visited twice and stayed the weekend once. It was a test to see how we'd all get along. So far, so good. He got very emotional when he saw David Patrick. He was so grateful that I called him last August, to ask him to walk me down the aisle. It hadn't been my idea. It was Ryan's. Ryan said, "Why don't you call him, Keri? Why don't you ask him to come to the wedding? He should walk you down the aisle, don't you think? Anyway, I'd like to meet him."

So Dad and Ryan get along well. Last time Dad was here, Ryan took him fishing. Dad bought us a new 70" smart HDTV. He said it was mostly for David Patrick, so he could watch "The Polar Express" and "Frozen."

Of course Big Pete comes by and wants to baby-sit. He looks like a giant when he holds little David Patrick in his arms. But he's a gentle giant, and a gentle giant of a friend to us.

Ryan still occasionally goes out to fish with Charlie. I wish he wouldn't, but I'm not going to tell him that. I was surprised when he said he wanted to. He said he missed it. He said the sea didn't scare him, despite what had happened to him. So, I just kiss him and tell him to have fun, but I worry like crazy until he returns. I still have bad dreams about that whole event.

I often think about Sophia and I will always miss her. I know she'd be happy for us, and sometimes I imagine her in heaven, laughing her butt off when she looks down and sees how it all turned out—how Ryan and I met, and fell in love, and how happy we are.

I can hear her say, "Keri, be careful what you write in that diary. You never know who's going to read it and where it all will lead."

Oh... Ryan's coming down the staircase. He's calling for me. I must have left my phone in the kitchen. I've been so distracted today. I think the event planner is here. She's early. Got to go. Bye for now, diary. More later.

The End

Made in the USA
Coppell, TX
06 September 2020